GW00471457

Killing Hapless Ally

Anna Vaught

Patrician Press
Manningtree

Anna Vaught has a BA and MA in English literature and is an English teacher. She runs a company offering mentoring and one to one English tuition and is an occasional freelance journalist. Since her teens she has been a volunteer at home and abroad in a variety of roles with children and young people. She has self-published two previous books and now writes poetry, as well as working on a new novel and some short stories. Her novel draws on many real episodes in her own life. She is upfront and robust in discussing her own mental health challenges these days; to be otherwise does a disservice to those who have not yet been able to recover and find appropriate support.

Anna is the mother of three young boys. Her husband, Ned, is from Georgia and theirs is a lively Anglo-Welsh household with three cats and a gang of rescue chickens.

Published by Patrician Press 2016
For more information: www.patricianpress.com

First published as a paperback edition by Patrician Press 2016

E-book edition published by Patrician Press 2016

British Library Cataloguing in Publication Data. A catalogue record for this book is available from the British Library.

ISBN paperback edition 978-0-9932388-4-0

ISBN e-book edition 978-0-9932388-5-7

Printed and bound in Peterborough by Printondemand-worldwide

www.patricianpress.com

For Ned. For everything.

And for those who struggle with mental illness in its many forms.

'The millstone has become a star.'
Patrick Kavanagh, from 'Prelude'.

Prologue: A peculiar life

Shall we start at the end? Friend; sympathiser; co-conspirator: read on.

Until recently, for worse and not for better, I had a habit of characterising myself as an accident prone, slightly unfortunate character called 'Hapless Ally'. I would, for example, write travel journals and, in them—I'm looking at *Hapless Ally's Subcontinental Travels* right now—inscribe the amusing tales of how Hapless Ally fell down an ill-signposted hole in Chennai, how Hapless Ally was attacked by a holy cow in Varanasi and how Hapless Ally once fainted on a train in Bihar, fell backwards and knocked over six men and a Sadhu: down like dominoes they went. It was impossible to venture anywhere without causing some sort of calamity; it was just funnier when it was her and not me. And people liked Hapless Ally more.

Of course, Hapless Ally wasn't just tottering about abroad: she had her foot in the door at home, too. She was reliably funny at family gatherings, distractingly eccentric and larger than life when required. It was tiring, toting her around all those years. So enough! I wanted to excise her; to scrape her off and be plain Alison and see if the scenery collapsed and the sky fell in around me. Could it be that, after all, it wouldn't? So, the moniker had to go and taking away her name was the first step in her demise. I wrote it on a piece of paper, scratched it off and stuffed it in the composter; saw yesterday's peelings begin to suppurate on the little jag. A continent away, the Sadhu picked himself back up, with a wry smile or two. I think he *knew* what I was up to.

The killing was going to take a while and I didn't know how it would go yet.

Hapless Ally had amused me and caused me intense pain in turns; I imagined that she gave colour to adventures and added the sparkle and dance of a prism in light to what was a dull, trying personality. For I was an individual who should, as my late sweet mama said of me, have been left in a hospital bucket at birth, not dragged up to dance on the grave of her beatified parent, Santa Maria.

And Mother's housekeeping song went like this:

'Little bitch. I will watch you dance on the turf as I lie below, all broken up.'

'But Mama: you know I can't dance.'

Slap and funeral eyes: 'I might have known you would answer me back. Pod those broad beans you little slut and afterwards go and thin your father's leeks.'

'Does Dad hate me, too?'

'I can't speak for him. Get the preserved gooseberries from the top shelf and don't knock everything down this time.'

Crash. *Inevitable.* And Mother went off to pray to the

almighty she called God, who was Dead if He ever Existed and I cleared up the crushed glass and the gooseberry ooze.

And still we had such a splendid lunch. That was the odd thing. It was partly the lovingly grown vegetables, topside of beef and billowing Yorkshire puddings that gave credence to Mother and Father's pronouncements. Grandmother at *The Hill* (a place of no hope where lived and haunted the egregious paternal relatives) was all tripe and spite; all mould and chintz; couches and chairs clear plastic-covered for the dirt; the hecatomb of eyeball pickled eggs and rancid-looking umber pickles in the damp pantry. *That* made sense of the curses in a house of such desolate proportions. But Mama, ladling out the best gravy and sweet carrots: *it had to be me*, didn't it? I was the smut; the little canker on the pod; on the silken corn husk. In my dreams, the corn smut was *huitlacoche*, which they eat in Mexico as a delicacy. There, I was prized and devilled up with ancho chillies. There, in the markets, I was as startling and free as Mrs Kahlo: I was *delicious*. But that was only a dream. At home I was neither beautiful nor a dish to covet. *You would spit me out.*

So sometimes Hapless Ally—because on occasion it was hard to decide not to be her—drove me into the bathroom as a child (post broad bean podding and leek thinning) when she began to hate me too; thus, she would laugh and mock a spit. *Out bad thing.* So I—or rather, *we*—would apply Mama's scarlet Chanel lipstick again and again, round and round, pulse skittering and looking like a clown, red slick smeared across a face. What I saw, job done, reflected back, was properly the monstrosity I was.

Hapless would shout, 'Do it now and do your worst, wart!'

'Okay, I know I deserve it. Maybe things will be better, when I'm properly punched?'

So I would hit my head with my fists, as hard as I could and until my ears were ringing and the passionate beat of my heart and pulse let me feel less alone. Calmed, I would venture out alone and ask if I should help with tea or tidy the shed, or did they want me to hang myself from that rather fine damson tree, out there in the orchard? Hapless Ally became me: I couldn't tell where I ended or began any more, but I knew that I learned to grow an appealing comedy that obliged the onlooker to accept me. Or, should I say, *us*?

You see, one of the vagaries of a lively psychiatric history such as mine is that not only might you co-exist with an alter ego, a different version of you more attractive than yourself, but also you baulk at living in the moment; everything is loaded with nostalgia, dripping with it in a way that is tiresome and enervating: you can't see the live oak for the Spanish moss and boy do you *hate* that moss, tumbling down and catching your shoulder in the breeze as it does. And the nostalgia is not kind. I mean that you look at a shimmering Christmas bauble and yet you see *another* pretty Christmas bauble of times past. Its prettiness—fugged with the familiar scents of cinnamon and cloves and all the season's spice—will soon have you tensing your muscles as you remember the underside of the carolling and the wassail: you knew you weren't wanted and you swallowed up the curses; you went into your room, having been told you didn't deserve the presents, and you longed to expire, immolated in your fit of self-loathing. You let people who bore you gifts do the most appalling things to you and didn't tell anyone until a kind lady called Dr Crook, who wrinkled her very professional nose (because she wanted you to be happy and on your feet), teased it out of you over thirty years later and you fell on the floor, onto the prickly carpet at Pink Pantiles House—the tremendous-gabled Victorian house, whence they send *Those Who Can't*—and you had to be helped up.

I know, I know, it was just a bauble, but some minds work like that, skipping from thought to thought and unable to see something, just now, for what it is. I can tell you that, over the years, I have experienced delirium over pickles, torments over toffees, cabbage, gooseberries, spotted dick, caravans and those lines in Dylan Thomas which tell of a picture or a shroud saying, 'Thou shalt not'—*oh yes*. These were things I saw: in sweetie shops where Mother pinched my hand and I tried to rock shut, away from her; in intense vegetable-boiling kitchens, through spat kindness, at funerals and in beastly, vaporous dark pantries. While 'Thou shalt not' hung in paternal grandmother's house at The Hill: once, with typical incongruity, above a picture of blue-tinged kittens playing with wool; thus, again, below a depiction of a particularly dark and evil dead aunt, whose scorn slid down the wall and onto the sateen cushions below. From both shalt-nots, spoke out a thin, dry voice:

'Thou shalt not' cry or laugh; 'Thou shalt not' spare the

nasty little child. 'Thou shalt not' tell everyone you don't really believe in God but just fancy yourself as an Old Testament pedagogue.

And the thin, dry voice spoke to a little girl. She was me and I was so, so scared.

I am Alison and I am glad to be sharing my tale with you. I will tell you, as we go, about the venerable doctors Crook and Hook who got me to a better day. Oh—and I have a *stack* of unusual imaginary friends. I still have some of them, you know. There's Frida (the brunette one) from Abba, Albert Camus, (not often connected with Swedish super-groups), Mary Anning the fossil collector, Sylvia Plath, John Keats and Dolly Parton (now there's another odd yoking!) plus Shirley Bassey and a few more flirtations along the way.

But after the end, which is about both death and first breath, I offer you the beginning. Not just the beginning when the ink of her name ran rivulets in the composter: the beginning of *me*. Do you want to know how it was? Hold my hand, now, while we traverse lines and move over into the third person while I share this. Both would help me to keep the tale straight.

1

The Hill: avoid it

The girl is standing on a soft bank in a spring breeze as the laundry blows high above her there in the orchard. The breeze blows cold, but there are currents of warmth about her legs as the day decides whether it will whip or kiss. She is wearing a long, chunky necklace that she had made of wooden Galt beads, a pink hand-knitted jumper and a pair of knickers. It's the kind of outfit difficult to carry off once you're a big girl. But sitting now, legs akimbo on the bank, she sees the faces of the yellow celandines open to the sun, the hedge full of primroses beyond the whirling laundry and she is happy. She knows she can bury her face in the violet patch and lounge there with their sweetness. That is, for a short while, because this child knows that after such delicacy come *penalties* and *consequences*.

Dozing now, in the day that is definitely kissing not whipping, the girl feels something against her elbow. She doesn't open her eyes at first, but now she feels it shuffling towards her cupped palm: it is a thought—insistent; warm; compelling.

Here came a voice now and the voice screeched, 'Alison! Down here now and finish getting dressed! Hopeless dirty little child!' (That was her mother.)

But also, the thought again, curled up in her palm: 'Don't worry, be a *Hapless Ally* whenever you need to. *Make something new: to cover up you!*'

The little thought in the palm continues to nuzzle; it won't give up and so Alison suspends disbelief and decides that there might be an alternative to feeling skin-off vulnerable; unwanted. Now she had a new name to put in her pocket. She didn't know what 'hapless' meant yet, but she figured it sounded clumsy; clunky and *less* of something—and yet *useful.* The funny thing was that it came to fit: right, like a well done sum. It was a red letter day: an invisible amorphous thing in the hand had given her a moniker.

And into the house we go. Mother, ah Mother! Jesus wept: she was such a saint. That's why, of course, Alison called her Santa Maria.

'To do list: ironed apron on; stoke the stove in the house I do not love; teach a class; be a pillar of the community.'

It was the same with her husband; he just said less, unless he was lay preaching, quoting from *The Book of Revelation* or cursing badgers. Alison had, periodically, reflected that to spill the beans would be quite satisfying when people sneered at her, having told her what a saint her mother was. But let us try to be sympathetic; try and see where someone else's unhappiness might take them, for Mother was acutely frustrated, so this is how the cooking went; its attendant feeding as a sort of virtuous violence:

'Bang' to the oven,

'Crash, cruciferous bastards' to the sprouts,

'I hate living here' to the father. 'It is all too *too* much. And most of all I hate *her*. Was she your idea? When is Number One Son coming home? At least he listens and isn't actually the spawn of the devil like that little bitch. I blame it on your weird slit-eyed family, all locked in up on The Hill.'

Ah, The Hill. We meet it again; a bleak little eruption; a hamlet of wall-eyes sat atop a plain, where the wind whipped up and the people turned sour and gnarled. Its name precipitated in Alison a fear of people *up there* where the ground swells up (*see also fear of buckets*, below); a cold and leering folk, standing around with pitchforks, occasionally performing crop dances or evil singing like that scene in *The Wicker Man* when they burn Edward Woodward alive. Always the fuck-wit indigents stood, staring nastily at people from away. No wonder a little girl should be scared. Also, a myriad fears floated about in a single day or with a collection of words in the world of Alison. Because of the influence of Santa Maria and the little thought in the orchard—for it is understandably hard not to be taken in by a prevailing saint and a talking, nuzzling thought—Alison also had to keep telling herself that she was just Alison and not altogether 'Hapless'. It had all got a bit complicated and the Hapless bit had really started to stick, so that it was sometimes hard to know when she was acting out and when she was being herself. There was so much to think about: batting back so many terrors at once.

In a truncated childhood, old before young, there were a few events that stood out. We will lump a few together and call them 'The Winters of our Discontent'—silent bronchial times when Santa Maria was bedridden; her activities brought to a violent halt by influenza, chest infection, pneumonia and grumbling mitral valves. Which was why, as she had not infrequently intoned, Alison was lucky to have been born and not left aborted in a bucket.

Or she would say, 'Ah! I should have left you in the bucket after birth because I saw you and just knew. You are forever Baby in the Bucket!' (Which felt worse.)

'Why did you never want me?'

'Shut up! I'm making fondant icing; it has to be *just so!*'

'Please tell me what it is about me—and I'll try to change it, I really will!'

'This is exactly what I'm talking about. Yapping always—and now you've broken my concentration and buggered up the Christmas cake. I can see the fucking marzipan through the icing!'

Yes indeed: that was a hard one to hear and it stimulated many years of bad dreams about buckets and abandoned babies. Even as a very big girl, with babies of her own, it still continued—and ended with the dreamer coming to consciousness, reaching out and crying herself awake. Fortunately buckets, after all that effort by the NHS, were eventually no longer entirely an object of repulsion or the stimulus of a phobic reaction. And the two harpy friends of Santa Maria, who said the same thing, over tea and fondant fancies, are also dead. No more Mr Kipling for you! From time to time Alison entertained really bad thoughts, expecting to have Santa Maria pop back, alive or dead, with another slap and some broad beans to miserably pod, all the while.

She would dare, aloud, 'I—I've got a Bakewell tart next to me right now. Ah, the Witch of the Women's Institute; the Troll of the Town Council, Doyennes of our Community: didn't Alison turn into a nice little girl?'

Or, 'Ha! Can't be that Hapless if I've managed to stay alive with *my* level of stupidity and clumsiness! And, you know, I always knew I was lucky to be alive. I never thought otherwise! I just could have done without you all mentioning *The Bucket*. I had such a lively imagination. A surgical bucket: look away everyone!'

But the spirit of the dare did not sustain her and she was claimed by the snarling winters: they were colder inside than out; even the radiators managed to radiate cold. Silence sat over the house; everything began with a closed door. Alison would scamper in—determinedly larger than life and determined to be helpful. Trying to be *that Hapless thing*: bang-crash-visual-comedy: but everyone loves *her* better, don't they? Impossible, of course: riding the skirts of her father's stress, watching the pulse throb angrily in the temple; trying to be the Alison she thought they liked, she would endeavour to boil potatoes and make tea and end up creating an enormous mess. It brought only a shout and a child rushing out to the beech tree—the wishing tree in the wood, with its kind heart and tender trunk.

Alison would wrap her arms about the tree's velvet neck and say, 'Make me fly!'

Or, 'Make me just me and not *her!*'

'Make me a tree!'

Or just, 'Make me not be.'

And somewhere nearby skulked a shadow who might have been Hapless Ally, waiting to adhere: to stick back on Weird Kid and make others like her; make 'em laugh. On the other hand, it was a big wood, by the lane through the village, so the shadow might have been a wandering Bible Billy, the oldest man in the village, with a beard you could hide your ferrets in; he fancied himself as Tiresias, except he wasn't blind or particularly prophet-like. Or it could have been Pervert Pete, who liked nothing better than a lurk and to steal pants and pegs from washing lines. It was a strange place; its beauty compromised by menace and perversion. This time, however, the sylvan skulker was Hapless Ally, after all. A stark reminder that Alison had to keep up the act, *or things would only get worse.* Hapless Ally was a figment in the head, but occasionally she stood as a shade beside Alison; you had to watch it. And Alison made a poem for herself, its starting point some lines she had once heard:

'Stone walls do not a prison make,

Nor iron bars a cage.

And Mother dear can do much worse

Than populate your page.

And Bucket Baby has to try
To mollify their rage.'

Alison contrived the idea that everyone must think she was
malevolent to people with heart conditions, pneumonia or
those compromised by infarction; or that she had wickedly
brought on others' ailments, disfigurements or sneezes by
being this burden: the cruel little idea flew into her head and
would not let go. And she thought that if she *really* tried
to be less herself and more *Hapless*, then perhaps less harm
could be done. The heart raced: while she was out there
tree hugging, might at least one person in the house die and
she would be found responsible, aged seven? What if other
people would die because of things she did in times to come?
To keep hidden from charge a while she built a den inside
the creepers near the beech tree; a crawl space. And, with
a gentle, warm blush of light, Alison became three people
because it was there that she first romped through the snow
in Sweden, in a long fur coat, chased by an amorous Björn
from Abba: yes, she was *Agnetha-Alison* (the blonde one) and
she talked to her best friend, Frida (the brunette one), about
love and Sweden and kissing men and how she felt girlish
and kind of coy that everybody was crazy about her. With a
pleasure that embarrassed her, Alison was no longer alone.

Frida was *always* understanding. Also she told Agnetha-
Alison that this little bucket-girl-maggot was pretty, did
really cool things with her eye make-up and fawn coloured
knee boots and that it wouldn't be her fault if anybody died.

'What's with all this guilt, sweet kid? You know, the man
before Benny—ya he was a Norwegian; I knew I shouldn't

have dabbled—well ya, he fell through the ice on a frozen lake, right next to me: eventually came back up looking like a fish finger! Well, was I responsible? Ya, no. I'd been wearing really pointy shoes when I was dancing on the ice, but the hole, I did not cut.'

The crawl space was a good idea: no-one could find Alison if she snuggled up inside, plus she had a big bag of Marks and Spencer tomato ketchup crisps, a pint of milk and a banana so she could stay fugitive for some time. She thought Frida would console her when it got a bit colder and darker because Frida was used to cold and dark, being from Sweden. Alison ate the crisps; Frida declined them because she was dieting to look super svelte for her wedding to Benny and ate only herrings and crispbread.

'Look, my little friend, I'm not going to join in with this Hapless thing. You're just Alison to me, so be Alison to others. You're a fine kid; you're going to be super hot! Stellar, baby. And, ooh, ya: look at your long eyelashes! Wanna be my double date and chief bridesmaid?'

'Frida, will you always be there? Visit me even if I go to prison as a murderer and everyone points at me and laughs?'

'I will always be there and I will bring my glitter, do your eyebrows and paint your nails. Ya, I will be your Swedish prison bitch.'

There were so many more winters of discontent: the best were iced with a macabre comedy and so fast forward to Cyclamen Terrace in Gateshead, the rain and November. Nothing promised but dull days; memorable days, withal, though, because here was a nasty bit of jest, ending on a dying fall and a suck at the morphine pops. In this case, the sucker was Helen, Alison's godmother, the only one of her father's siblings to be accepted by Alison's mother. She had got away from The Hill, gone off to the Sorbonne and been extremely clever out and about in France. She smoked in a cool, languorous way and said that Alison could come and live with her, get—*'I'm not your mother so I can say inappropriate things'*—some proper shagging in, have adventures and travel the world. The only pictorial record Alison had of someone looking motherly to her as a baby was Helen, chic in a tweed Chanel ensemble, holding her and gazing at her lovingly. So that was great. But Helen moved inexplicably from Montmartre to Cyclamen Terrace, got dumped by Santa Maria, developed a brain tumour (two events which were not related although Santa Maria felt there was a link) and got married to Terry. If you've ever seen the Fat Controller on 'Thomas the Tank Engine', well that was how he looked: with a further roll or two over his collar and marginally increased facial expression. By coincidence he was an enthusiastic train spotter.

He told them, puffed-up proudly, 'That tumour's the most aggressive they've ever had on Tyneside. She's a case for the history books is my wife, although it's a crying shame she can't teach her piano lessons, what with the confusion and all.'

There was a silence. An excruciating one, when tumbleweed and a sort of bored, listless apocalypse blew against the window.

Down by the gas fire and squinting through his mammy's

enthusiastic gusts of air freshener and the puffs from the Glade plug-ins, they sat. Helen was upstairs in bed; Terry and Mammy were downstairs, fussing about the kitchen. Mammy was laying the table for her son, pulling his chair out and patting him on the head; Alison and Santa Maria perched on the edges of chairs while Father *did* for them outside. Terry was not in the least practical and also rarely went outside, preferring the two-bar fire, 'Countdown' and Mammy's commodious breast. Occasionally, there would be shouts of pain and cries for morphine from upstairs, but generally all you could hear was the sound of Terry chomping on his cabbage or spotted dick and the chirrup of Carol Vorderman in her earliest days. And that ominous twittering sound, before the thinking time's up, when you think, 'My life is shit.' *De da, du da diddle de da! Ping!*

Now and again Terry would call up, 'No morphine yet, pet. Can you hang on until one?'

'I can't stand it any more. I can't, I can't...'

'I could pop up with some paracetamol in a bit, pet. Mammy and I are trying to decide between vowel and consonant at the minute!'

Dad was outside trying, she thought, not to cry as he dug and pruned savagely, then got on a ladder to repair the flat roof out back. Santa Maria sat rigid within. No-one spoke. Terry had an extraordinary appetite and tended to dribble.

On the day of the funeral, on the sixth day of Christmas, the scene changed to Gateshead, rain and December. Occasionally there was grey sleet: Alison could feel it falling into her soul when she was not trying to stifle inappropriate laughter. It was a burial you might not forget (or at least remember more than other burials, should you get about much to that sort of thing: there are folk who love to caress a silent hearse) with Terry weeping by the open grave in a strange ecstasy, throwing in red roses and a picture of their Airedale Terrier. He also threw in his wedding ring. The grave next door had pictures of a nasty-looking Alsatian and Rottweiler propped up behind its rigid plastic flowers.

'God forbid,' said Santa Maria, who absolutely did not believe in God (Who was Dead if He ever Existed).

'I don't suppose you have a tube of caulking for further DIY, Terry?' spat Alison's father with the starkest incongruity he could muster, as the undertakers started shovelling.

Terry had perked up considerably by lunchtime. There was dinner cooked by Mammy, but just for him, so the funeral crowd dispersed while he tucked into his baked meats. He sat at the table, with his napkin tucked in around his fat neck, and enjoyed being waited on. It was Friday, so he knew it was stew and dumplings, but they broke from tradition and had spotted dick again; twice in one week. Spotted dick was *Monday*: crumble was *Friday,* but a lot of suet was consumed that day because the lad needed comfort and Mammy believed in the restorative powers of lard.

Santa Maria said, 'I hate him and never want to see him again' and also that the reason Terry had thrown his wedding ring into the open grave was so he could go back to being married to Mammy. They drank PG Tips and ate mince pies and after lunch Terry and Mammy settled down to start a jigsaw from his extensive collection: it was of a Spanish holiday resort, complete with big hats and festive tissue paper and cardboard donkeys.

Mammy purred, 'La! Look, pet! I got you a new jigsaw roll. It's got a super velvet back. Ooh: feel it!'

Terry fingered the soft material thoughtfully, 'Oh yes, Mammy: that's lovely.'

'You mustn't be sad, my lovely little troll-boy. Mammy's got you now and the other will be in heaven.'

'Ooh yes, I know. Have you got any custard slices in?'

'Yes, pet, and Mammy's little troll-boy can have two with a cup of tea and a Garibaldi on the side.'

'Oh Mammy—you're my favourite girl, you are.'

Alison's father expectorated loudly outside. The dog had mysteriously disappeared.

The Gateshead and grave in winter experience got even cheerier because, on return, Dad went to The Hill to visit another sister: not, that day, sister Evil Plant Emily, but sister Mad but Nice Andrea. The latter took the news of the funeral well (the former was at bingo, which took precedence because she was on a roll), but then she got out of bed and threw a console table at her brother. As a ten-year-old, Alison could not quite grasp what was going on sometimes; for example, why she was never left alone with Terry, why her paternal grandmother's pantry with its huge jars of glowing pickled eggs and onions scared her so much, or why Mad but Nice Andrea didn't get out of bed for five years, apart from to gibber and jibe at the traffic, hurl objects and take overdoses of something. Alison also wondered, guiltily, whether her aunt threw other furniture. There was a Welsh dresser verily laden with plates and Toby jugs: that could *surely* go down with a mighty crash and anyway the jugs were gurning, hideous things. But generally Mad but Nice Andrea picked small items.

Alison desperately wanted to ask her, 'Auntie Mad but Nice? *Can you hear me?* Before you were a lunatic, did you have imaginary friends and an alter ego? I've got a friend like that; I've got a second me; I think I'll get more of both. You see, I've been trying to be someone else so everyone wouldn't hate me. I can be myself with you because you are mad and also my favourite auntie apart from dying Helen.'

Mad but Nice Andrea might have croaked, but with a startling clarity, 'You are great. A bit eccentric, but that's fine. Get away from these people; get away from Hapless. Go be you! You can be happy.'

But instead, when Alison caught her sweeping eye, Mad but Nice Andrea, shrieked, 'Fuck off, fuck off. Why is this shopkeeper here?' and threw a bottle of cologne at her niece. Alison replaced it, at a pace, knowing that the liquid was vital for keeping the smell of bed sweats down. The child tiptoed out, dodging a flying hot water bottle in a bunny cover, its ear flapping—and feeling all hope had gone.

'We are going to Clevedon to listen to the brass band play on the pier. Get me my fur coat and my muff!' shrieked the voice behind her.

Funny and funnier things happened at The Hill: hangings, tumours, enormous rats with giant teeth, an unexploded bomb, repeated lightning strikes, cats with Old Testament names—Simeon, Rastas and Tiresias—locked rooms that no-one ever went into and, according to Santa Maria, Grandmother merrily stoking a huge bonfire of Alison's father's books to punish him for not collecting his things quickly enough after he had married Santa Maria and cut the apron strings. There was cruelly boiling tripe with its gusts of steam and laundry-smell; the pantry of frightening pickles, stacked like eyeballs in Grandma's dark chamber of horrors. You felt in your bones the damp and the crawling mould. It was a combination of Peggoty's dark store-room, so frightening to David Copperfield with its smell of 'soap, pickles, pepper, candles and coffee, all at one whiff' and the Salem House schoolroom, with its smell of 'mildewed corduroys, sweet apples wanting air and rotten books.' And, to accompany the odours, there were the stories, recounted over sausages and mash, about the bizarre ways in which Grandpa's brothers had been killed.

'And say—do you remember what 'appened to Uncle Ralph?' While he spoke, in his broad Mendip-voice, Grandma's tripe for tomorrow slapped against the sides of the boiling pot.

'Well, I…'

'Ah well, what's that? Say you don't? Now, Uncle Ralph, now 'ee hit 'is head on the way up from the quarry, got trepanned and that were that; Uncle Harry were squeezed between the buffers of the train at Bristol Temple Meads, though I can't say which platform and Uncle Percy went out with the tide at Weston Super Mare and 'is hat came back on the mud; people said the body were washed up at Portishead, but we never claimed it. Dear old Uncle Reg, clumsy flatfoot bastard, now 'ee fell off the back of 'is horse and were trampled to death in front of 'is fiancée, who ran off in 'aste with the grocer, which Mother said served all three of they right for carelessness. Mother! Bring pickles from the pantry!'

Off the dark hallway, seeping red cabbage waited for the hard-knuckled hand and downy arm of Grandmother to scoop and slop and lay down with less than love. No-one here would have even noticed whether Alison was just herself or being the more palatable Hapless Ally; besides which, they hated everyone. It was almost a relief for the child. It didn't matter who she was, did it?

Here, all the skewering and squishing death-stories were told as gentle reminiscence, horrible endings so comforting over an otherwise silent dinner on the huge table by the old range with the clothes on the Sheila Maid hanging overhead. Frequently, in this exposed position on The Hill, the wind would whip up, Grandpa's chickens screamed like banshees, timbers creaked and doors quavered and smashed shut: perhaps the unquiet souls of the dead, disliking the cheery retellings of their worldly extinction. Grandpa was nearly blind, but compensated verbally with story after story, determinedly still driving his red Morris Minor van to 'The Hollow', the next village along, to go bell ringing with his wall-eyed, big-foreheaded friends: if he killed someone on the road, then clearly they should have known to move and anyway, tolling bells stopped for no man. He was a fine poacher and trout tickler and handy with an axe or chainsaw, with no maiming or fatality up to that point. Had he lived longer, propped up by tales of incompetent oncologists, chiropodists with shaky gin-hands and mental asylums, doubtless he would have expired horribly, like his brothers. Disappointingly, he went quietly, not far from The Hill, in an old people's home, which smelled overpoweringly of wee, talcum powder and the pungent boiled cabbage smell Alison associated with Terry and Helen's house. The day he chugged off, the grandfather clock kept going, but the staked dahlias wilted and the cats howled into a place behind the pantry door where a dead grandmother must have lurked as she waited to slop and slap the sludgy umber pickles at future despised grandchildren.

Grandpa had never been able to read very much, but he could recite poems by Tennyson and Arnold and the whole of Browning's 'The Pied Piper of Hamlin'. Those were the spellbound, golden moments. And it was hard to imagine Arnold's 'Sohrab and Rustum' told with anything other than a broad North Somerset accent, a bit of a dribble and a touch of snuff on the lip and septum. It wouldn't have made sense, which Alison remembered years later sitting in a tutorial in Corpus Christi College. The esteemed professor declaimed assorted lines and she thought, 'Wrong! I don't know what yer saying!' It should have gone, 'And firs grey o' morning filled eeest,/And the fog rose out Oxxxxus streeem' and not, 'And the first grey of morning fill'd the east,/And the fog rose out of the Oxus stream' in received pronunciation. But, however it was said, here's the thing: words can heal. They can make you soar, whether read or heard. And you cannot take them away once brought into the world. Sometimes they are good even if a bad person said them; because the words can exist independently of the mouth that uttered them or the horrid geography that spawned them. *It is magic.*

Mad but Nice Andrea had a husband called John who terrified animals: anything ran when he appeared. The cats would howl and sprint; Grandpa's chickens scattered. Dad said it was because John was a vet and they were instinctively nervous of him; that he must smell of chloroform and antiseptic, but Santa Maria said it was something else; something black and sinister—just typical of folks round that way. When he came in, after dinner and terrible deaths, for crumble, Alison eyed him suspiciously. Did he vex cats or sacrifice chickens for pleasant diversion? Pets regularly disappeared around here. Alison looked outside to see whether the rooks in the elm tree had stopped their chatter. It certainly looked still out there. A robin fell silently off its perch.

'Wow, festive. Hark the fucking herald.'

When they popped by with sedatives and a hypnotic on the way home, Alison watched Mad but Nice Andrea from the corner of her eye; her aunt had retrieved the hot water bottle and was ripping off the bunny cover and chewing its edges. Someone sat next to her doing needlepoint vindictively and Alison couldn't be sure if it was another relative, or maybe a kind of minder. Like Grace Poole in *Jane Eyre*, only in a fifties bungalow rather than the attic in Mr Rochester's stately pile.

Alison thought, 'How would I explain my family to anyone? But Frida will understand and at least I can be Alison and not Hapless Ally with Auntie Mad but Nice because she doesn't know a bunny bottle cover from a ham sandwich, so it's all the same. There's always the risk that she'll kill me, but it's probably okay.'

Alison had overheard mutterings in the kitchen; she heard phrases such as *personality disorder, manic depressive* and *psychosis*. She heard the voice of Uncle John, saying of his keening wife, '…And Mother, I did think when I married her she might have been a sociopath, but she was cheerful enough then and anyway folks don't mind that at The Hill.'

Alison thought, 'What's a sociopath? It sounds cheerful anyway. Kind of chatty.'

So a curious but normal Christmas break and Alison went back to school with the customary sense of being just a bit separate. To get away from mad women (who lived in depressing slapdash-mortared bungalows, which after all weren't interesting in a pointy, Gothic sort of way and where there was no hint of left-behind Caribbean heat on the top floor), she furiously and hungrily read and re-read that bit in *The Wind in the Willows* (it's at the end of 'Dulce Domum' if you care to look) where Rat manages to make a cheering little feast for Mole and the field mice who have come to sing carols at Mole End. For added reassurance, she read 'The Wild Wood'—with particular emphasis on the moment when Badger opens his front door and the two animals tumble in out of the snow. There are hams hanging from the ceiling, a big fire, the plates wink in a kindly, anthropomorphic way and when the famished animals are fed and ready for bed, their sheets are coarse but clean and smell of lavender. To

Alison, a hybrid of the two chapters connoted Christmas; the word *cosy*; into life came a wafting amorphous thing which some might have called *happiness*. And best of all, no Baby in the Bucket. Here, Hapless Ally could stay away because her host didn't need improvement and could just slough her off and relax. *It's okay, baby girl. It's okay.* Because in *The Wind in the Willows*, the creatures veritably fall upon one another in a riot of being pleased to see you, which felt like an unfamiliar construct beyond the books. Well, with the exception of how Helen made her feel, but Helen was gone, with the wedding ring—and possibly the Airedale—to a grave in December Gateshead, leaving a shelf of books in French to Alison. *Ooh la la!* Alison thumbed the books and missed her so much in a world that made fuck-all sense.

One Saturday afternoon, as Santa Maria and her father bickered in the kitchen, Alison started Camus's *L'Etranger (The Outsider)*: she liked the picture of Albert Camus on the back; he looked sort of confident—had an attractive hauteur about him—and he was leaning against a wall like he didn't give a toss whether or not you liked his book. Of course, the writing was not comprehensible to Alison yet, but we'll be meeting its author good and proper when Alison is a little older. With an *Oh yes. A very big yes*: because Albert Camus was very much present at the first sexual experience *seule bonne femme* and most likely no-one could say that of *The Wind in the Willows*. It is terribly inappropriate and infra dig to think about or write the word *wank* in the same paragraph as *The Wind in the Willows*, but now and again euphemism loses out when an orgasm's at stake.

At home, the Christmas tree came down early and Dad had a big bonfire. Alison's parents always had bonfires when there was tragedy. Or just indecision. Or Tuesdays. Alison—trying very hard to be kooky, daft Hapless—dared a grown-up dialogue with her father. 'Are you ever so sad? Are you crying?'

'Bugger off, you little cuss.'

'I mean, about your sisters?'

'Aren't you listening? I've got work to do, fuck-wit.'

'I mean one being dead and the other chewing off the water bottle cover and being a sociopath and a lunatic. Are they the same thing?'

Her father stared hard at her with his watery grey-granite eyes; he was so strong; with beautiful, muscular forearms and shoulders like Atlas. She wanted to be scooped up to rest there. To have him say, '*It's okay, baby girl.* I'll keep you safe. You're fine just as you are,' but he snorted in a derisory way and kicked sparkles from the bonfire; the miniature stars should have been pretty, but were angry and ugly. Alison threw her advent calendar on the bonfire and stood for a moment watching it curl up and little green flickers come from the purple plastic bit which had contained the Cadbury's miniatures.

Daddy. My daddy.

Ah, 'The Twelve days of Christmas' and The Winters of Discontent. Such larks and lossocking, for the season brought with it much anecdote that is only (and darkly) amusing in hindsight. There was the time when Alison's brother—an umbrageous much older sibling (hereafter known as Brother who Might as Well have been Dead) who had informed her she was brought home and found to be the wrong baby, but Mummy didn't have a receipt so the horror couldn't go back—impressed upon her that she had brought on the deaths of her parents. At night the child would wake in a wet bed, with no-one to tell, crying, '*They are coming for me because I am a killer. I am a wart; how could I be otherwise? I am Baby in the Bucket.*'

Brother who Might as Well have been Dead took her out for a walk at twilight in a papoose on his back; such an early memory, forged in fire. At home there was a dark and shadowy wood—darker than the wood which contained Alison's wishing tree—and in that wood he picked the darkest tree of all and left her behind it, upright in the metal-framed papoose. She could hear the laughter as he walked away, knowing that wart could not extricate herself; he retrieved her past darkness, silently; she had been too scared to cry because she believed wolves came when the day fell.

Alison said, 'I will tell someone.'

And he spat, like his mother when she was pulling out her daughter's hair over bean pods and sink, 'Ah, but who would believe *you*?'

Inside, the tree twinkled and there was a 'Fourth Day of Christmas' feast, sour in the mouth.

Another Christmas, Santa Maria died alone in an armchair during 'Neighbours' while elsewhere, and free for a while, Alison was chasing the moon and the stars in a little corner of South Asia—and on return (a retrograde step) Alison found comfort in the arms of Sardonic Steve, who liked weird sex and hated most people and all religion. There was 'The Fifth Day of Christmas' when Alison got into Cambridge and felt, for the first and last time, a sense of having done something that was actually condoned, making the five gold rings both glister and tarnish at the same time; which occasion preceded the one with the hideous parting when Sardonic Steve left her, 'You've wrecked my life, you selfish bitch' notes; not enormously festive, but at least he put pen to paper and had drawn some ironic holly, next to a picture of a bleeding heart with a steak knife in it. He'd also come round and stuck scissors into cushions: her embroidery scissors protruded from the hideous heart-shaped felt one.

Now *that* was a man who, if he'd been inclined that way, could have turned his hand to farce and black comedy, but Alison retrieved all the scissors and cried and cried because she had been proved (again) bucket-worthy. Also, she was slightly jealous of Sardonic Steve's talent for melodrama and punchy visual indexing. Scissors collated, Alison reflected on the first Christmas after Dad died. She had swooshed in, deliberately bang crash look-at-me-jolly Hapless Ally; that was a better bet than giving anyone pause to accuse her of seeing the old bugger off. So, in her cheerful weeds, Alison was Hapless Ally and she really tried, but put too much tinsel on the tree and cooked the giblets, still in the plastic bag, inside the duck and Santa Maria and her porcelain doll-faced, pillar of the community friends shouted at her for screwing it up, ad nauseam; she sat snivelling and full of headache through the Indiana Jones film thinking, 'I bet Harrison Ford doesn't have this kind of trouble.'

She even thought about writing to him:

'*Dear Mr Ford, did you ever have a really shit Christmas? Like one where you cooked the giblets in the bird and everyone hated you? When you decorate your tree does everyone say, "Ooh a triumph! Just enough Hollywood shine and festivity"? Were you left upright in a papoose as a kid in a dark and shadowy wood where you thought the wolves would come and eat you? Did you ever have an alter ego; something to stick on so that people liked you and so you weren't loathed by your family? Like Harrison...and...Comparison: that could have worked.*'

What was it about this time of year? She recalled yuletides when Sardonic Steve sulked all day because he was so hungover and thus invited his friends over to smoke pot and throw the stubs in the fireplace: Alison went out crying into the wind and running to escape—and fell over on the ice. Even the ice had something to say, but everyone was too stoned to notice the wet and muddy idiot in the room. These were also the years when Sardonic Steve would not allow a Christmas tree owing to simply too much festivity and the scale being all wrong—but I expect Alison asked for it, did she not?

Shall we leave Christmas for the time being? Instead, it is time for *the colour table* and to reassure you that the revels do get better because later on—precipitating tumultuous events with Hapless Ally—Alison meets the drawlin' travellin' Dixie Delicious. And some proper fun is had along the way. Having said that, aren't things that are, well, a bit shite, a bit (again) infra dig, those that are so much funnier in retrospect?

Thus, 'Oh and it was twenty for Christmas dinner, we had an idyllic afternoon walk and a lovely time with Grandma. Just perfectlovelytralala.'

Pollyanna *fuck*: would it sound sneering to ask, '*Where's the comedy in that?*'

If the perfect family and the well-crafted Christmas truly exist, may the Lord strike us down for saying it ain't so.

2

Scary ordinary things

Now, in Alison's room there were two essentials: the colour table and the little books containing the rules of the room. The colour table (all set out on a pretty little wooden stool later presumed lost as tinder for one of the parental bonfires) became an essential part of the room's structure and hue. Alison changed the colour table weekly. It was *hers*—even if she might have been little cuss, fuck-wit or Baby in the Bucket. A memorable table was the pink one: that contained a pair of salmon-pink silk knickers borrowed from her mother, a polished stone from a craft shop, a rosy cameo brooch of uncertain provenance, a scallop shell with a rim, the pink ones from a packet of refreshers, a Barbie-pink wafer biscuit, a necklace and—depending on the season—some damask flower petals. She set them all down tenderly and at the last minute added a tiny amaranth-tinged gone-off bottle of perfume that had come from the Avon Lady.

Alison rearranged the treasures regularly; refreshed them if need be—and an important thing was that she formed navigable gaps between them. So that, if you were *really* small, say, you could walk along the little roads between the petals of an aster and the cameo brooch. This was the secret bit: the colour was pleasing to any onlooker, but the order, traced round and round in the curlicues of a little finger—of Alison's little finger—was the private bit.

'If I were a miniature me, I could spend all day basking on the petal, looking up at the gemstone rock' or,

'I could climb on the pink wafer and jump down, sliding across the pink knickers.'

It may appear to you, reader, that this was an overly detailed way in which to see something; or a recollection that cannot possibly be. But it *was* and *is* so. Such a commanding impulse: to arrange little things in groups and trace a finger round the gaps in between; a microcosm that is intimate and seen only by its author.

In childhood, it was the one area where Alison could say, 'I can be me: make things with my hands! And I didn't knock things over or break things.'

True. All the items on the table stood still; didn't wobble, knock each other over or fall on the floor at her clumsy feet. In these still hours, Alison and her alter ego were divisible, so the former could be at ease: briefly, Alison was in control. At such decorous times of arrangement and rearrangement, you couldn't hurt her. Little matter, anyway, if a pink shape fell, because she had a drawer of reserves—such as a lovely little gold clock—with cherry blossom painted on its sides and fine enamel face; the clock tied in elegantly with the colour table and rounded off the proportions of the microcosmic world.

There was ritual to be observed here, again and again: three little steps by the pink wafer; turn around three times and say the first lines of *The Secret Garden* four times.

' "Chapter one

THERE IS NO ONE LEFT.

When Mary Lennox was sent to Misslethwaite Manor to live with her uncle, everybody said she was the most disagreeable-looking child ever." '

When the table was set, the rituals performed just so, Alison reduced herself, like Alice, so she could travel its roads and, at other times, she made the *Rules of the Room*. The rules: nothing complicated there. There were laid out lots of little strictures in very bad spelling which we would struggle to replicate now, all set out and neatly underlined in tiny books she had made. Alison imagined the room as a world to travel in, so the books were partly a guide: the bed was the island, the wardrobe the ship, the chair was the cave and *don't touch the floor: mermaids could get nasty*. She had bad dreams about them, with the faces of Santa Maria and her two harpies, the porcelain doll-faced friends with whom she consorted and who would advise her on suffering the dreadful martyrdom of being mother to such a child. Alison's books contained the rules of the world and the room.

'Friends can come in.'

'Doll-faced people cannot.'

'There are jellies and After Eights for tea.'

'The room is only lit with candles.' (Which, unfortunately, were not allowed by decree of Santa Maria.)

Also, 'Do not touch the colour table.'

'Do not chew gum.'

'Share things.'

And sometimes, 'Let me be just Alison and not the two of us.'

Or, startlingly, 'I am scared I have killed people.'

And, 'No Mummy allowed in my room.'

The books had blank covers and were stapled together badly, because she was a bit young to be a dab hand with the stapler just yet. She lived in fear of Santa Maria finding them and so moved them around periodically. Every so often, starting in childhood, and subsequently all through adolescence, Alison would wake shortly after going to sleep, hot and sweating and frightened: she would get out of bed and check the arrangement of the colour table and the placing of the miniature rule books: the expression of fear of which we spoke before—'Am I or will I be a murderer?'—haunted her for thirty years after that and never let go, leading her as a child to be scared that the police would come to the door and as an adult that she would be roundly caught in the street and charged by children and parents. It is what the good Drs Hook and Crook of later life described as a *ruminating thought*.

Once, after the nastiest crack up, Alison was at Pink Pantiles House with the Mental Health Recovery Squad (MHRS—and the S is really for *Service*, but Alison reckoned *Squad* made it sound more superhero). Dr Crook the psychologist said, 'Let the thought flood your head and feel what it does to your body. Now notice that nothing else has happened or has *ever* happened. This way, you will re-train yourself and the fear will diminish. It is groundless.'

Alison thought that this would, indeed, be marvellous; that she could give up the permeating anxiety about arranging and rearranging things and go out other than apologetically or in disguise. But she thought of buckets and the day everyone said, '*You did it! You hurt the lovely little girl!*' And she said to Dr Crook, 'How do you know? *You weren't there.*'

And there was a rambling, tumbling idiot in the room who was spitting out in a desperate and horrible rush for expression and to purge the long held evidence against her, 'When I was five, I was playing with a girl and she fell and cracked her head open. Everyone said I pushed her. But I didn't. I just **didn't**. She died when we were teenagers. It was her head. Santa Maria said her parents might have thought it was my fault. So I couldn't write them a card. They might come knocking on the door, after me, after me, me, murdering me and she would understand why. I have had nightmares about it all my life. It is like the Sylvia Plath story called 'Superman and Paula Brown's New Snowsuit', where everyone rounds on the girl who *didn't* do it—who *didn't* ruin the beautiful clothes of the popular girl—and the more the clumsy unpopular girl tells the truth the more everyone's faces say, "*Yes of course you didn't but you must ring that nice Mr and Mrs Brown and apologise and write a letter to Paula.*" And they all know and everything, everyone and the world have changed and her parents are so disappointed. And anyway everybody knows what she is like. Damn Sylvia Plath. No damn Paula Brown! Damn Santa Maria. *And fuck fuck fuck nasty evil me!*'

Someone was screaming in the room. Well, a fairly controlled sort of screaming, one doesn't like to exaggerate, but it was building to a crescendo. It came from Alison. There was a little blood on her palms where she dug in her nails. Gradually, came diminuendo as Dr Crook continued to meet her gaze; she was unwavering and determined. When the noise stopped, there was a long pause. Dr Crook left the room at a gentle pace and came back with Dr Hook, the trainee psychologist, and she said, looking intently and sternly into Alison's eyes, while Dr Hook put the gentlest of pressure on her hand, 'You did not do this. You never did this. It is not real.'

It was the most frightening moment of Alison's life. A dreadful confession of what she had been and quite clearly what she must still be: the ensuing silence was bitter and cold. Finally, someone spoke: the fragmenting words came from her own mouth.

'But how do you know? How? But... *You weren't there!*' said Alison.

And when Alison raised her head, she thought she saw Hapless Ally out of the corner of her eye. Previously, the latter had been smirking, waiting to adhere and improve on the little murderer; now she sat slumped in the corner, muttering quietly as the patient was stripped back to a core, and what she muttered was this: 'Bitch. You little bitch. You can't ever be just *you* now.'

'Dr Crook! Dr Hook! It's *her*. It's Hapless Ally. Can't you see her? Can't you? I have to have her and she has to stay because if I don't and she doesn't, what will happen to me?'

Dr Crook said, 'You are being a difficult patient. Shh now. Let her go. Be laid bare for the first time. Could I shove her out of the window? It's a way down and that might finish her off.'

It was a startling suggestion, but the good doctor smiled, from a place beyond words, and the other good doctor looked into Alison's eyes and, still, kept the gentlest pressure on her arm. Alison wasn't ready to open the window just yet, however.

Once, when she was nine, Alison had come back from Brownies to find a fire engine outside her bedroom and the fireman having a cup of tea with Santa Maria. One of them said something like, 'You've been a very naughty girl so we're here to talk to you and tell you off. Your parents rang us. *Aren't you the bad little girl?*'

The fact he guffawed and showed a gummy smile as he said this meant little, but sent Alison to the crawl space by the beech tree to turn Swedish and very blonde and commune with the ever sympathetic Frida. Did everyone know what she had done to the little girl? Before, she had been scared only of policemen; now it was the firemen, too. It was only after three visits by the fireman that Alison spotted the link with her father's enthusiastic bonfires in the wood and the whoosh noise from the chimney as he started a chimney fire. (Note from the future, from Alison to Drs Crook and Hook: *'No fear of fireman developed, only an ill-judged short romance with one later on. He had curiously oily, slightly sooty hands and smelled of toast. Also, wish you both had been there in those drab days to stop this all in its tracks and meet a good friend, Frida, before the love went all melancholy in Abba and poor Agnetha was forced to bare her pain in "The Winner Takes it All".')*

In the den Alison whispered to Frida, 'Mum says everyone knows what I'm like. That's why they look at me all funny. I'm not like other kids. I'm the wrong kid.'

Alison told her about the girl and how the memory she couldn't properly form was so scary. Said how others must see such sin in her because Santa Maria always told her they could: the kid was transparent—or translucent. Like a nasty little octopus containing a box whose markings you could see through that lucent flesh: THE WAGES OF SIN ARE DEATH. Alison always admired her mother's extraordinary similes; it would have been hard not to.

Like a box telling of sin and death. Inside an octopus.

Meanwhile,

In a dead room, lay a mad aunt who might also have been a sociopath.

In Gateshead lay a dead aunt, buried with a ring and an Airedale terrier.

At the half-dead Hill now shrieked the ghosts of dead brothers and the bad tempers of strange cats and the rats with big teeth and 'Thou shalt not' spat down the wall onto the plastic-covered couches and sateen cushions.

'Is this what everyone's life is like? I suppose it must be.'

And THE WAGES OF SIN ARE DEATH.

'Heave, ho, everyone: it's my little bitch daughter. I expect you all know about *her*. Look at what it says on the box: she'll die or go up in flames for what she does. It's a sin what she is.'

Dinner time.

Night or day, it felt as if the well-preserved porcelain doll-faces of Santa Maria's decent community-spirited friends pressed in on her with open mouths that showed more grimace than joy. And how come Santa Maria was so big on sin when she said God was Dead now even if He had ever Existed? Did that mean He had once lived, but had given up? He'd been extinguished somehow: perhaps He too had spent too much time on Cyclamen Terrace in Gateshead and got stifled by the plug-ins? But Frida's beautiful hands made an expansive and confident cat scratch and she scattered the smug albescent doll-faces as if they were thistledown. And Santa Maria and the nasty doll-faces were elsewhere and maybe God was not Dead, but had come back.

'Frida? Why can't I just play with Sindys like other girls?'

'My little friend! You are what you were meant to be. You just need somebody to help you chase your shadows away. Also, your relatives are as weird as all fuck, ya? Let us say thank you for the nice music and always, *always* remember that I'll be there, every time that you arrive. The sight of me will, ya, definitely, prove to you you're still alive, and when I take you in my arms and hold on to you tightly, you'll know it's going to be okay tonightly and that is for sure.'

'Oh thank you, Frida. It's two o'clock in the afternoon, though.'

As Frida stood by in a ready-to-chase-the-shadows-away sort of stance, Alison confessed her nervousness about *the others*. There was the orthodontist, for example. Santa Maria taught his golden son and when Alison had accidentally bitten down during an impression for a brace he had got cross and said, 'Your mother told me what you were like.' Also brandishing a miniature mirror, pink water and a pointy stick was Mr Fisher the dentist, with another creepy son who Santa Maria thought was such a gift. Mr Fisher had given her an injection with his big bold hands before removing some teeth (he was in league with Mr De'Ath, the orthodontist of considerable evil). Alison yelled and wriggled and he leaned hard on her in the chair and, while he mouth-breathed like a rapist and emitted unsettling wafts of Old Spice aftershave with a mint top note from the mouth breathing, he stuck the needle into the side of her mouth, missing the gum area by the pre-molars.

Setting his jaw *just so* he said, triumphantly, 'Your wonderful mother said you would be like this. I expect you always will be.' The extractions were excruciatingly painful because the gum wasn't properly numbed, but nothing to be done there.

Anyway, 'I shall tell someone.'

'Who would ever believe *you?*'

On the wall by the chair were merit charts and certificates

and pictures of the son, Fisher Junior, *summa cum laude*. Alison didn't get a sticker on the way out. There were none saying, 'I've been an awkward shit at the dentist.' Santa Maria glowed pleasure at the Fisher Junior memorabilia; imagining for a moment this was her pretty little son. If they had been for a girl, such trophies would have been earmarked for the likes of Heroic Alice, Alison's classmate, whom Santa Maria admired, momentarily and vicariously living the life of this child's mother.

Now the books and the colour table helped to impose some order on the world, but Santa Maria had ideas of child improvement and she had conceived of things to impose order and decorum and culture on her grubby child. Her friend's daughter was just the role model required. She wasn't a Baby in the Bucket Alison of course; she was *Heroic Alice*, fluent in all the skills of growing and pleasing her parents endlessly. Alison disliked her smug, confident little gait on sight, but did try to make friends during enforced playtimes, when Hapless joined in to make the base layer more entertaining, more vivacious. Alison was simultaneously enrolled for piano lessons, Brownies and ballet. *Wrong wrong wrong*. Heroic Alice had it all down to a T of course: diligent piano practice, pretty in a tutu and angora cardigan and badges all up her arm.

The piano lessons started amidst much howling and slapping and hair and ear pulling and spawn of the devil comments. Santa Maria was determined, however, and the fact that Miss Hamm the piano teacher did not appear to like children was not considered an obstacle. The teacher had a large wart on one side of her chin with a big hair sticking out of it. On the very worst days, with Miss Hamm narrowing her eyes in derision at Alison, the child would be scared that Miss Hamm would shut the clumsy, hateful fingers in the piano lid. Alison fantasised about pulling the hair from the wart. Snap! Yank! It is gone with one deft movement! Miss Hamm had very big teeth: like a big mean rat. Like Anna Maria the nasty rat in Beatrix Potter: the one who tries to eat Tom Kitten, unskinned, but covered in roly-poly pastry. There was nothing to be done though, save the lonely feeling of the stone sinking down, down, on a Sunday afternoon in the provinces.

Alison had no patience with the piano; it just would not agree to accommodate her, its keys remained resistant against the pressure of her fingers. After months of poor reports and an embarrassing turn in a little concert in Miss Hamm's house (made tenser by the arrival of the fireman at home shortly beforehand to put out a particularly recalcitrant chimney fire), her mother capitulated and told her she could stop. It was mainly because Heroic Alice had played so sweetly, a child graced by immaculate white socks pulled up to her knees, brushed hair and bobbles and no boiled egg smeared on her face. The angel even bowed with some expertise when she had played her piece and paused, so considerately, for applause.

The comparison for Santa Maria was too painful to bear, but the relief to Alison of being removed from scorn and properly attired pretty little girls was sweet indeed. And, anyway, Alison had a secret: she wasn't 'tone deaf', as Miss Hamm had pronounced, for when she closed her eyes at night, great patterns of notes would swarm and swoon behind her eyelids. They would become friendly, glide like water and, gradually, become still and compose themselves into translucent melodies.

'Hmmmm,' thought Alison: 'One day. *One day.*'

It took another six years until she picked up a flute, found it melted into her hands and became acquainted with Miss Ermutigung, the music teacher from Berchtesgaden who had found love with a British backpacker when she was acting as a tour guide in Hitler's bunker and subsequently come to live in Wiltshire and rescue Alison from the closed-in world of the terminally tone deaf. And anyway, Miss Hamm died; it was rumoured she'd choked on an eyeball pickled egg, which just goes to show that you should not snack while playing the piano. She was found, upright, egg in mouth and fingers rigor mortis under the piano lid, a nasty crotchet shouting at weary descending minims. Outside, a cat looked in through the window and smiled if ever a cat could.

'Ha! I learned about nasty pickles from Grandmother at The Hill!'

'You're not allowed to play at my house any more because you're weird and you're dirty,' Heroic Alice had announced (post-concert dénouement) giving her hapless fellow musician a kick. 'Mummy says so!'

Alison thought she would plot revenge on the little bitch one day. *But how?* And didn't the provenance of that thought prove Santa Maria's point: such a sin = death?

'Yeah: but it might be worth the risk. I had a bad thought about Miss Hamm and look what happened there. Result!'

After possibilities had clearly been exhausted with music, Santa Maria announced that Alison would, next week, start attending ballet. Mother produced the outfit and Alison hated it straight away: it had no pockets, for a start, and pockets were always required for interesting things you had found: funny shaped stones, small sticks to fashion into weapons: treasure from other folks' detritus. But her mother had the steely run for cover look on and it was raining, so Alison gave in and tried on the wretched outfit. She looked like an evil-tempered sugared almond. Because it was going to be a very public exposure, Alison also knew that she had to be Hapless Ally. She was going to be useless, so she had better be comically funny: that way they might laugh, but it was better than black looks and other people choking on their tea in horror at Baby in the Bucket.

The village hall, venue for ballet, had a highly sprung floor. Hapless Ally (as she was trying so hard to be) set off its squeak with her man feet from the first footstep in. Ahead of her, there were lots of sweet little girls in their pink ballet pumps, leotards, tutus and soft fluffy wraps. They were well-proportioned with delicate girl-child feet and they had looks of steely determination on their faces: they were ruthless cheerleaders. Of course, our girl had tried to walk in gracefully with a big buoyant smile, but it came with a thud and a creak and the girls turned. She realised one of them was Heroic Alice—and also that they were, en masse, looking at her with their eyebrows raised. But it was too late to run from the pretty, shiny hell-hounds.

There was a witchy woman in charge of the little girls; her name was Miss Close. As with Miss Hamm the piano teacher, it appeared to Alison that the lady didn't particularly care for children, regarding them only as rough objects to be trained and improved upon, with condescension and brutality, if necessary. So the best she could do was big up the Hapless.

'Maybe she'll feel she can work with me, if that's who I am?'

But Sophie could do every little move expected of her, including the mimsy scarf work; Emma could bend her leg up behind her back, while smiling and keeping excellent poise. Ah—the grace of Heroic Alice. Oh. Miss Close was smiling. Perhaps, like Miss Hamm, she just didn't like Alison (or her Hapless counterpart). But the girl gave her all, her fake character welded on as she thundered around the hall in vain mockery of the pretty movements the girls had been asked to perform. She was aware of the shame, scorn and embarrassment settling upon the room when she, elephant as she was, danced past the old room heater with its big wire guard. It rattled and croaked as she passed, with not a sound for the other ingénues.

This time, Santa Maria was so disappointed that she never sent her daughter to ballet again. As Alison left the hall, unbuttoning Hapless with her silly clothing, she could see Heroic Alice, now wearing a lovely little fur cape with a diamanté button on top of her ballet clothes, and speaking in stage whispers behind her hand to the other girls, 'Oooh yes:

that's the one I was telling you about. The one with boiled egg on her face and dirty socks!'

'Ugh. Disgusting, isn't she?'

But on this particular occasion it was too much for Alison and she ran back and kicked the ringleader in the shins saying (she thought the reference clever but was clearly alone in this), 'You're a bad nut and I hate you and hope the squirrels chuck you away.'

Alison ran off, shamed. But a further afterthought made her run back: 'And I know loads of rude words so you and your tutu can fuck off!'

Heroic Alice burst into tears; she had been crushed and stained by the dirty girl with the dirty words. Alison stood on the veranda of the village hall. It was strange: the building looked like a little hall in the Hill Stations of Northern India. She had seen these pictures in a book called, *People of Other Lands*. There was just time to glimpse the foothills of the Himalayas and for a reassuring chat with a handsome Indian man before Alison was belted by her mother. She called to him, 'I'll be back when I'm older and I'll help you on your tea estate! Really, could you hang on for me?'

The beautiful eyes of the man simmered love, acceptance and some definite possibilities of future fucking. Alison knew all about fucking from the piles of pornography under the bed of Brother who Might as Well have been Dead, with whom she had once been sent to stay, between the years of being left by him in a dark and shadowy wood for the wolves, and his years of popping back to organise funerals with considerable enthusiasm, breathing onto coffin plates and buffing them up with the edge of his jacket. Gone was the soft romance of the little girl; the sweet notion of holding the hand of a boy in a daisy meadow, for she had looked with horror at the images in the glossy magazines and internalised the language, wondering if what was painted there might be useful when picked on by the pretty little *girls that could*. But for now it was more sin and wages and a second belt before a shouty drive home. Inside the Hill Station hall, Heroic was still being consoled by her similarly distressed friends and Miss Close had come and expectorated a stern telling off against the car window as they pulled away. Later that night, Alison was forced to make an apologetic phone call to Heroic Alice's mother.

'It's for what you did to that nice, pretty little girl. You don't have half her determination. And change your clothes—you smell like...like...like an old dog! Oh, all I had wanted was a child of sweetness and light after the misfortunes I've had and now your father always being so close to death. Why why why?'

Oh Santa Maria, if only you had known. If only. If only you knew her *now*.

On the phone Heroic Alice's mother chirped, 'I am sure you will never understand what good behaviour is or be anything like my daughter. You are a nasty little waste of space.'

Alison lowered her voice so Santa Maria could not hear and whispered, 'Well, I saw you with Mr Melchizedeck the vicar in the bushes after the Christmas Fayre. What were you doing? *Collecting holly?* So you can fuck off, too. Oh: I killed my piano teacher with a pickled egg. And I know all about porn from going to stay with my older brother! He's got piles of Readers' Wives in his house! You'd be amazed at what I can describe and at the sex-vocabulary I know!'

And the phone went down. Alison sighed, for so much swearing was tiring, if eminently satisfying and effective. Sweetness and light it wasn't. And we weren't done yet. There was Brownies, the third tine of Santa Maria's three-pronged attempt, to mix a cutlery drawer metaphor: it was an accident waiting to happen.

Having already been forced into two arenas inhabited by Heroic Alice and the pretty little *girls who could*, here was another. The urge to rebel on the swearing-in day was strong, but as ever she was in fear of the words and Santa Maria's hair and ear pulling, so she chanted the Brownie Guide pledge, stepping from one chair to the other; over the apex of the two into a new realm of enchantment. Not, of course, as delicately as the other new recruits or with the right words.

'I think that I will try to do my best:
To love the queen (but with a capital Q)
And serve my God and his country (with a capital H)
And try helping other people
So everyone can manage to keep the Brownie Guide Law
And definitely do loads of good turns
Because it is the law.'

'Hopeless—but sit down because I can't stand listening to it anymore, so help me god,' said Brown Owl.

'Written with a capital G,' said Alison. 'Yes, like for God, who was, I mean is, Dead if He ever Existed.'

Brown Owl was gasping now, discombobulated; fingering the silver cross on her flaccid bosom. But then she never smiled very much; always looked mired in her own anxiety. Was there more to it than just having taken a dislike to Alison as the little wastrel shambled through her initiation into Brownie club? Over the next few weeks Alison hoovered up snippets of conversation. Alison was *always* eavesdropping on adult conversation: it was how she knew her maternal grandfather beat her grandmother, that Santa Maria wanted to go and live somewhere exotic (like The Cotswolds) because Somerset was full of heathens and hadn't been an improvement on South Wales, and that Mr Gibbs who did craft work at the school was having a torrid affair with the mother of Alison's classmate, Samantha Stokes (more fucking in the bushes; Alison *always* noticed fucking) and that last weekend they had gone on a hot air balloon flight together (possibly involving more of the same), having previously carried on in the school staff room while collating takings from the summer fête. Under the very nose of her husband, who was Chair of the Governors.

Alison learned that Brown Owl was not happy in her sterile—she said *sterile*; why was there so much antiseptic on it?—marriage; that she felt duped into the volunteer role but had cast herself, anyway, in the role of martyr. It was all especially hard because her prize poodle had recently been run over by a tractor. Alison felt a bit sorry for her so did her best to attain a badge: *that* went Horribly Wrong (written with a capital H and W). On badge day, Brown Owl brought Tawny Owl along; the latter was a sour-tempered owl who had, like Miss Hamm, warts with big hairs in them. The catering badge was, as one might have predicted, a disaster. Notes on clipboards stated that there had been '*Too many spent matches. 1) An entire roll of kitchen paper was wasted. 2) There was considerable mixing up of food and non-food substances*' and, worst of all, '*3) The inappropriate use of water in a tiled area leading to unsafe floors and, potentially, mild peril.*' Santa Maria paled and Alison knew that soon she had better run for Frida and the crawl space.

'*And the child is unsuited to structured and responsible activity! That can be point four on the clipboards!*' intoned the owls, with victory in their eyes, as Santa Maria and her unfortunate Brownie left.

Alison dived for the back seat before her mother could belt her and pelted for the crawl space as soon as she was at home. Frida, who was wearing a very glamorous floor length fur coat and matching muff, laughed throatily at the turn of events.

'I'll give them one, two, three and four! Oh, for sure! I've never liked owls. The owl-kind are not kind. *Jag anar ugglor i mossen!* Bastard owls! But you are a rock star and Björn is just crazy for you. Don't worry about those cupcakes, ya. Would you like some Ryvita and lox? Or we could do "Waterloo"?'

Alison still had a stash of tomato ketchup crisps, so she ate those, pondering that she could likely stay out for hours. She could see chimney smoke, so her parents were settled inside and had possibly locked the back door by now anyway. But then her palm itched; an angry, unremitting itch; she scratched it, but the itch would not subside. Up came the feeling from the day she turned three and sat in the warm grass of the orchard: it was the little thought in the palm, nuzzling; insisting.

And it said, 'I've got plans for you, Hapless Ally or are you just Alison? Can you even remember when you were just Alison? And do you understand the name I gave you yet? You feel it don't you? It is coming, Hapless Ally. *Coming*.'

Frida heard it too and shrieked, 'Get out ya, bitch or boy hound! Leave her alone. *I* will be her Waterloo and not you, little fuzzy thing in the palm.'

But at that moment all the scratching and every chord of the best friend she had in the world could not clear Alison's hand.

Ah, point five on the clipboards: *Baby in the Bucket! Just watch the consequences of being born, and not reading the writing on the wall...*

3

Crap holidays; lusty blacksmiths

We've spoken about The Winters of Discontent, The Hill and a little about miscellaneous Christmases and the leisure time that wasn't really leisure. What of the holidays, or the summers of childhood. Those halcyon days of which we are told?

Before most trips, Alison's father would say to her, '*You are only here under sufferance.*' After this announcement, he would methodically slap her three times to get it out of the way before the journey, then blow his nose and adjust the car mirrors. It was part of the routine. But the words caused confusion for some time because Alison was not, as a child, entirely certain what *under sufferance* meant. That she had to suffer and grin and bear? She surmised by her father's tone that it meant *we have to suffer you,* so it wasn't the most festive start to a trip. It was at times like this that Alison couldn't bear to look at the palms of her hands. She was too frightened that she would find the itchy scratchy dark thought there; too frightened to remember anything.

In the Brecon Beacons, there was the same campsite always and the same stream churning through. It was lovely though: rich malty earth and the farmers calling to their sheep. But there was a caravan involved: if there was one thing Dad loved it was his caravan. And if there was one thing that Santa Maria hated it was his caravan. The caravan led to a couple of funny but sour anecdotes in later days and was also the cause of *The Worst Parental Swearing*.

Herewith caravan anecdote one. When Alison's father retired from his own pillar of the community job there was a feature on him in the local paper. (Nobody ever said he was dying; Alison was supposed to have worked that one out: as he'd only said, 'I've got a lump on my leg' it sounded to Alison like a job for antihistamine, though in retrospect it did appear odd that he'd pulled over suddenly in a lay-by to point this out.) The article in the paper stated that, 'the family's main hobby was caravanning.' *Was*—like they'd all been squished already. Santa Maria regarded it with scorn; meanwhile Alison felt uncomfortable about the word *family*. Then Santa Maria said, 'I hate Fucking Caravans.'

There was an awkward silence.

Not so long later, by the time Dad was shuffling and gasping about the house and the caravan sat outside on the drive, green with algae and with little patches of moss and grass sprouting here and there, Alison decided she had better heave ho and be Hapless Ally: make him love her before he gasped and shuffled off to God who was Dead if He ever

Existed. She wanted to bounce in, clumsy but funny; cause a few splashes, but make it look like new for him. Even so, she was sure that his condition was reversible; that he'd be up, oiling tow bars, pretty soon. That particular day she had to wait until Santa Maria went out because she thought (rightly) that her mother was probably hoping the Fucking Caravan would suffocate and moulder away, or be buried by trees. But the power washer, assorted soaps, T-cut and a shammy did the trick. Alison—all bouncy Hapless Annie and 'Daddy it's me!'—went in to her father; he was drawing spring flowers in a sketch book with some felt pens. It was as if he were having a sort of sentimental dotage, or maybe a second childhood. And she interrupted to say, 'Go and have a look.' He stretched up like a meerkat sentinel, suddenly oddly alert on caravan patrol. And he said, slowly and deliberately, 'Don't you ever touch my Fucking Caravan again.'

And it is strange: Alison's sibling, Brother who Might as Well have been Dead, condescended, out of the blue, to send her a CD of family photos. (Proving he wasn't dead, although you never can tell.) Pictures of the maggot-child were outnumbered a hundred to one (and when she was in the picture it was to gauge Fucking Caravan perspective) by pictures of flax, periwinkles, cows, vegetable rows and a flotilla of petrol lawnmowers. And tender shots of the caravan: France; Spain; Holland; Porthcawl; Rhyl; Aust and Magor services. They were generally just of the caravan from all possible angles, but several featured Santa Maria, glaring and standing in the doorway, wearing a range of unattractive headscarves as if in protest. It was hard to understand why these, with a clear image of simmering anger, were included in the archive.

The Fucking Caravan had taken them many times to the Brecon Beacons. There were silent but beautiful walks in the mountains; Kendal mint cake and Bounty bars eaten by Llangorse Lake and Alison sneaking out to kiss a boy from a trailer when they thought she was idling on a swing. Once even a proper lying down snog with a boy in a barn and some advanced kiss chase in a spinney. There were many angry cooked breakfasts, viciously spitting bacon and eggs, her father's spectacular snoring close at hand, and Alison running away to gather sheep wool on the mountains, determined that she'd gather enough to make something fantastic. Of hours washing the wool in the stream, trying to stay away, as Santa Maria and the Fucking Caravan-fancier dozed or bickered. She remembered that, with some regularity, badly packed bottles fell out from overhead cupboards onto her head and there was a painful memory of a bottle of vinegar mixed with her blood. Everything stank of bacon fat and portable toilet disinfectant; behind the chintz curtains, it was hell and you were released from it with the smell of fat clinging to you and the chill of the disinfectant in your nostrils: it put a barrier between Alison and the outside world, so that nothing scented as it was: the world stank of the inside of the Fucking Caravan.

One pretty time, Santa Maria ripped off her ugly caravan headscarf and let fly, pounding on Alison's back while shouting, 'You little bitch! You little maggot! You don't even know what violence is! I grew up with violence.'

'Mummy, should I cook the bacon? Mummy, isn't this violence?'

'No this is not violence!'

With the un-pounding hand, Santa Maria fried bacon in the warped and blackened pan. More fat. Dad disinfected the cramped little toilet. The pounding spent, the afternoon segued, incongruously, into tea, bacon sandwiches and a box of Mr Kipling's while Alison's parents listened to Alastair Cooke's *Letter from America* on Radio 4. It was, as she reflected in later years, a childhood replete with incongruity. She just didn't know what the word meant yet. While her back throbbed, she ate a second cake. Outside, the stream thundered on to the kind and distant sea.

'Oh, I want to dip my hand in that icy sea like boy-Dylan Thomas. I want to be in the sea town away from monsters and throw stones at cats and meet Mrs Prothero as she beats the dinner gong. Her daughter Miss Prothero would look at me kindly and ask if I'd like something from her bookshelf to read because Miss Prothero always knew what to say and I would say back to her, "Oh yes, I would and I would and can I come up to your bedroom and we can talk about all the books you have and I can borrow and come back? Can I maybe stay forever? You could read the *Mabinogion* to me! Oh, I would and I would!"'

There was another time; a fine time, she hoped. This was the project for her and her father to walk, in stretches, the whole of the Pembrokeshire Coast Path. To this day, Alison thinks that this is the finest coastline she has seen, though it holds such piercing memories of St Bride's Bay on a fine day and setting out on a voyage around her father: really, it was *his* project; she just happened to be there, but it would definitely beat bad-tempered crochet with Santa Maria in the Fucking Caravan. Up and down, climbing over the rocks; occasionally, or at least this is how it was remembered, perilously close to the cliff edge, or along thickets of gnarled, lichen-covered trees, they did a different stage each day. She climbed on rocks at the water's edge, took the face of the wave in her face, coming up new for a while and chewing on bladderwrack seaweed. The cormorants eyed her suspiciously, sleek and stretching out their wet wings to sun and breeze. Out there in the bay, she could see the great tankers waiting to come in to Pembroke Dock or Milford Haven, or perhaps they were setting out for balmy climes. To *where?* Somewhere tropical perhaps? Out there, to the heart of darkness and down a deep wide river that was an inscrutable force of nature, old as time. Looking far out to sea, it always felt to Alison that the tankers carried a tinge of the supernatural with them; they might have been cresting warm waves weeks ago, visited by flying fish and graced with cinnamon and warm spices: these were soft nuances they carried into colder waters.

She imagined herself like a pretty little mermaid on the rock: 'But sailors, sailors: *take me with you.* Take me away from this. I will grow up on your boats and cook for you and not break anything and when I am old enough and big enough maybe you will fall in love with me with my long shining hair! And I don't mind if there has to be fucking although I already promised the handsome Indian man at the tea garden outside ballet.'

The coast walks were, apart from visits to The Hill and jobs in the garden, the only time she spent with her father. You'll notice he didn't gain a moniker. That's because, to Alison he was then, as he is now, incomplete; shadowy; an unknowable figure. Alison could have told you everything about his accomplishments and his hobbies and about how hard he worked, though: so that had to be *knowing* enough. He was a silent man (apart from the episodes of badger cursing and shouting at anything, human or feral, which got near the Fucking Caravan), but teacher; woodsmith and wordsmith; creator of fires; fine cricketer; lay preacher: many lives in one. He had survived The Hill, was mad for petrol lawnmowers with their craft and their finely calibrated maintenance, chainsaws and the correct manner of cleaving logs (done with mathematical precision). Yet he was intensely accident prone. He had cut off a big toe in a lawn mower accident, twice severed his thumb in the workshop—once as Alison watched.

On the toe-lawnmower day, she heard the hideous shrieks before she saw the shredded Wellington boot and heard the scream of the mower (and of her father): 'Fetch the frozen peas, you little fuck-wit. I'm holding my toe on.'

'Why would you put your toe in the peas?'

'Now! It's come off!'

Alison rifled, with great anxiety, in the freezer. No peas. She settled on a bag of frozen gooseberries. 'Could it go in here? Put it in and I'll take it back to the freezer.' It was an odd place to store a toe, but Father was puce so she said no more.

On a quiet but thumb-severing Sunday, Alison's face was hit by the ricochet of blood; one other Sunday, as the light dimmed, he felled a tree and ran the wrong way so the tree felled him. She pulled him out. An apocryphal tale had it that during military service he had fallen asleep, standing up, under the inspection hatch of a plane; it fell open against his head and he lost most of his teeth. The plates stood, at night, weirdly yellow and majenta candy-coloured as they fizzed in glasses in the bathroom. Also, he had never, in his whole driving career, cared for using the indicator, but this had never, as far as she knew, led to any mutilation, amputation or fatality. That didn't mean it hadn't happened; those at The Hill would have killed and pickled any witnesses for one of their own, so it might have done.

But who he was, Alison did not really know, although she had felt his blood on her skin. So, in the teenage years, as they walked, she would try to talk to him about thrift, seabirds or whether the cormorants that had scrutinised her on the rocks could be trained to dive down and fish and come back up and drop their catch, like she had read they were in China or Southern India. And once, particularly daring, but really against her better judgement, she asked him A Difficult Question. She said, knowing that her parents spoke so highly of Number One Son—of how easy and gentle he was, while she stayed Baby in the Bucket, 'Dad, can I ask you something. I, I want...for you to tell me something?'

'Oh! What is it *now*?' The watery grey-granite eyes looked past her.

'I think I want some reassurance. I mean, I'm sorry, I mean that I know Mum doesn't like me and that I am a trial and that The Wages of Sin are Death and all, but—'

'For Christ's sake, get on with it. I want to identify those birds on the rock there and can't if you keep talking.'

'Well, when you talk about me, do you say that I'm, that I'm, well, okay?'

His answer was blunt. 'We prefer to spend time with Number One Son. He listens to us; he likes to be with us and he never says a word. And you should know you are here *under sufferance*. Now pass me the bird spotter.'

'But I listen. It's how I know you like cormorants and thrift and caravans.'

'You are talking.'

'Dad, I *want* to talk to you.'

'Be quiet, you little cuss.'

Alison always remembered this conversation. And she would remember the advice she overheard him giving to parents: 'Never crush a child's spirit' being an important phrase. But the *sufferance*, the plainly preferred sibling, the palpable disappointment in and plain dislike of the daughter; it rankled on the clearest day: 'He never says a word. You are talking.' She couldn't keep quiet because the words were so beautiful, whatever risks they brought with them.

Maybe her father felt delight, of sorts, at the academic career later on, but always in terms of her doing, not being and that is a significant distinction. In later years, while lifting him from the bath, rescuing him from the bathroom, hosing out fires, rescuing his caravan from peril, the words would come back and visit.

Their last conversation ran, 'Remember to put out the bins. Try to get something right before I die, won't you?'

She forgot.

He said through clenched teeth (and with much with the same staccato diction as the *Fucking Caravan* line), '*You. Have. Let. Me. Down.* I will probably die before you can get anything right. I am at the point of death now. It could happen at any moment.'

Not, 'Ach, you forgot, you idiot. Oh come on, run for the bin men, there's a good girl. I'll try to pop off after they do, so we're square.'

Instead, always and innocently, there breathed the syntax of damnation. It was there rattling the bucket with the tiny, mewling form in it and graced by, some years later, the vision of her mother coming to consciousness after a life-saving operation and saying, 'Why are *you* here? Where is Number One Son?'

Ah, but Brother who Might as Well have been Dead had somewhere to get to, didn't he? It's like in Auden's poem, 'Musée des Beaux Artes', which reflects on how, in Brueghel's 'The Fall of Icarus', '...the expensive delicate ship had somewhere to get to and sailed calmly on.' And that was fine. It is odd and jarring to be so brief on the description of a sibling, but *hear ye, hear ye*: FAMILY IS A FLEXIBLE CONSTRUCT. It might be that you have a more meaningful relationship with the man who services your car.

And anyway, when her life went tits up, to quote Auden again, 'For him'—for the one who is supposed to love you—'it was not an important failure.'

Sometimes you lean on the family you store in your head. Funny, later on, to find that you're related to Albert Camus... Sometimes people do not love you. Sometimes they did and they stop. To them, that failure might not be as important as it is to you. It might not even matter at all if the wax melted on your wings as you flew too close to the sun and down you came to die.

But from a garage to feathered boy to chapel of rest we must go in one easy bound, for when Alison's father died, he was wedged in a very yellow coffin, under a periwinkle blue nylon quilt which gave her a small electric shock. But that was not what she saw most: it was the lilies. He hated lilies. He hated them—*had* hated them—with an irrational passion and now they were clustered round him on the catafalque and below his hands. They appeared to be spitefully multiplying. Alison sucked in the sweet, ponderous smell of the Victorian sick room with its nuances of the newly-dug tomb or vault hanging heavy in the dismal municipal room. These odours mingled with the cold anonymous smell of the chapel of rest; perhaps it is the no-smell of embalming fluid. Does embalming fluid have a smell? But here was something she could do and this time—for the *only* time—she would get it right. She kissed the waxy face and said, 'Please take those lilies away from my father. He hates lilies.' And also, 'I loved him. Why did I fucking well have to love him?'

On the halcyon holidays, whether it might be Bavaria, The Beacons or after a day on the Pembrokeshire Coast Path, in the lonely evening, Alison would settle into the hammock bed in The Fucking Caravan, draw the curtain and pray for a very long time either not to wake up at all or to be a brand new person on waking: a person who was new to them. So, in her dreams she swam in a lagoon, a long swim in a fine azure lagoon, and she found a tunnel, like a breach between worlds, coming up through the water to a new place. There was warm sun, nothing fell on her head or itched her palm, there was breadfruit rather than smash and tinned stewing steak and the girl's shoulders dropped with the relief. Gone was the stench of bacon fat and disinfectant and she felt comfortable with her name, without the moniker for a while; she was just Alison, before returning to the world and The Fucking Caravan. Plus encore.

Moons later, there was an ill-advised trip to France à la caravan and so *Herewith caravan anecdote number two.* Alison was *under sufferance* all the way and her father's driving was erratic; the four toed foot unsteady on the accelerator. It was the illness; the elephant in the room: metastasis on the motorway. Outside Paris her father had a panic attack, clawed at the windows, and wove a dramatic pattern across the road; he had been stung by a bee in the car as they slugged along on the heavily congested autoroute, which was readily made more congested by the *Rosbifs* who had plugged it up with their caravan. For an eternity he did not move but started muttering and then, with hardly a crescendo, to scream.

'That bee! That bee! An end-time bee—it came for me!

Why would it be in the car now? It is the bee of Abaddon sent from hell. The bee of Apollyon! There in the book: *The Book of Revelation*? Yes, isn't it? Isn't it? I am dead! Dead of abominations! God does not want me! Things are sent! It is too late!'

Alison held her breath, tried to make herself invisible and decided not to correct her father: not bees, *locusts*. She wondered about whether she should try, extra hard, to be more Hapless, as her thoughts wandered over the familiar paradox: *I am too sad to cry.*

Now, they had pulled over to the side of the road and Dad was screaming, 'Jesus help me! Help me Jesus! Come now and help me! The bee!'

And, 'This is hell on earth. Help me, help me; Jesus help, me! I am at the point of death, but help me! And please Jesus help my Fucking Caravan!'

Alison thought they were all about to die, right there: at the sting of Apollyon's bee. Either that, or she would have to drive them all herself along the autoroute, without having had a single driving lesson. That day, God really *was* Dead if He ever Existed and Santa Maria sat rigid in the front passenger seat, clenching and unclenching her hands, with the side of her head pressed against the car window. Alison could not read the expression on her face. Eventually, as though the near-death incident had never occurred, they were on their way, in silence, for half a day until a site was found for lunch. The inconstant driving sallied on and, somehow, her father misjudged the gap between two trees and wedged the caravan fast. Alison laughed accidentally and caught the full force of her father's slap across her face. They were going nowhere. Her father started whimpering and crying; her mother still sat rigid, like she used to do when Terry dribbled while eating spotted dick.

'Go to the village. Do something, little cuss! You're not close to death like I am!' shrieked her father. A requiem played from the car radio. It was Fauré's.

The dying man had screeched both vague and dramatic instructions; commanding a not wholly sensible project for a seventeen-year-old girl in a crop top and miniskirt. But he had also made a reasonable point; she wasn't as close to death as he was, so off went Alison, trying to be big and bouncy, to do that *Hapless* thing, tripping over the tree roots and walking to what appeared to be a conurbation. Dad was, once again, shrieking about Jesus and picnickers were looking on.

She could see a blacksmith in a forge. He dropped his tools and swaggered over. The burly looking man was dripping with sweat.

'*Nous avons une grande problem, Monsieur! Voulez-vous aider des touristes en France?*'

It took a while to explain a caravan being stuck between two alders, but he followed into the wood with hacksaw and cut the caravan out by sawing off its double glazing. It wasn't a pretty sight. Alison's father still sat whimpering in the driver's seat but Santa Maria came out and offered some money.

'*Merci mais NON, madame. Peut-être votre fille?*' growled the blacksmith. And in English, 'But I will take your daughter?'

The letter R reverberated at the end of *daughterrr*; it sounded feral: rebarbatively sexual.

Alison dropped Hapless, said, 'Go away' to her and saw a chance to run towards the light. For a moment she wondered whether Santa Maria would settle on such a bargain and the two of them could carry on their sojourn alone. She thought about it herself; he looked a powerful enough man, with strong forearms and an apron with manly looking tools in its front pocket. Plus, he was Gallic and Samantha Stokes (the one whose mother carried on with creepy Mr Gibbs, who did wicker-work craft at school—and she whose parents had what was called a *porn collection*—starring each other—in their garden shed) had said French men were always extremely hot in bed. Staying in France at the forge would certainly get her out of A-levels and she wondered whether a really hefty and risky shag over an anvil would make her feel better. But the moment passed and ended with a Gallic shrug and a flick of a black apron.

Still whimpering and palpably at the point of death, Alison's father turned the key in the ignition. As they drove off, towing the very ragged-looking caravan with the blacksmith shuffling off into the distance, Alison felt the stone drop in the heart. She did not know, until adulthood, that not everyone's holidays were actually like this. But what she *did* know was that the leaden weights in her heart and somewhere around her solar plexus were despair.

There were, however, more and rather more consoling adventures with blacksmiths on that particular trip to France. Alison's father had eventually parked up without fatality or further use of hacksaws and they had headed off to the fête at Chinon in the Loire. Alison's parents wandered a while and then, with terminal cancer and failure of the mitral heart valves between them (which made them snappy and a bit breathless and caused her father to overreact to bees and autoroutes) they went back to sit in the car and listen to the World Service with a picnic of rice salad and *rillons de porc*, followed by a diazepam each. Alison was most definitely not allowed to talk. In the end Santa Maria said, 'Bugger off and go for a walk.' It didn't sound hopeful, but off went her daughter.

And *what* a walk. There was money enough for cheese, wine; for slabs of pork from the hog roast. Hot *so hot*. Walking for hours, for too long; sloughing off the trailing despair by ducking into alleys and small, dark crevices to explore between the tall houses. She knew Dad and Santa Maria would be furious and that she would hear no end of how selfish she had been, but it was said commonly enough. The slap in the face and a pinch she would take. Even the loss of a handful of hair (Santa Maria had a very good grip): a bargain struck.

Alison stood and watched a production of Molière's '*Tartuffe*' for a while and she felt a hand at her back. It was firm and strong, but she sensed that the caress of the thumb across the palm of her hand made it unlikely it belonged to a pickpocket. The hand drew her out away from the theatre crowd and she met its owner. He was broad-shouldered, verily covered in sweat and soot, bare-chested and wearing a black apron. It was Denis the Lusty Blacksmith. The man had followed her periodically during the hours; stalking her sweetly. He was fine of face and his eyes were dark and limpid.

He said, 'You are the most beautiful thing I have ever seen. I do not know how it is possible. Come with me. You are the chance of my life. And I am no *hypocrite*.'

And is a truth commonly observed, I think, that when a Frenchman speaks to us in English we want to fuck them: right here, right now. It's just one of those true things, like not being too *soignée* being sexy, or Napoleon writing to Josephine, '*Ne te lave pas, j'arrive*' knocking you out *en français* and sounding dim and grubby in English.

'What is your name?'

'It is…' She had to think for a moment, 'It is…just Alison.'

'Oh, my lovely Just Alison. Whirl and dance this way to me and away from this Molière! You are the chance of my life!'

If you had to look back and pick some stand-out moment, then I suppose this was one. It is possible that it was a cheap seduction, but we will choose to believe otherwise and not spoil the story of Denis, in the medieval streets, glistening with sweat, begrimed and holding some blacksmith's tongs, with which he gesticulated happily and wildly as if they were an extension of his hand. Ooof! *Hot*. Alison had no conception that someone might think she was beautiful and she walked through the streets with him, stopping for Calvados, cherries, to smoke. She saw his street-side forge, felt the fire; met his mother. He kissed her and time, as they say, stood still with a long and smoky kiss.

In fact, up came the poet Louis MacNeice to comment now: he liked France, too, and he whispered in her ear, 'This was a moment, Alison. Time was away, and in this moment, life was different. Go. Change. Run towards the light.'

But her stomach suddenly lurched. She had been out for hours.

'I have to go, but I will be back.'

'*Promis?* My Just Alison?'

At that moment, Alison was entirely convinced that she would just grab some things, her passport and run for it; back to him and *towards the light*. But when she got back to the car, her parents were asleep. Deliberating what to do, she looked at them and experienced a wash of tenderness that was not commonly felt. No-one ever said any smug guff at home about love or washes of tenderness. When a man told her he loved her once, she couldn't stomach the expression, so paused and said, 'Right, thanks. And quite. And indeed.' Moreover, Alison instinctively felt that those who were full of the lexis of love were not those to be relied on in a crisis because everyone who had ever told her they loved her had, in fact, fucked off in a crisis. But here it was: *the rush of love* for them. And so she got into the back seat and cried silently and painfully for an hour, missing her hot blacksmith. When her parents woke up, they said nothing to her. They just drove off, mute.

Alison never told anyone about this event, but it remained, for many years, peculiarly and inexplicably painful. He was a strong man who could have carried her through the streets. Or maybe we will say that he was just a cheap encounter. But I don't think so.

But oh how funny what the years draw to you, for years later, when Alison stood knee-high in monsoon water on a Kolkata street drinking *chai* with the boys on the stall, a kind looking man with deep brown eyes asked her for directions and later followed her to her hotel, rocked her in a hammock and read to her until she fell asleep. That was when she surrendered the memory of Denis the Lusty French Blacksmith to the past. You will meet Dixie Delicious later. And you will be rewarded for your trouble. Technically, we would have to wade through Artefact Nigel, the two troubled and coked-up Americans, the swinging Canadian, Professor Pobble, poet and academic, Tom the Brilliant Cellist who frowned like thunder and went away and Sardonic Steve. Well, actually, we're being economical: Alison didn't keep count. Nor did she actually realise she was having a relationship with some of them, until she went, 'Ohhhhh', courtesy of the crash course in self-awareness and interpersonal relations, as delivered by psychologists, Drs Crook and Hook in days with the Mental Health Recovery Squad. But then along came Albert, more incendiary than the forge of any blacksmith. How could a girl resist?

4

The mis-education of Alison

So let us tramp more through the forest of ardour later, and tell now of Alison's schooldays. There were a few things worth the re-telling, but these days are really about *The Books* and *The Ideas,* so forgive the story if we keep the distinctions between *Alma Maters* necessarily vague. How can it be that fourteen years of learning and the rest can give us so little to crystallise on the page? But let us try. For Alison—especially Alison wanting time and world to be herself (whatever that was) and not to spend it as Hapless Ally—the books performed vital functions, curing, as Larkin had it in 'A Study of Reading Habits', most things you might go through, but not school: school had to be endured. Nonetheless, the books were always a vital salve and it is impossible to describe these days without them.

Certain chapters in *The Wind in the Willows* had, we have heard, the function of creating home and hearth; Alison was not sated by the pastoral pleasures of 'The River Bank' (although the hamper sounded a fine thing), but the tramp through 'The Wild Wood' was read frequently because the place where Mole lay down to hide sounded like the crawl space where Alison communed with Frida. Looking back, all the favourite bits were the descriptions of safe havens, burrows and long corridors where Badger shuffled along with a candle and carpet slippers that were scuffed and very down at heel. Alison imagined herself in a tartan flannel dressing gown, rusticating happily by a fire in a sett in winter. She stepped gingerly through the descent to Mole End from the open road; the episode prompted by Mole sitting down, crying and giving way altogether to his emotions, because he scented home. Alison had no particular sense of how *that* would be (although the colour table and the crawl space in the wood did a pretty good job), but read and re-read significant chapters, ruminating on place and on the home and the welcoming hearth.

Alison grew up in a beautiful place, but a sense of safety and comfortable enclosure were best achieved through the pages of a book, so she turned to 'The Wild Wood' (knowing that Mole would escape its dangers in a hollow and with the aid of Ratty with a stout cudgel), the home of Mr Badger and the snowy journey through the fields in 'Dulce Domum'. The chapters on Toad and 'The Open Road' were best avoided because they contained a Fucking Caravan but there was one chapter which caused a shiver, without a clear understanding of its cause. It would make her cry and feel helpless and lonely as a child and yet she wanted to read it again and again: the world of our subject was never tidy in the way that the world of, say, Heroic Alice might have been (although, of course as adults we discover we never can tell: for the glossiest girl might be inwardly crying, 'Help me! My bespoke underwear is holding up my soul!'). Alison's world, with its itchy palm and its *sufferance* was messy and confusing and caused headaches and head banging. And so she would run for places: for dug outs or soft meadows, whether in real life or in books.

Once, after lingering on stories from *The Wind in the Willows*, Alison canvassed her classmates on their opinions of the book and thus it was that a peculiarity arose: none of them remembered a particular chapter—and this caused her to wonder whether it had been imagined in a dream by day or night: 'The Piper at the Gates of Dawn.' It wasn't the notion of the child otter having wandered off, held safe by the great creature, the friend and helper, and found again by his father, but rather that it is about mystery: of something deeply felt but, faintly, inchoately understood.

On hearing the pipes of Pan, Ratty knows he has found the *place of my song dream* and when the moment is passed Mole, '...stood still for a moment, held in thought. As one wakened suddenly from a beautiful dream, who struggles to recall it, and can recapture nothing but a dim sense of the beauty of it, the beauty! Till that, too, fades away in its turn, and the dreamer bitterly accepts the hard cold waking and all its penalties.'

To Alison, it was like Caliban who 'cried to dream again.'

She certainly understood *cold waking*—had many nights of that, frightened, alone and convinced of appalling sin, wetting the bed in her fear. *Penalties* were part of life; sporadically most of life, and definitely the consequence of happiness, as she had instinctively known that day in the orchard, caressed momentarily by deferential celandines and the warm threads of breeze. Alison would yearn to find this place and its feeling, of sadness, but also of inscrutability and throbbing, growing faith. And so into the nearby landscape, she would run, early and before anyone noticed, to the fields and the weir. Bounding out so early, unusually chipper and comical, she might have been Hapless Ally, trying hard for buoyancy and comedy. But she wasn't: she was just Alison and she was looking for something only she could see. Strictly speaking, running out early was not allowed, but it was worth the gamble. Yet would she ever find the kindness of a great creature there? Of a great *thing*? Hope almost exhausted, she would lie down in the wet grass and weep there, knowing that the land retained a memory, sweet and sad and buried, of something extraordinary there in the sods, by the pounding of the water. One day. O*ne* day.

And so we turn from a tear falling on the grass, to a funny little girl at school. There, everybody was reading *Charlie and the Chocolate Factory* and acting out scenes from it; they were crazy about it. It didn't do so much for her. For Alison, the book added little to her internal inscape but was more use for the caricature you created to cope: she thought of the nasty, elegant little ballet girls as resembling spoilt, demanding Veruca Salts. Augustus Gloop was worryingly like Terry in aspect; Augustus just drank from the river of molten chocolate rather than imbibing of the multitudinous spotted dick, tripe and onions and any kind of pie and probably didn't watch 'Countdown' in a tropically-heated house on Tyneside. Alison hoped that if she were one of the children, she'd be Charlie Bucket, a nice kind of kid—and she would have liked to own a grandparent called Joe. Alison was not unfamiliar with the concept of relatives who never got out of bed (although Mad but Nice Andrea tended to wear her duffel coat in bed, not pyjamas), but for her it would have to be Frida as your golden ticket companion. Or Helen, before Cyclamen Terrace, the rain and the short interim before the brain tumour and bonkers, with the smell of the cabbage wafting up the stairs, but she was probably being a bit busy having affairs and smoking in the cool way; sashaying in her knock-off Chanel suits and cute pillar box hats. Adventures that never lasted and which they never shared. Alison didn't know yet that the bequeathed Albert Camus was the gift that delivered.

Now, while the peppermint grass in Willy Wonka's factory was one to remember as you plucked a blade and sucked, for her it was a swig of cider in *Fantastic Mr. Fox* that provided the correct dosing of comfortable and cosy. Something about the illustrations of the fox's lair, with the table of plenty set out; something about the way Mr and Mrs Fox were clearly crazy about one another in a truly foxy sort of way struck a note with her. A note that spoke of hope and possibility. Another from this canon, *Danny the Champion of the World*, might be a book for Alison to read securely now in adulthood and as a mother herself, but as a child the fine evocation of the joy between father and son was unreadable; the book scratched and itched, however much you liked the concept of pheasants being dosed with medicated raisins. Moreover, they lived in a caravan. And we know about them. Also, Alison's father had remarked that Roald Dahl was known to have disliked children, which placed him on the same dais as Santa Maria and Alison's father and she could never get past the first bit of *James and the Giant Peach*; not just because of the ghastly, mutually adoring aunts, but because of the prefatory blunt description of death. Death, in Alison's consciousness, was always a-knocking at the door. In books she wanted feasts, cosy spaces, secret gardens with high red walls and gnarled trees; she wanted safe dark rooms with tall drapes and haven hedgerows of red campion and honeysuckle. She wanted all that and to be warm, silent and extremely small. She did not care for a mauling, trampling or skewering of the parent kind. She could get that at home, with plenty of gore—particularly over tea at her grandfather's house. So what was needed was the comforting detail of 'Concerning Hobbits' in *The Lord of the Rings* (a winter book), or the straggling but lovely roses of *The Secret Garden* (a book to be read in bed, but only when it rained—and in the autumn).

Back at The Hill (thus interrupting the vital reading programme) Restless Rhonda, Alison's cousin, had died of mysterious causes while apparently potting on in the shed and there ensued much shuffling and whispering about the dark, old house with the creaky gate and the old plum tree that had been struck again by lightning; at the funeral, no-one cried, but raised their waxy faces to the altar beyond the waxy face in the open coffin and sang the hymns quietly through cold, pinched lips. And in The Place beyond the Sea (which is to say a corner of South West Wales), cousin Lewis had died by his own hand, leaving his mother, Mfanwy, turned inward and mute for decades, looking one way across the old churchyard where her son lay and the other across the sea to the islands. The Sound was a place where Alison loved to be on the boat looking at the whiskered seals, but it became tinged with the melancholy of a mother, looking out across the water and thinking of her dead son; local people referred her to her as 'Muffled Mfanwy' as her voice never came out properly again—for she was stifled by an inexpressible sorrow. Then Maternal Grandma turned her face to the wall and Santa Maria responded with an angry bitterness: there was a late phone call and she said, 'I am going to watch my mother die.'

It sounded like a play at the theatre; like Beckett: Theatre of the Absurd. Alison hadn't the faintest idea how to comfort her mother; her carapace was hard and shiny and so hugs would slide off. Anyway, Alison didn't really know about hugging; she saw her relatives extend their hands and brush an arm stiffly with fingertips, looking into the middle distance. That must have been their hug. But she saw other people do something different. Even kiss. To Alison, a kiss was what happened before a man fucked you and what, once, Helen planted on her forehead, all puffed up with tumour and morphine in bed.

It had gone like this: 'Love you, my little one. It could have been so good, you and me.'

'Please don't die, Auntie Helen: what will I do without you?'

'You will "lie down",' said Helen, between pops of clear breath, ' "where all the ladders start/In the foul rag and bone shop of the heart". It's Yeats, you know. You remember?'

'I know, Auntie; he's on our bookshelf, although we haven't talked to one another yet.'

'There will be time, my darling.'

'It doesn't sound very good, though. The foul rag and bone shop bit—and in the heart, too.'

'*Au contraire*, my little one. It is where you will begin. Where you *must* begin. And you will survive and be happy.'

'I don't know if I can do either of those things.'

'*But you can.* And take the Camus from the shelf before it's chucked in the skip when I've shuffled off. Terry doesn't read French and I wonder—but I love him; *I do love him,* pet—whether he thinks the examined life is one best avoided. Don't tell anyone I said that. I've got to stay at Cyclamen Terrace now, so you take Albert. Look: isn't he handsome, too? Maybe he can look after you now?'

Helen *knew*. She knew everything about Alison. And she gave her the knowing look: the one which said, 'You will become *the girl who did.*'

'One day,' thought Alison, 'perhaps I can begin and do what she described.'

Helen kissed her.

'What did you just do? What was that thing?'

'I kissed you. Because I love you. It's what we do.'

Home was silent. No kisses. No ladders. For reasons that weren't explained, Alison was not allowed to attend Maternal Grandma's funeral. That being so, the girl, true to form, wondered if she was implicated in her grandmother's death and that was why she should not attend the funeral. It was frightening and shaming and Santa Maria spat angry tears when her daughter tried to help.

'I want to make you feel better. And I thought, if Muffled Mfanwy was at the funeral, I could help her feel better too.'

'The best thing for me is to be nowhere near you. I am grieving for my mother. Go away, you little fuck-wit. Go to your crawl space.'

Alison shook and felt cold and sick.

'You, you...know about the crawl space?'

'We know everything and if you're not careful, we will cut it all down.'

'Did I...did I hurt Grandma?'

'Probably. How could you do otherwise?'

Thus it was that Alison turned to her *Important Acquaintance* with Mary Anning and her treasures: because she felt she couldn't be implicated in anything there and quite liked digging things up. And who could she hurt on the beach at Lyme Regis?

Mary Anning was the carpenter's daughter from Lyme

Regis, she who collected many fine fossil specimens and found the first ichthyosaur. Acquaintances now, but the friendship was coming along, although Alison was always in the way on the beach. There were some hitches, though: Mary had a cunning little Jack Russell called Tray and Alison hated him for his perspicacity. When Mary wasn't looking, Tray became a leering little black dog who said, like the itchy scratchy sometime thought in the palm, 'Better watch out. It's going to get you Alison. Or are you Hapless Ally? Which is you? Which is better? Wait and see. Woof ha ha woof!'

Alison was desperately clumsy and could do a lot of damage when Mary was cleaning off major specimens with all her little tools and brushes, so there were lovers' tiffs and consigning to storerooms to cause less damage. But Mary behaved as if she were fond of her and when Alison closed her eyes, she would imagine that she and Mary were walking along the Jurassic coast, towards Golden Cap or Black Ven. Mary would tell off her foolish friend for knocking over the 'curies', the abbreviation Mary gave to the *curiosities,* the fossils she collected.

'No not like *thaaaat* (in her gentle and flavourful Dorset accent), you are just hapless—and go gently through Father's shop. Step away before 'tis broken.'

There were some fine things, tumbled onto the floor by her clumsy friend. Things that, 'Ah! Things that could have reached a pretty penny with the folk in London, if you hadn't have been and knocked them on the floor. Ah! Anyone ever told you were haaapless, Alison?'

Well, that was ironic.

Mary had extraordinary faith in herself. She didn't care whether other people were interested or not; she was just led by her eye along the beach, knowing what was worth the collect and what was just *beef*. She told Alison that her vigorous way had been formed by—a story many folk in Lyme Regis knew—being hit by lightning as an infant. She had been under a tree and three women with her had been struck dead, while the infant Mary survived, thrived and bloomed. Alison watched her in awe and thought that, if *she* were struck by lightning, it would be more as it was in the Stevie Smith poem, where a girl contemplates how it would be nice to get hit by lightning and killed while she was just walking across a field, not that anyone would be bothered. Alison, struck, would be fried and dead, or all raggedy and alive and Santa Maria going, 'What have you done now, you little maggot? Haven't I been punished enough?'

Mary Anning was the first and last person Alison could imagine was pretty in a grubby bonnet, stained by the blue lias—and a dirty apron over the plainest of grey dresses. And her little dog, Tray, skipped joyfully behind her, but growled, skulked and strolled behind Alison, when Mary bent suddenly to dig. Mary was light on her feet and she had the great love of her father. There were men, important men, who loved her too, later. Or at least that was the gossip Alison would hear, whispered in the sea breeze on the Jurassic Coast. She thought she wanted to have Mary's clear and unwavering gaze, but instead she fell over the rocks and picked up the wrong stones. And, in the end, Mary dumped her for the more sophisticated Miss Philpot and that was that.

She shouted as Alison left the workshop, jars tumbling behind her, 'You really are haaaaapless. Ha ha ha! Take thaaaat! Duck now: 'tis a bezoar!'

Mary had thrown a bezoar—a coprolite—at her: fossilised dinosaur shit. Another face and voice to mock.

Her mother had bought her the book and now quoted Charles Dickens on Mary Anning to her, 'Look: here's something that could never apply to you, hahaha: "The carpenter's daughter has won a name for herself and has deserved to win it." Heroic Alice or Mary Anning you will never be.'

Alison knew that this was a fair observation, but it felt pointed and, useless palaeontologist that she was and would ever surely be, the quotation stung. Now, on the bedroom shelf, Mary was laughing at her throatily from within the book and her laughter had been joined by the more sedate chuckle of Miss Philpot and the laughing, goading raised eyebrow of Santa Maria. *Bitches.*

'I wish I had a coprolite to throw! Santa Maria's right!'

After this humiliation, Alison put the book *Mary Anning's Treasures* to the back of the shelf, behind the Bible full of God who was Dead if He ever Existed and went back to spending more time with Frida in the crawl space, while it lasted. Frida said, 'Oh ya, fossils and mud. Not good. I'd like to see her survive a Swedish winter. Bonnets and aprons? Not *not* hot. How about ice skating with me? Björn could meet us. He's still mad for you and has written 'Fernando' in your honour. You could borrow my fur muff, if you like. *Muffs are hot!*'

In addition to the friendships, there were many love affairs over the years. Sunday afternoons, even as a child, would find Alison's mouth full of Porphyro's marvellous jellies and fruits from 'The Eve of St. Agnes'. For her, the identification of the author was a little like that of Pip at the beginning of *Great Expectations,* deciphering what his parents might have looked like from the graphology of the stones. Except Alison decided who and what John Keats was from the beautiful ochre leather-covered book, its spine and title pages limned with fulsome gold. She had a sense of who he was even before she ventured inside and saw pages featuring the most winsome picture of John Keats, with a frontispiece of autumn fruits, putti, roses and waving grasses. The font was beautifully rounded and the words *Keats Poetical Works* looked like they might be edible. Certainly, Keats didn't look as if he could build a wall or do anything really manly, but he was her first blueprint of what a sensitive man might look like and possibly the first man she fell in love with, aged ten. Clearly, Alison's attachment to John Keats (or 'JK' as she liked to call him) was not what you might call a normal first crush. The shirt was loose at the neck, white and flowing, and the eyes were intense and sad. There was absolutely no doubt he would have understood her, unlike her actual boyfriend Stuart, in school, who touched her chest under a table in the school library and said, 'Look your boobies are developing.' JK would never have stooped to that. He would have been too embarrassed and tried euphemism; harked to The Ancients. But Stuart moved to Barnsley and she went back to lounging about with Keats and never returned

Stuart's letters. He kept writing, 'I love you' and, 'I bet you've got big boobies now' and enclosed some black jacks and a rainbow chew. But what did *he* know about Greece, urns, autumn, plants or men in closets with spectacular feasts while a soft amethyst light was gently falling on their beloved's breast? (Or boobie?) But JK wrote, 'I wish that I were alone and in your arms or that a thunderbolt would strike me.'

Lines were declaimed with the stroke of a nascent breast and a hot cheek. They did well to stay hidden while, on the other side of the sofa, Alison's parents scowled their way through 'Songs of Praise'.

'Look, dear! Those fuck-wits are miming. Obviously *miming!*'

Keats stayed with Alison for some years; her Sunday afternoon love affair, there by the bookcase, on the scratchy carpet behind the sofa. Sometimes poor old JK had to stay entirely in the book because he had something called consumption and needed his rest and some wet cloths over his face, but that was part of the romance. Mind you, he did get a bit demanding, asking her where she had been, could she alter lines in her letters to him—which she wrote when she was away in The Fucking Caravan—here and there so they were warmer and kinder and she got cross once or twice and told him she wasn't going to fanny around with that sort of thing. He would cough and his pupils would dilate spectacularly and tragically and she would assent to his requests. Much later on, however, Keats was moved to the background as someone altogether more manly stepped forward. Not for this *homme* a lie down in the afternoon, but a manly growl after lunch, some Gitanes and a Marc. Step forward Albert Camus and also the story of becoming an existentialist on a campsite. Not Albert; oh no, no, no: he was far too cool to be seen in a Fucking Caravan. It was Alison, trying to translate the world into something that made sense.

We have already shared fateful tales of The Fucking Caravan, of the entrapment between two alder trees and, on the same trip, tales of two blacksmiths. However, on that same 'holiday', parked up by the Seine and sitting under the willows for days (with her parents somewhere else; they didn't say) Alison began a roaring and extraordinary affair with Camus. It was a reading summer, between the two sixth form years. All around was the sense that people were dropping like flies and the deaths of Dad and Santa Maria must surely be imminent; she just hoped, ever practical, they didn't happen when the two were out in the car, or maybe driving on to the cross-channel ferry, with everyone hooting furiously behind them. But the reading: for days on end by the river: Sartre's *Nausea*, Genet's *The Thief*, and, best of all, Camus's *The Plague*, *The Fall*, *The Outsider* and *Selected Essays and Notebooks*. Also, at speed on the journey home, Simone de Beauvoir's *The Force of Circumstance* and, cheerily, *A Very Easy Death*. When she got home, Alison devoured Gide's *Straight is the Gate* and *Fruits of the Earth*: 'Nathaniel—I will teach you fervour!' Fervour: Holy Fuck—*what was fervour?* What was lust for life? Were those things somewhere in the unknowable distance, just visible beyond the bacon grease of The Fucking Caravan? She was intoxicated: dislocated entirely from her surroundings. The dislocation did not provide a new or unfamiliar sensation, but *this* kind of dislocation was one in which she was on fire and in splendid company.

'Come. Come away with me now. Tonight,' said Albert Camus.

Now, one could dwell on the literary qualities of Sartre and Simone de Beauvoir, but the most impressive thing for an adolescent Alison (she whose constant companions to date had been imaginary Swedes in a crawl space) was the sense she gained of Sartre and de Beauvoir's love affair; that they wrote and argued and shared and, of course, smoked (like Helen) in the cool way. And when de Beauvoir wrote about her love affair with Nelson Algren—not to mention sharing bricks (*bricks: Ooh la la!*) of raspberry ice cream with him—Alison had a peculiar light-headed and heavy-hearted sensation. It was, we would have to say, the first knowledge of the erotic. And it hurt, because it didn't exist in any part of the real world, where there was just getting off and, for some girls, an early, clumsy, grasping fuck. When Simone de Beauvoir wrote of their 'contingent lovers'; of love affairs, known about by both but clearly allowable and part of happen-stance rather than a dedication for a lifetime, it sounded both painful and delicious. How entirely entrancing for the teenage Alison that de Beauvoir and Sartre wrote and expressed an intensely creative life to one another. This was something Alison could never quite get out of her head. And when she tried and failed to engage something which might look like it, the stone dropped in her heart and she was scared to open her hand in case the frightening thought was there, pressed into the palm, waiting to open. And she was scared of being herself: *Just Alison* (as Denis the Lusty Blacksmith had it), while in her heart remained the appalling leaden feeling and the acute sense of being separate; eldritch-girl, possibly a killer; not inclined to the magazines and spontaneity of her female peers: missing the point always. *Wrong* and *Weird Kid*. She willed herself to live on in a way that was meaningful and hoped that she would find people to discuss these feelings with; that she could know someone who understood about absurdity, existence precedes essence or the frightening experience Sartre's Roquentin has when, in *Nausea,* he touches a door handle and comes face to face with jarring, sickening anguish: that anguish lived alongside Alison permanently. At five, it had started somewhere after Saturday morning cartoons, as the day unfurled; at sixteen it began after Weetabix and before the first application of lip-gloss.

'This I understand: it is when the scenery collapses,' said Camus.

He made it sound exciting in his low tone. But it wasn't in real terms: at least, *not yet*; instead, it was terrifying and yet Alison had a timorous sense that from that terror came only a beginning. That definitely made sense. Good God: intellectual heat; the erotic in its most subtle form; a notion of how to live with hope, when God quite clearly does not exist and we must travel to the frontiers of our anxiety to understand where to start. Alison was not asking much in a man, then.

Ah—but one ready day along came Albert, ready for action. If you have ever read his peculiar, flat, sparkling, cold story of Meursault in *The Outsider*, then there is little to express. But if not, imagine a wandering, solitary individual, not inclined or feeling the pressure to act as expected. Not cruel, but mercenary because appetitive; plainly erotic in responding to his needs as and when they push forward, articulate of who and what he is and yet without what would feel like morality to us. He did not cry when his mother died; he shot a man on the beach and did not express regret, only annoyance. For the teenage girl, it hit a nerve. The description Camus had of his protagonist as a solitary and wandering individual; as somebody entirely alone and on the edges of society, now, *that* was the truest description of her to date. It was—and there is no other way to say this—a first orgasm. Not only with the plainness of the character and Camus's prose, which Alison gamely attempted in both French and English, but also because of the man. Let us describe him. Alison had to get over Meursault first, a man both in love with the world and separate from it. Camus told her of how his protagonist was inspired by a stubborn passion, for the absolute and for truth. His truth remained a negative truth, but it had its own beauty and without it there could be no adroit comprehension of ourselves and of the world; no self-containment. Meursault's life was that of a foreigner—a stranger—to the society in which he lived, and he wandered about on the fringe, in the shadows of others' lives: plain, but deeply sensual. Such descriptions made Meursault enormously attractive to Alison and made her fall more for the man who wrote him into being. Such a telling of the outsider, the wandering foreigner living and breathing a negative truth, pierced and had a difficult heat for her because, of course, that was Alison. We could say she was Weird Kid—plenty did and probably still do—but *L'Etrangère* would sound altogether more arousing, non?

Alison had photocopied a picture of Camus: it was of him, apparently sitting on a rather lopsided sofa, and leaning forward with his hands tensed, his mouth slightly open, his eyebrows raised and his trousers showing his socks as he inclined towards a co-combatant to advance his argument. He was so fabulously French; so fabulously exotic because he came from Algeria, that he carried off the sock thing with élan; socks were not normally a detail of erotic piquancy. Camus might have been describing how brilliant it was that William Faulkner had pulled off the language of high tragedy; that a man from Mississippi could find language that was simple enough to be our own and lofty enough to be tragic. Or perhaps he was dictating something for the Resistance magazine, 'Combat', of which he was the Editor in Chief. But, to a teenage girl, under his spell, he was also evincing arguments for 'Come away with me.'

And, 'Let me show you.'

Or, 'Let me show you how to live in the face of despair. Sit on my knee and we will begin.'

And, occasionally, when the Oran sun roused his temper, 'Come here now. Stand against this wall. *I will take you.*'

Was this what Helen had meant, in gifting Alison the Camus as she lay on her Cyclamen Terrace deathbed? It was a jolly long way from a few drunken fumbles in the dark when *they*—the *boy-kind*—mistook her for someone else.

Albert's cadences were delicious: he was declaiming phrases of profound, shattering erotic power to Alison's ear. And he had enough style to be vulgar, if he wanted. Camus had a history of manly pursuits, too: goalie for a prominent Algiers football team; a fine swimmer and athlete. She had a sense of his being a consummate *man*. Funny; brave; a demon in the bedroom—if you ever got that far, because what are walls, floors and furniture for? And, unlike JK, he could have built a wall or changed a tyre. On the occasions when Alison went to other girls' bedrooms, she saw they had pictures of The Cure, or Bono, when he was ragged, young and angry. *She*, meanwhile, had a picture of Albert Camus next to her desk. People said, 'Who's that?' and she said, 'My godfather.' The notion felt entirely, naughtily fitting, for the Camus books, *en français*, that Alison possessed had been bequeathed to her, as you learned earlier, by her godmother Helen, studying Camus at The Sorbonne. Perhaps Helen had been similarly intoxicated (which made the Terry the Fat Controller, the unexamined life, Friday-pie thing even more depressing). So the honorific chimed as fitting. Plus it felt like Albert leaned over Alison in a proprietary and manly style. *L'Etranger* was inscribed with the words '*Helen Griffiths, Paris, le 19 Janviér 1962*' and Alison had always hoped that, in leaving France for Terry, Mammy's pie and a new life in Tyneside, Helen was able to say, like Camus's protagonist at the point of death, that she knew she had been happy.

She hoped it was like this for Helen especially when the morphine gave her respite from pain and the unexamined life downstairs, punctuated by the sickening puffs of air freshener from the Cyclamen Terrace plug-ins.

Now, in all their years together it never mattered to Alison that Camus had been dead ten years before she was born: he was there on her wall now.

Godfather. Most louche, brilliant, gorgeous godfather.

She saw in his *Notebooks* that he wrote, 'I loved my mother with despair. I have always loved her with despair.' Albert even understood the paradox of *that*! It was exactly how she felt about Santa Maria. And by God (although He was Dead if He ever Existed) Albert was brave: he would stand in the face of despair and say that now he was free.

Ah, the growingupsexthing. Alison had hopeless expectations, really, for while Camus smouldered away behind her closed eyes, real life was, shall we say, more a damp inconsequential thing than a smoulder. There was Johnny in the barn. Always, 'Let's go to the barn,' a bunk up against a bale: no use *there* expecting conversations about Proust. She asked him about books and he said, 'Why would anyone want to read boring books?' But in school, there was an important dalliance with D.H. Lawrence. It was *Sons and Lovers* and she remembered mostly Paul Morel's loving: not the bit which was like a communion (with Miriam) but the bit which was 'too near a path' with rather racier Clara. The evocation of Paul's mother, however, as he drifts back to her—and drifts to his own future death (as Lawrence himself had it in his notes on the text), now *that* was a theme best avoided during these delicate years. Besides which, no-one would have got it because at that time boys just wanted to get you drunk and feel you up in a dark room when the parents are away. Only in reality, they were feeling up someone else. Like Heroic Alice. *Oh yeah*: Heroic was still around; jiggly tits, cool-thriving and diving and looking on her hapless (again, ironic, though *note lower case*) counterpart with scorn. She had the best clothes and hair; told the kind of jokes boys liked. When she moved upstairs, the party moved with her, while Alison stood downstairs thinking about existentialism and, 'I'm a misfit and nobody fancies me.' Alison was definitely *Weird Kid*. Good job she had Albert.

Not long after, Alison discovered Sylvia Plath: now *there* was someone with an embolus of fear and an itchy, scratchy little thought in the palm. Alison would act out scenarios of meeting Ted, based on the diaries she had read; they would meet, drunk and—again—smouldering (she liked smouldering) at each other at a party and she would bite his cheek. The room would hum harder and all was in a brandy glass whirl; the blood ran down Ted's face and along Sylvia's arm. *And oh Lordy: the poetry and the sex.* In class, the girls would say, 'Uggh! She is mental.'

But Alison would think, 'Sylvia: oh my God, you're gorgeous! Look at you, rocking your fifties swimsuit, your twin-set and pillbox hat. But you put your head in the oven and I am so so sorry. You know, I head bang and cut myself and think all kinds of dangerous things. Your father might be full fathom five, but my parents? Well, they are pillars of the community. We are a middle class family and that, Sylvia, is how they get away with it. Everyone's looking at me Sylvia: they're saying they know what I'm like and that's why my parents are dying. You say you tried to rock shut? Well so did I: when I was fourteen I took a big dose of paracetamol and I tried so hard to die and come up through clear water as someone else. It's crazy, isn't it? I even made a big mug of tea to go with it and lay down with no note. I told Santa Maria; didn't want her to find me, but she said, "Oh well that's just typical of you, you little bitch." I never went to hospital, but I survived. I was always sore—but I survived. And it was so so selfish. I'm sorry that you lost Otto so young and that your mum didn't understand you and that life went wrong with your Ted and that you ended up getting a bit obsessed with bees and water. The day you died, February the eleventh? I will always remember you...And I think you were a fucking genius.'

Alison reflected that Sylvia was the new Frida. She certainly had some unusual imaginary friends. Frida had been stylish, cheeky and coolly Nordic; she had always known how to distract. Sylvia was a bit trickier: she wrote in a frenzy, declaimed that she was a genius of a poet and made jam in between times. Her diaries and texts were full of compelling and weird images—mirrors, bees, foot lampshades, candlesticks, panzer man, eating men like air, Hiroshima ash, more jam making. She was both whore and domestic goddess. She was a roarer of a girl in an immaculate twin-set;

at once a plain, resourceful woman and, as Alison's classmates had it, *mental*. This wasn't going to be tidy—plus Frida wafted about Sweden, had a house in the woods, did a bit of painting; was calm and quite the yoga buff. Plath was unutterably, horribly, by her own hand dead in the gas oven and poor handsome Ted was getting a rough time at the hands of the Plath acolytes. But Sylvia had the uncanny ability to put into words some *thing*; some concept or anxiety that Alison was trying to give shape and form so that it was less frightening; in this case, the words with the tireless hoof taps that meet you on the road years later.

'Oh,' said Alison, 'the words. How they pierced and how they pierce today still. I wish that I had a way of muffling the words when it hurts me to hear them…But they're indefatigable! Always.'

Alison dabbled in Beckett too: *Waiting for Godot* needed to bide its time, but *Happy Days*—Winnie buried up to her waist in a mound of scorched earth in the first act of the play and her neck in the second half? We were getting somewhere.

Once, in those days, a boy came up to her in a pub and said, 'You're weird. You dress weird. You've got crazy hair and a big nose. You're really fucking ugly. Heroic Alice said you were!'

There was a crowd looking on; no-one said anything either to disagree or agree, so she was trying hard to think of Denis the Lusty Blacksmith seeing them off with his tongs. Or, 'What would Albert Camus do?' Of course, he would laugh, in a hot, derisive, Gallic way and the youths would scatter like thistledown, insubstantial in the presence of *A Man*. It didn't work this time: Alison couldn't summon him up for circumstance pressed down too hard; she couldn't even summon up the alter ego to laugh, 'Look here's Hapless: the better part of me. You'll like *her*.'

And where was Hapless when you needed her? Somehow, she couldn't be called up to adhere. Alison thought only that she was Winnie, in the second part of *Happy Days*, except that, unlike the brave and bellicose Winnie, the only word Alison could say to the boy and the crowd was, 'Sorry', then leave to sit down and punch and scratch herself with Hapless Ally, who had now sauntered in, apparently quite independently, and was energetically egging her on. Alison realised with a horrible prickly jolt that the latter appeared to be developing a cheerful autonomy: popping out to do things separately.

'It is this way that madness lies?' asked Alison.

'Oh yes. And Boo!' sneered Hapless, now skipping off with a popular boy who thought her lovely. She had that familiar, 'I'm about to get off with someone, but how about you?' look. The one that curled about the lips of *the girls that could.*

Absurd.

After this painful and pivotal incident, Alison considered whether a relationship with divas might be more germane: Dolly Parton and Shirley Bassey—heroes to this very day. Dolly and Shirley will meet you again, later. They are gently competitive these two: you'd love them for it. Va va voom!

Now, in the growingupdays there were days which, at the time, gave the promise that they were eternal: these were the Cambridge days. But the thing with the dreaming spires and ivory towers is that there are untidy people under the spires and in the towers. There are archives of beautiful things; there are, indeed, dreams and the reveries that come with absorption in something that is brilliant. But there are also desultory cackles and fingers that point: it is like life and it is not one thing. Alison always struggled with the question, 'Did you enjoy university?' because the answer would have taken half a day: '…well, yes and no and story and anecdote and dusty shelves and accidentally living in the seventeenth century so I wasn't safe crossing the road and oh—the clever folk and the light on mossy Cambridge stones and college bells at dusk and *exeats* and climbing over Magdalene Gate at three a.m. and suddenly Dad (hereafter *Vaguely Dead Dad*) was dead on the bathroom floor at home—and Santa Maria was blaming me—and bedders and porters and dinner in hall…and of course some days I unravelled…'

Besides, she had a relationship with three universities in the end because of the ill-advised research projects that came in later days. There were Cambridge, Oxford and another fine institution that we must leave unnamed for reasons of its name being too painful to write or say aloud and because it was shit. Life in university days would have been so much easier if not befuddled by roads less taken and kerfuffle and, well, very funny turns. The kind of thing where you hear the beautiful chapel bell ring: it is autumn and dusk. Outside the city the birds fly low over the fens; there is a faint mist over The Backs. It is fine indeed, but Alison would hear the mellow tone of the bell and in a second it would be alive and mocking, pulsing and frightening—as the stones of the old paths rose up to hit her face and she thought for a moment of the story called 'The Yellow Wallpaper', by Charlotte Perkins Gilman, where madness falls to rise as the patterns on the wallpaper animate and quietly terrify their watcher. In those times, it felt like there was another figure, watching her from rooms on the first floor: it was Hapless Ally again, beginning once more to detach more confidently: doing her own thing and laughing at her host. When you are not wholly well, the very ground you walk on can do that too, chanting mockery and perhaps spitting venom. And all around, the mists and mellow fruitfulness abound: but not for you; no, *not for you.* You don't know then that things can be different. Alison didn't know it for a very long time.

Books and more books were eaten up at speed as she came face to face with her extraordinary ignorance and the more she read the less she came to realise she knew. There were Latin and Greek to try and understand; the whole canon of literature before the seventeenth century, as the mis-education to date had not even touched on it. Alison had spent a fevered summer in a static caravan (oh the irony) in Pembrokeshire stuffing her face with books when she saw the course contents for the first year. In tea breaks, Camus would visit to discuss the reading; on walks, he would pull her by the hair and bite her lower lip; taking her into a sea cave, when 'Time was away' and when it was, happily, somewhere else. Sometimes, boy-Dylan Thomas was on the beach, on holiday from Carmarthenshire, but still dipping his hand in the fish-frozen sea and Albert would say, 'Oof—he has potential. He is not afraid of *paroles*. Now that is a man I could *tangle* with.'

Alison countered with, 'Where were you Albert, when the boy shrieked of my ugliness in the pub? When Hapless Ally joined in? You're my godfather and you're supposed to be there.'

'I was in the desert. I went away from Oran to think and took only dates and anise.'

Existence precedes essence could be a right selfish bastard if it so pleased.

Such sojourns aside, and alone again in the caravan, there had been a solo introduction to Chaucer, Langland, and The Gawain Poet—a desperate and busy rush to fill in some gaps. For the first time Alison read Arnold (although she had heard it declaimed by Grandfather at The Hill) and Tennyson and felt a wild urge to get started and also the fear that she did not know very much. She didn't. And yet the world inside her head was the only world she fully inhabited, because there had lived Frida, JK, Mary Anning and Albert. And those days were heady and frightening. They were a helter skelter rush from her parents dropping her off and sighing at the pretty view of the punts on the Cam, a sudden collapse by her father, groaning on to her bed in his endgame, Santa Maria's admiration of everybody else and then suddenly being alone. Alison felt that she must make a life there while, at home, everything was dying. There was nothing for it but to buy a packet of cigarettes and steel herself to it. Start on the rituals:

turn around four times, walk three paces, recite the first lines of *The Secret Garden* four times. And do it all quickly.

Indeed, Cambridge looked to her a forever place, although she must also have known that this was not possible. Alison felt helpless in the face of a crush on Germaine Greer: she had never seen this kind of confidence before; plus she had humour and was most definitely clever-hot. The historian David Starkey would visit: a severe, surprisingly funny and brilliant uncle—before he became media Don and everyone started being nasty to him on Twitter *#inthequietdaysbeforesocialmedia*. Upstairs in Divinity College sat Doctor Llewelyn, who always showed the students at his own college the exam papers the night before they sat them, although Alison rather gathered that it might not even have been all of them, but just the acolytes with whom he shared flagons of gin and possibly a biscuit. He made good tea, though; his cleverness was incendiary; he once cried while reading Dante's *Inferno* in lectures and introduced students (or perhaps the shiny happy students, who were everyone but Alison, and who already knew of such) to Walt Whitman, William Empson, and counting with utter concentration in the observance of rhyme and rhythm. Alison was terrified of him, though: his intelligence laid her bare, both Alison and Hapless; both suffering from a poor education and, not, apparently, the intellect to set that right. Alison would sink, on Friday afternoons, into the big armchair in Dr Rabbithole's parlour because he gave the impression that he was sympathetic to Weird Kid: he listened intently, offered sherry (while she noted how disarmingly strong his wrists looked, as he poured) and once said, shortly before finals, 'You're brilliant but, for the first time you're lucid: you must be scared.'

That was the picture in other rooms and across other quads, 'You're clever but we can't disentangle what you are saying or who you are! There are no signposts.'

'Signposts? Ha! How do you have signposts when the scenery has collapsed: there are no real landmarks: it's just a heap of detritus, now.'

Albert Camus on the wall kept a watch on proceedings, Godfather with her real-time own father very much having played his endgame after screaming all night. And Alison's night was not always very pretty, with its clangings and jungle sounds and screeches. Albert could not save her from it: probably, he thought she had to feel the despair to be free.

Her night said, in resonant voice, over the low tones of Albert, 'I am you. I have no signposts. My essays have no signposts. They are all laughing at me. *At you.* Dante is consigning me to the lowest rung; Whitman is telling me to stay away from his *Leaves of Grass*; not to "loose the stop from your throat" but to keep it in there: not to speak.'

In her dream, the poets looked at each other, looked at her and looked at each other again, the corners of their mouths contracting into a sneer. Santa Maria stood behind them. Virgil was refusing to be Alison's guide; Whitman told her he was not for her as he loafed upon the grass, 'For what did *you, aberrant,* know of how it is to be lyric with self-reliance?'

'But I know that I contradict myself and that I definitely

contain a multitude—friends others can't see, alter ego and all.'

William Empson, looking askance, chimed in, 'What I wrote: it is beyond you, so give up now. There is no ambiguity about what I said, so don't look for it, worm. Now go.'

Santa Maria nodded in agreement, laughed and barked, 'Told you so' and Alison woke up to the cold world. Still, holding the feeling of the dream in a pocket or in the palm of her hand where the bad thought would come, Alison carried on reading and carried on having desperate and unobtainable crushes; clever men left her aflutter for three years, regardless of whether they were gay or not. Maybe they could be turned with a jiggle of tits and a declension or two. Ah—but not by *her*, of course: it would have to be a mighty show of Hapless Ally and even so, trimmed of too much vivacity because its excess would have made them stare in this socially articulate world. While she simply did not have the confidence and the hauteur of the Heroic Alice-like girls from public schools (or maybe just those who weren't repeatedly hearing, 'I should have left you in a bucket') it still sometimes felt just like one long three-year fuck: from time to time an actual coupling, but generally just a theoretical one. Lexis, rather than praxis, as Aristotle might have said if he had written about different sorts of fuck. And I don't think he did.

The fractured days were, dreams and hard spites withal, tremendously, scarily exciting. Exams were managed only after the little rituals had been performed and even then her large, looping script was punctuated here and there with the tears she tried to stop up. And as for the excitement, Alison, melancholy sort as she was, judged that to be a symptom of its very mutability; the prelude to a universal 'Fuck off!' But how about we just focus on Professor Pobble? For a while, he looked like a keeper in a mutable world. Ah—but as what?

5

Professor Pobble and a big wobble

Professor Pobble had a kind and open face; for the last year under the spires, they would talk for hours. He was supposed to be her supervisor but more important was that he was Alison's best friend. For a while, she took down her picture of Camus and put up some of Professor Pobble's poems in his stead. He had a gorgeous growl of a voice and he was sad and in the wrong place. *Oh* how she grasped the idea of being in the wrong place: she had been in the wrong place since the day she was born: being in the wrong place emerged in the gossamer memories glimpsed before sleep: *the memories I have of before I could remember*—the soft, tentacular nocturnal memories. *They dressed me and fed me and looked at me but they didn't want me.* The inscape was always swaying and could go at any moment, she felt. It might go with Professor Pobble, but perhaps he was man enough to catch her.

They would talk for hours about Irish poems; the word

immram was delicious when he spoke it: the journey; the quest. It was because of him that there was a summer best described as *happy* in the archives of King's College library, reading the letters of a certain Anglo-Irish poet, feeling their heft and struggling to comprehend that here he was, writing of Auden, Betjeman, the BBC, Oxford; drafting poems for his friends, for love lost, for love won: Oxford, Ireland, *Thalassa*.

She would arrive at his rooms: 'Ah! Shall we then embark again?'

She would return from holiday: 'I went to Borth. They said it was better than Prestatyn, but it was shite.'

'Ah, the sea; always round the corner. Now, that is how it seems to me.'

Alison would spend the weekend in London with a distant aunt or two: 'Well then I am glad that London contains her—I mean, I am glad, *I am really glad*, that London briefly contained you.'

'Really, Professor, why?'

It was a gift, their borrowed language; what and how he told her, his 'broken comrade': the replies and passing comments came in the lines of poets as argot. Professor Pobble was an expert, of course, and it was the first experience of sharing books at length, pulling out lines from poems, creating a world in the room, dining on the words; it was magic, a private currency, but always with the dark undercurrent of their key subject's work derided by others at the university. Alison wondered why something couldn't just be safe and accepted and unstained and would wander home across the quad feeling darkly, palpably sad. Why so sad? *Immram, immram, immrama.*

One time, on a Professor Pobble day, Alison tripped on Clare Bridge. She had been to a party and decided to be Hapless Ally, bursting in bright colours and humming. The room had gone a little quiet.

'Oh, you're Alison, aren't you? Yessss I thought so,' said the pretty redhead, her words trailing off, suggestively.

There was the hard little smile she was accustomed to seeing; it was the smile on the faces of her mother's porcelain doll-faced friends. Alison wanted to say, 'No, actually, I'm someone else' (which was partly true) but instead faltered with, 'That's my name, don't wear it out!' which was the least sophisticated thing she could possibly have uttered. She went home as soon as she could and on the walk her palm itched: she knew that it would, for there was the little thought shuffling in the palm, ready to eviscerate: ready to disentangle *you, Baby in the Bucket, wart, maggot girl.* Alison, having sloughed off Hapless on the walk home, gripped the stones of the bridge and tried, desperately, to focus on the mortar, the lichen, the Cam and the punt passing below. It was hours—hours. Santa Maria (now, hot on the heels of Vaguely Dead Dad, a Dead Santa Maria, although that didn't seem to make much difference), the lovely redhead and even Hapless Ally—again looking on separately this time—came into focus on the riverbank. Look: they were having a picnic. They had beautiful blankets and candles in jars like glow worms in a green night: they were happy together. Dante said to the gathering, 'I have a guide for you' and they looked at him with pleasure; William Empson sat separate, but happy: pastoral with new friends. To Alison, as the laughter from the riverbank floated up to her, came lines came from Sylvia—this time from *Johnny Panic and the Bible of Dreams*. Sylvia was on a bloody bridge, too—a bridge, *the very same bridge* in Cambridge and she had written that every now and then would come a moment when the neutral and impersonal forces in the world around us coalesce in a hideous judgement. That was a terrifying prospect. Sylvia told of a feeling of panic; of being condemned and of how the outside world mirrored the inner. In February, in snow, she had walked on Mill Lane Bridge, feeling lost and lacklustre; a creature whose vivacity had been lost and who did not stand easily and comfortably in the world, but still smiled a smile which lacquered over a fear of words or looks from others. She was set upon by a group of snowball-throwing boys. It was just a simple thing, but it carried with it sadness and judgement. Sylvia told of how, 'with a tolerant smile that was a superior lie', she had walked on.

That was it. Smile at the world. Lacquer it, but inch-thick, not with a mist. Make a superior lie.

I am two people.

I am one.

I don't know who I am.

Alison walked home, stiff and cold; oblivious of the surroundings, but back at her room she appeared to come to. The pretty girl opposite smirked at her. Hapless Ally was behind her, separate but whole again: Alison slammed the door in her face but Hapless, being a sort of ghost, went through it. She had been gathering her own identity—particularly today. *A snowball.* Alison went into her room, clawed and clawed at her arms and legs and scalp; she smashed a glass on the floor, took off her socks and, with infinite concentration and with infinite awareness of sensations, walked firmly and slowly on the glass, coming to a little more. Hapless Ally, supposedly the crafted self to stop Alison being excommunicated, fetched the first aid kit and urged her on, bastardising lines of Samuel Beckett just to spite her: 'I can't go on, I will go on. I can't go on, I will go on. Look at you! Look at you, maggot, wart. Making a bloody great fuss about tragedy and comedy and other trivial detritus! And who would trouble about you? I'd say you'd be better on your arse than dead, but ha ha ha—except in your case; then, maybe both. Ha ha ha. Look at the little simpering Baby in the Bucket!'

Scratched and cut, Alison stood still and saw out of the window a punt on the river: a boy with his girl in the moonlight, so romantic, *but we are not for you; no-one is for you.* She staunched the blood, diligently put Savlon on her arms and legs, rubbed her sore scalp and made some tea. Her actions tended to be calm and methodical once she had hurt herself and seen the blood. She did not let the kettle fully boil. This was just what she had done when she was fourteen: when she had laid herself down to die and her mother had hoicked her up.

'UP, little bitch: get off the floor; there is work to be done, if you care. Look at me. I am ill, ill, ill. I have taken a pill. But I am still podding the beans and fetching in kindling.'

'There's wood enough within!' said Alison.

'How *dare* you mock me and pretend to be Caliban!'

'Mummy, I have done something stupid and I need to go to hospital.'

'No—you shouldn't have left there in the first place. You should have stayed—'

'Yes, I know: stayed in the bucket.'

But she didn't die; didn't know well enough how to do it: Alison failed. She didn't want to again. It was time. No more snowballs thrown. No more superior lies or lacquered smiles. It was like a recipe, taken down.

'Now, the water must not be too hot, so make tea in a favourite mug and add plenty of milk and swallow down just so the handfuls of paracetamol.'

But something—what was it, that *thing*? —compelled her to act further: she got a taxi, arrived at Addenbrooke's Hospital and said, 'I have done something stupid' and no-one called her maggot or fuck-wit. And it was not the desperate clawing to life that did it, that made her stop and call. It was more that someone would be cross or upset to find her—and she couldn't bear the thought of Muriel, the bedder who kept an eye on the student rooms, finding her cold in the morning: Muriel had enough problems, with her drunken philandering husband who didn't love her and never had and her wayward son with the heroin. *That was what it was*: she didn't want to make a sad person sadder.

At the hospital they told her that there had not been enough to finish her off or qualify pumping and she had been spectacularly sick, which had been of great help, but could they call someone? She said no. The tentacular memories were there, in the hospital bed, just as they had been on the bedroom floor when she had once laid herself down to die as a kid; the long fingers, touching her gently, but with an ecstatic cruelty. On Clare Bridge, she had wished to be rubbed out in some way. Everyone must laugh at her; Dead Santa Maria had been right about the bucket. Alison was there, at Cambridge, *under sufferance*; whose she didn't quite know, but there was no doubt she was, as always, a fraud. She had been let in because they felt sorry for her or owing to clerical error. Alison's school and some of her friends' parents had said as much: *you were lucky. You got away with it.* Years later, she met one of them on the road. Well, in Tesco; it was just before killing Hapless Ally and just after the birth of Alison's third son, and the delighted crow, pecking away, said, 'Oooh look at you; I would never have recognised you. Oh yes, my Joelle is doing brilliantly but *ooooh look at you.* It must be all those children. Oh and your poor mother...She was a saint, lovely, important, was Santa Maria. We all said so, we did—and then there was *you.* Yes! Ooooh look at you!'

Her shark eyes had the cold gleam of someone who enjoys delivering bad news. *Schadenfreude. Delicious.* Alison did not have the nerve or tenacity to shove her into the freezer; she just stood by the 'Asian Foods Frozen' section, trying to focus on the okra and fenugreek. BUT (evil laugh and note from the future as compiled in the hefty folders of Drs Hook and Crook of the Mental Health Rescue Squad at Pink Pantiles House), '*Bring it on next time. And shift it bitch sister: or you will be named in the sequel, oh nasty Sponge or Spiker. Because Alison, worm, has turned.'*

But back in the day, a little way off the dreaming spires, and sat bolt upright with Hapless Ally on a hospital bed, the world around was in a foul mood, nipping at her toes and chanting, *Alison, Alison, Baby in the Bucket; girlie with imaginary friends.* The faces she had seen were not those of the snowballing boys, but of everyone she had met, ever, smiling and tolerant. *You are here under sufferance.* She dug her nails into her hands, felt the acid in her mouth and a dull ache in her abdomen and went home on the bus. Alison was terrified with a tolerant smile that was a superior lie. She tried to see Father Chasuble, the chaplain, but he was busy having a port and Stilton party with the un-Weird Kids; she thought about Professor Pobble, but he was so kind, so clever, so shiny with it—she could not disturb him. She sat in her fine room, with the view across First Court and wondered where on earth she was going next. More lines from Sylvia were reverberating. Alison reflected that, while Sylvia was able to transfigure her—Alison's—very experience into lucid prose, there was a yearning for the crawl space and the days of Frida. Not so much, Sylvia's friable longing to permeate the substance of this world, to become anchored to it through tending flowers in the garden and the diligent housework of quotidian routine, but Frida's spirited glitter-song of how the show must go on. Could she meet Frida somewhere else, one day? Could her platform-shoed friend scoop her up and say, 'It's okay, baby girl. It's okay. I've got you.'?

But, you know, there were others besides Frida, whose presence formed after hers: women who are still there: big luminous icons who might also have helped the sad girl on a bench in the park whom Alison glimpsed at dusk as she walked alone, two days after Addenbrooke's. Meeting the girl, another drifting soul, now *that* was a pivotal point: it made Alison think about what was rot and what was not. But *the girl*—Evelyn—who was cold and half alive on a bench at six o'clock on a fine but chilly evening, inappropriately dressed for December, with not even a jumper on, was full of pills and cheap cider, and Alison knew what had happened instinctively and scooped her up; found herself in the ambulance with Evelyn, who was whispering to her, 'Let me go. No. No! Let me go. Let me, let me, let me go…'

There followed another night in Addenbrooke's hospital until Evelyn's parents arrived, strange and stiff. There was no hug for the girl. Their distress was palpable, shocking, for sure, but there was no scooping up, holding fast and battening down: just resistance and three hard shiny carapaces, all lost at sea. Evelyn desperately fingered her bracelets and looked only at Alison. Watching the girl's parents, it was horribly like Vaguely Dead Dad and Dead Santa Maria: nobody here was fit for purpose. But Evelyn survived and so it was a life saved.

If you had to list the good and bad things you had done, then Alison told herself insistently that the saving of a life, even if it were the life that someone did not choose to live, must be listed always *always* as a good thing. If Evelyn is alive now, would that she, too, has set the darkness echoing and a soft jumper to retreat into, when it's cold. Or imaginary friends to provide solace.

'And the rot,' said Alison, 'the rot is everything that *is not*. And everything that *is*, begins with imagination and poems. It's what Helen said, isn't it? Lying down "in the foul rag and bone shop of the heart:" that's "where all the ladders start." I just don't know how to climb them yet.'

So what of Professor Pobble? The poet; the lover of poetry? Well thereby hangs a tale. There were walks in botanical gardens, dinners out and talking for hours and hours. And tracing the Professor and poet through two more universities and PhDs started and abandoned through deaths, happenings at The Hill (more hangings, séances, explosions and untidy feuds) and weeks and months when time should have been away, but wasn't. But Professor Pobble was always there, with soft voice, reassuring her that she lived in important times, that 'The millstone has become a star', that she was there, woven in and out of the content of his books, and, most of all, as he wrote to her in their dedications, ' "Time was away", when you were here.'

Alison reflected, a few years later, that sometimes she was remarkably unobservant; that's why the attentions of Drs Crook and Hook were so important. Because she sat up in bed late one night, pulled from sleep with a piercing thought, and said, 'Professor Pobble *loved* me.' But by that time, time was not away and it was too late.

Hapless, Alison.

6

Hanging out with the Holy Rollers

At the university, Alison had tried to talk to God; tried chapel and praying: she had been trying since forever. But nobody came. It didn't work. Oh dear: *Alison and God who was Dead if He ever Existed.* Now there's a title. The God thing had *never* gone very well. Alison even tried to force it on some occasions later on, in her working life, by doing school assemblies and even—Holy Moly and *Ave Maria*—Sunday school, but the subject always came back to a thirst for something quite out of reach and memories of Jesus looking indignant and sniggering.

When Alison was fifteen, she had struck up a friendship with a boy in a Christian fellowship. They used to have what she considered were extremely dry romps in the back of his Ford Escort and he was a great fan of the Conservative party, which Alison, writing a Christmas card to Tony Benn every year and sending him rock cakes, asking Glenys Kinnock for advice on politics and boys (Glenys said, '*Neil and I advise sticking with Labour and only courting the Welsh lads because they've got fire and sense. Tidy*'—which was fine by Alison), and making mufflers for the women protesting at Greenham Common, instinctively had a hard time reconciling with being, well, *of God*.

The boy's parents were kind and thoroughly respectable, but had an unsteady relationship with immigrants, gippos, lefties and feminists, all of whom they tended to besmirch over a Sunday roast. But the boy—let us call him Ichabod—and his respectably fascist parents brought her along to the Sunday morning gathering.

Then, as now, Alison was repulsed by Christian rock, being more of a fan of the censer, the dirge-like hymn and the furiously non child-friendly service. It is like a scene in the comedy, *Father Ted*, when Mrs Doyle reminds the priests that she doesn't go on a pilgrimage to enjoy herself but to have a truly miserable time. This is exactly what Alison wanted from a church: to be penitent, uncomfortable and for it to be very *very* long and with clouds of incense. She thought that all the twangy guitars and baggy bass were simply too joyful: it sounded like a Bon Jovi concert, but it was less funny and entirely lacking in camp and Jon Bon Jovi's tight arse. And as for 'Kum ba ya' with an acoustic guitar! The hairs on the back of her neck stood on end—and not with pleasure. There was much groaning and mumbling from the congregation, however, so Alison launched herself into the song, feeling sick but still wanting, in some way, to feel the same happiness the others appeared to feel. But it didn't work.

The service worked in crescendo and diminuendos and with each ascent and descent, arms were raised, tears were shed, frequently a body writhed on the floor and had to be helped up and everywhere people were speaking in tongues. To hear and speak the language, if we call it this—a gift of the spirit—excluded her. She had no sense that she would ever *ever* be able to do such a thing. She plucked up the courage to ask someone about it and was informed that this gift could come to her if she truly believed. Like a child she screwed up her eyes and willed herself to, but no: week after week, nothing.

Ichabod took her to his pastor, who sat her down on the velour sofa after tea and custard creams, with more Christian rock gently and painfully playing in the background and said, 'Prepare, sweet child, to receive the Holy Spirit, as Ichabod did.'

All Alison could hear was the traffic outside and all she could think of was the fact that the velour sofa was a bit slippery and a bit squeaky and also that she had sat on a rather damp dog toy and it was digging into her arse.

Opposite her, above the gas fire with its fake stone fireplace, there were several wooden ornamental *Name of Jesus* jigsaws. Alison knew, in glancing at them, that the jolly little wooden ornaments irritated her. It wasn't their fault: what she would have preferred, rather than this bright and optimistic room, with its zealous central heating, was a sepulchral cold and damp, a hard seat and some properly

Catholic pictures of Jesus bleeding from the crown of thorns and holding up the stigmata. Pine Christian knick-knacks and all the rest of the twee God stuff just didn't hold or enthuse her in the same way, but she found it hard to discern whether that was owing to an aesthetic predilection or a spiritual one. Perhaps Dead Santa Maria had been right about the Baby in the Bucket, because her daughter now entertained this ungenerous kind of thought.

'Who do I ask? What can I do?'

Alison had a brief conversation with Dante; he had rejected her before, absolutely refused to be her imaginary friend, her head friend, but she asked him again, 'Who will be my guide? How will I go and what will I see there?'

And up came Dante into the stuffy room, gently telling her to make the journey and come back through her weird Alison and Hapless Ally world to glimpse something else: 'Yes I am here! I give up! If you will leave me alone afterwards, you can borrow Virgil; he will guide you. Remember these words, Alison, as you go: these are the last lines from my *Inferno*—and may they help you. There is a secret for you to discover:

"The Master and I went upon that hidden path,

To return to the light of the sun,

And without taking a moment's rest,

We climbed on high, he first and I second,

So that through a circular opening,

I saw some of the beautiful things in the sky.

From there we went out to see the stars again." '

Suddenly, with Alison thinking of how it would be to see something beautiful and know that it is okay for you to look at it, Dante was gone and the hand on her arm was not that of Virgil, but of a pastor, sweating, urging and mouth breathing heavily like the nasty dentist of her childhood.

'You might feel it like heat, or get a buzzing in your ears. But feel it you will.'

There were no stars to see, no hidden tunnel to find and access or aperture to behold as the pastor spoke tongues and hissed all over her. Alison shuffled on the sofa and tried to shift the dog toy from under her left buttock and wondered if the pastor was making the whole thing up. The tongues sounded more like Esperanto than, say, Hebrew or what she imagined Aramaic might have sounded like. But she felt mean for having the thought and tried to dismiss it.

'I know you feel it. I can see it in you. I am your guide; your conduit. Do you feel faint, loose limbed or dizzy? Ohhhh Spirit we welcome you.'

It sounded more like the séance she had once been to after a village show at The Hill and the 'Ohhhhh' recalled the orgasms she'd seen on forbidden late night telly and tried to emulate with Albert Camus. Now Alison was getting restless (plus she was suppressing a snigger), so she said, 'Yes to all those things' as the glasses shuffled on the sideboard and the pastor announced that the Holy Spirit had been in the room with her and had entered her and we must all now rejoice.

The pastor laid her hands firmly on Alison's head again and announced that again she might feel a kind of heat, or maybe the buzzing thing. Then she abruptly released her hands and it was all over, with a lie. Well, she *had* been very hot but that was because the central heating was jacked right up.

On the way out, verily skipping with the Spirit's presence, she recalled painfully a particular section from Philip Larkin's 'Faith Healing' and walked home, feeling lost and all the way there dreading a holiday, to begin that night, in The Fucking Caravan. She wished that hands would come, 'to lift and lighten'. Alison became acutely aware that this early adventure with the Pentecostal church did nothing to dull the ache she felt. It was the same lonely thing that had her scurrying for the bookshelf and *The Wind in the Willows* when she was younger or, for that matter, tracing through adequate space between the objects on the colour table in her bedroom. The impulse had been the same: to put at rest the aching feeling of being all wrong; external to circumstance; unwanted.

She pictured Larkin's line of people awakening briefly, with the laying on of hands to,

'… all they might have done had they been loved.

That nothing cures. An immense slackening ache…'

The hands give only a hiatus; a breath when all is well, as tears break loose and the dumb idiot child in them awakes, only to be exiled back into a world which they cannot transliterate. Perhaps it would have been better not to glimpse an alternative. Later, in attempts to understand and feel what the others feel, Alison tried regularly to go to Church of England services, but there was a sense of a club; a group of people with whom she could at best flirt and acquiesce. Some of them were terrifying and territorial women who didn't like her children. Or possibly just didn't like *her*. She tried with a muscular but ultimately impotent insistence to be one of them: to feel the presence of God. Sometimes, it almost came, but always it shifted. *Elsewhere*. She tried to understand the Bible from an intellectual and theological perspective; she met immeasurably kind true believers, but nothing shifted the *immense slackening ache*; at its best it was watching the comfort derived by others that kept her trying—but were they deluded? Just desperately clinging to something that Camus would have suggested you slough off and that, after such terror of a universe devoid of meaning, there should come liberty?

There came a moment of panic. She was taking a school assembly at a primary school: trying to do her bit, willing herself—and them—to believe. A child put up her hand and said, 'I don't believe any of this, so how you gonna convince me then?'

And foolish Alison wanted to say, 'Well I entirely agree and I'm not going to convince you and I can't because I'm not sure I believe in any of it either. Let's hang out, kid.'

She thought of afternoons of Camus sex, and of embarrassment and faith and doubt with JK behind the sofa and reflected, 'I know. Let's go and embrace our negative capability!' But to the child, she was the idiot—dumb, inept and her interlocutor knew it.

Yet was it possible that the cure should come in doubt?

'*You may feel faint*,' the pastor had said. Nope: Alison just felt a bit sick and a bit disappointed in herself. She wasn't disappointed in God, if He *did* Exist, mind you. Even Santa Maria's passionate loathing of God must have come from somewhere; from an awareness of Him, so that she could deny God and hate Him and say He was impotent and say He was dead. But Alison just felt foiled by her own weakness and, in all her years, she would still try to find faith: at Christingle in a old church with its childish oranges and sparklers, in the Catholic services with the Missionaries of Charity, in the stiff-backed parental simmering (of dead, undead or live parents, though you never can tell) on her wedding day, in listening to the murmuring of her husband's prayers—and in the night, if she should wake, questioning, with clamped jaw and wet eyes. Still, '*The immense slackening ache.*'

And,

'*That* nothing cures.'

7

Meeting Dixie Delicious

Oooh: *the Meeting of Dixie Delicious*.

Alison was running or fleeting, as usual. An elderly lady she had once met at a bus stop had gifted her some pearls of wisdom: those gems you receive when least expecting them; insights gained when your small talk with a stranger by the cleaning products in a supermarket morphs into something altogether more profound, or when chat about inclement weather as you stand waiting for the bus shifts to some consolations of philosophy. The lady told her to remember something: when you are stuck on the horns of a dilemma and want to effect change and run, in the act of running, seek to know whether you are running *towards* something or *away* from it. Talk about a useful maxim! It had often been used since but, through stupidity, also ignored and repented of at leisure. Because the thing about running *away from* things is that they have a habit of returning, deferred and angry, and then biting you comprehensively and savagely on the arse. Alison knew this, but she was still running and running away from: from a disquieting sense of confusion over Professor Pobble; from an entanglement with the unsuitable boyfriend, Sardonic Steve, and what to do *there*; from Dead Santa Maria, who was even more cross post-mortem, and also from whether or not she (Alison) was supposed to be at her desk, getting on with a PhD thesis on the poetry of Richard Lovelace, a mid-seventeenth century Caroline poet, camp as tits, who liked dancing and garments and bona robas and hunting and The King.

The chosen subject had posed a problem; part of a canon which comprised many a cheery genius, Lovelace was fascinating but clearly not as good as the others in said canon. He was also a staunch Royalist and if Alison had had to choose she would have done her best to look kindly on Commonwealth. And yet, Cromwell? Well, *he* was a bit reckless with artefacts and heads. Charles I was soaked in privilege and sweetmeats yet, then again, the poet and parliamentarian Andrew Marvell had reminded her that *he* (the king) *nothing common did or mean*. Alison knew that thoughts and opinions—and her own identity—could be split or balanced: sometimes precariously so. Holding that dichotomy within herself—holding it so tenuously—her head ached because she was obliged to come down firmly on the side of Mr Lovelace to prepare her thesis for the press: she should have stuck with Louis MacNeice and The Greeks at Oxford. (Another project overturned by dark days and the itchy, scratchy thought in the palm that would not settle.

And there was the *lack of the signposts* again). Our girl had chosen the wrong subject for the thesis because, *one:* Lovelace was annoying her; *two:* having already gone through two supervisors, neither of whom was particularly interested in what she was doing, she had lost all faith and decided that she'd even forgotten how to write, with Dead Santa Maria chuckling and echoing all possible doubt; *three:* there wasn't any need to write any more on the subject; *four:* she was plain terrified about being found out as a fraud again; into the club of clever people by clerical accident. And Professor Pobble was there again, winking at her knowingly in lectures about rime royale, *terza rima* and the like; there had been another fine collection of poems with once more a dedication to her. He had written, 'Alison: you are very important to my books; you are woven in and out of the pages,' yet she had taken years to understand what he felt for her. He had been kind and decent throughout, which made the pain of it more piercing. Now, could it even be? Or, even more tentatively and decidedly riskily, *how* could it be? He absolutely belonged to someone else. But oh: the awkwardness: now he confessed all; articulated all—and all as a fond impossibility. The ground had fallen from under her feet as she sat there thinking, 'What do I do? And what do I do again?'

They had been sitting in a restaurant, neither up nor down, but eating salt cod and potatoes *dauphinoise*. Lovelace sat in the corner with King Charles, eating cake and occasionally looking over, irritably, with a flouncy sleeve gesticulating rude argot. Suddenly, a man was at Alison's table, saying over her head, 'Warm congratulations, Professor, on your new book and on your poetry appointment' and in the disturbance, with both of them sitting there, rigid, pulling at napkins, she got up and started to run away. He followed her to the bus stop, touched her arm and said, 'Sorry and sorry again. I'm sorry and for everything and time is, time is still away. Isn't it? Couldn't it be? Please say that it can be? *Immram, imramm, imramma*—remember...? Please say you remember...and we can go back, can't we?'

And so there was an ending: bereavement. It wasn't his fault. She blamed herself for being too stupid to notice what he had been saying, and for years. Alison, as we have gathered, could be mightily unobservant. Her punishment is to miss him for a lifetime. She reflected that he had always thought she was particularly clever: what if that had been only refracted through love? Just a distortion of the facts—and that, instead, her turn of thought and phrase were decidedly pedestrian? That is a question pondered to this day. The difference in the present, of course, is that thanks to the kind hands of Drs Crook and Hook at the Mental Health Rescue Squad, it doesn't stop her writing things. And also these days she can leave the house without a complex ritual to be followed to the letter which would go: read the beginning of *The Secret Garden* four times (*this means it's okay to leave the room*); check gas three times (*this means I am not a fraud*); taps off four times and one for luck (*I know enough about poetry*); check windows are shut six times, turn around on the spot after the last check (*I will not be shamed in the street; Santa*

Maria, dead or alive, will not point at me in a crowded place and screech 'BITCH DAUGHTER' and no-one will stare and laugh.)

Having revealed just a little about Professor Pobble, it may appear that little has been said of Sardonic Steve, but some things must remain hidden. Sardonic was a dark lord; an object of ill-advised fascination since Alison's pubescent days and he wanted to control and he *could* control her because, of course, he knew the things he could do and say to lay her out. It could be that she would have deserved it; we are sinners, all, and broken. But the thought of *it, them, the words* frightened Alison day and night; also, he knew about Hapless; about the self to stick on in public: to sanitise, impress or perform whatever vital function was required. If he knew that, she was both laid bare and had her artifice exposed and he could tear her into tiny shreds and go, 'Ha! I'm cleverer than you!' Alison kept quiet and apart the secreted embolus of fear; she tried not to think of it or look at her palm in case the shadowy thought came up at her and felled her. These days were a work of vigilance: of trying not to be annihilated, while naked and in the street. But bide your time and know that all this brings us, through these (*five*) mightily disjointed reflections, to Kolkata. *Of course it does. Ek, do, teen, char, panch.*

So this is how we got to this particular street: with signposts she didn't see yet.

Alison had travelled many Indian streets, running to or away from. People who suffer from depression, from anxiety, from despair and self-loathing, may take risks: throw in jobs and let themselves go to see how far they get. Yet what is someone's *reckless,* may be another's incandescent *brave.* For Alison, India, its great mass, its colour, was refuge and adventure: in Heathrow, she could get on a plane, riddled with nerves, acutely aware of all sensation, and go somewhere aflame with difference: she could feel courageous and hope more confidently that she was sane. And when the fear came, then there was Hapless—for emergencies, although uncomfortably so.

Today, in this particular street, water was up to Alison's thighs and she appeared to be the only whitey silly enough to be out in it. It had been a hard monsoon; there was, they told her in the street, an abundance of standing water, all full of bacteria. People were struggling with dysentery and yet it was, still, a street of joy; a place of festivity. The street was populated by the tea boys, whose ablutions carried on, at dawn, under the municipal pumps; by Banana Man who worked the street each day and dumped the last of his haul in her lap, not for free, of course; by Abdullah the rickshaw fellow. He might have been eighty, but she reflected he was probably nearer fifty; laughing always. He gifted Alison a spare rickshaw bell and she tied it, back in Albion, onto the dashboard mirror of the Vauxhall Astra. It was, it must be said, a time of intense happiness, whether or not there was running to or away from.

Alison was able to become—as always on her travels—a little more Alison. Because 'Time was away' and she hoped that Hapless Ally was held in that skein of hours. For a while,

Alison was free. At first, in fear of being just herself, Alison had tried to put on her Hapless clothes:

'Wouldn't it be better if it were her here? She's still bigger and bouncier and more attractive than me. How could I travel and live here, just as me?'

Once, being ever so Hapless, as if she were the prettiest veneer and the way to be safe, Alison had propelled herself onto a busy train. This was an event noted in 'Hapless Ally's Journal of Subcontinental Travels'—a travelogue of which you heard as you first began reading this story. On the KushiNagar Express, steadying herself and feeling over-hot and about to faint, she (as Hapless) was comically unsteady as the train lurched to a start and down she went, pretend-amused, and behind her down went the six men and a Sadhu.

There was a pause before everyone got back up and laughed. Or rather, the men laughed, the Sadhu didn't.

'In our foolish lives,' said the Sadhu, 'when we fall, we get back up as someone else.'

He looked at her squarely, old eyes wrinkled at the corners, knowing and wry.

'Oh—I'm just so silly! I do it all the time! I also fell down an ill-signposted hole in Chennai and was attacked by a holy cow in Varanasi. These things happen to me; I'm funny like that! You can call me Hapless Ally.'

'No.' said the Sadhu, '*Not funny. That is not your name. And that was not you.*'

Words to startle, aflame with truth on a train in Bihar.

But back to the important street. That summer, in the prodigious flooding of West Bengal, people stumbled in gutters and the boys of the chai stalls raised their kit on boxes and hoped for the best. Everyone who lived on this particular street had found enterprising ways to elevate their home, too. The suds from the washers at the pumps joined the floods; Alison had her dress tied around her knees, so it wouldn't get too wet or torn on underwater obstacles. She was on her way to the bookshop. Just to browse. There was, as usual, a plethora of Penguin in India books and amongst them she found an immaculate copy of Eric Newby's *A Book of Traveller's Tales*. Having always been a fan since her encounters with the engaging Newby in *A Short Walk in the Hindu Kush*, she bought it and took it back to the dormitory room, past Abdul, grunting and cursing in his half-sleep. Alison found that the book was signed by the author with the words, 'To Ted and Vi, in memory of a happy walk on Dorset cliffs. Yours, Eric.'

Dorset cliff/Kolkata pavement.

'Time was away'.

Alison wondered, without knowing why, if this book had been left as a clue. And she thought, 'Have you lost your mind?' But there was something about the combination of the author, striking out happily along the Jurassic Coast and the book ending up here, in a bookshop by the post office in Chowringee. It sent a little shiver along the spine and awoke in her, again for reasons that could not be fully understood, the urge to walk on for a while, in the street in the flood. Downstairs, Abdul was awake and gave the familiar leer; it might have been a smile, but Abdul had a lot of problems with his teeth (and with his wife and children, which might have been why he was so grumpy).

Alison visualised some strange things: on impulse and just in case, scenting a pivotal moment, she pressed her hands to the sides of her head and warned Hapless Ally, 'Stay in there. *At the back.* Come near the frontal lobes or set foot independently in this street and *I will fucking kill you even if it means the death of me.* And the Sadhu saw you, you know, and knew you were not me! And does it really matter if I couldn't set things down straight and write a PhD? And does it even matter anymore if I'm Baby in the Bucket?'

Slowly, she put a hand on her solar plexus and scratched a finger across the troubling palm and said, to the secreted embolus of fear and the sometime dark thought, as she held herself, upright and calm, 'Sit: stay here with Abdul, you little bastards: you are *not* taking this one from me' and went out.

Abdul murmured, '*Baba choda rendi.*'

'What was that, Abdul?'

'I was saying, I am like a father to you.'

'I don't think that was quite what you said.'

Alison thought of the wise old lady at the bus stop and said aloud, 'Look: I'm doing it! I'm running TO!'

There was a man on the other side of the street, wading through water happily and going in the opposite direction and he called across to her, 'Excuse me, can you tell me the way I could get to the Blue Sky Café?'

Alison was startled because he had chosen a sentence with pleasing internal rhymes (though its tetrameter was imperfect) and momentarily thought she might have imagined the man.

She said, 'Go straight ahead to the corner and you'll see it there.' To have attempted the beckoning symmetry of meter really would have been a shade too far. Anyway, what she should have said was, 'Turn round and go straight ahead and you'll see it there' because the man whirled, lost in the watery street. Thus the ability to give inaccurate directions for the simplest of journeys was a point he raised with her later that day when they met on the same side of the street. And still he followed her (with his own directions), alter ego, embolus, itch and all to Albion and the funny old house and came to visit a while and then never left.

And she told the man, 'I forgive you for the broken tetrameter.'

And he said, 'Your directions suck and why didn't you just point to the signpost?'

And she said, 'Signposts and I have a difficult history.'

His name was Dixie Delicious.

Alison met him, as if in a story, stumbling across a book by a familiar author in an unfamiliar place—and this was, truly, how it was, after the day in the flooded street in Kolkata, Eric Newby, and the very wrong directions which turned out, in a funny sort of way, to be the right ones. Dixie Delicious had a calm eye; he didn't wake in the night, sitting bolt upright, like Alison did. He had faith: he had it in the palm of his hand and the heel of his shoe and she looked at it and saw possibility and she followed him, just as he followed her. Sometimes, they fell over one another and laughed as they travelled on. And in another city, Alison watched him go out and imagined what he saw, single and indivisible: this was how it went.

Benares, Varanasi, one of the world's oldest inhabited cities. It was not his city, but she sensed he felt at home there. He sat by the river at dawn and a multitude was there, bathing and praying and offering up what they could. *Look at him. Look at how still he is. How does he do that?* The sun hit the water and he watched them quietly, not able to offer a libation, yet content to watch and bless vicariously. He bought tea and set it by her bed. Then, later, mangoes, limes, tomatoes, onions and some olive oil from an ayurvedic medicine shop so that he could make a dressing of sorts. He begged a small hillock of salt; his eyes said he hoped she would be proud of what he had done. On the balcony of the room, the light was dazzling. There, he assembled the breakfast for her, called her out from her room. With his call, though, she sat at ease; he smoothed her hair, put on her hat for her and gave her what he had made. They said little as they ate and watched the sun, still in its ascent. The colour of the Ganges changed from white and gold to the more familiar muddy brown. Now, he stood up and told her that, from now on, he would stop running, stop travelling *away from* and start travelling *to* a destination. Whenever he put one foot in front of the other, it would be with her. She understood and that was that. There were smiles of complicity.

'Stay with me.'

'I don't know if I can. I am broken; was never made properly—and there is more than one of me.'

'And you think any of *that* bothers me?'

In the lanes below, the monkeys chattered. They could smell the food he had prepared and were ready to steal. He spoke a prayer. The heat of the day was becoming pressing already and the yoghurt sellers a little further along the street were doing a good trade from their trestles full of clay cups, filled with the cool, sour yoghurt.

'And again and again, I don't care who you are and if you are more than one,' he said.

'What about my dead mother? Dead Santa Maria?'

'We'll ignore her.'

'And Brother who Might as Well have been Dead?'

'If he Might as Well have been Dead, does it matter? He's nixed anyway, isn't he?'

'I hurt myself.'

'I'll stanch the blood or maybe just tie you up to stop you doing it.'

'That sounds alluring,' said Alison.

Then, 'What about God who was—or should I say *is* Dead if He ever Existed?'

And Dixie Delicious said, 'He is alive. He was down by the river.'

When he was ten, Dixie Delicious happened to be in an elevator in a hotel in Dallas, Texas. In walked a tall man; the boy looked at the man's shoes. From there, it was a long way up, but look he did. The boy saw that it was Johnny Cash. No, he must be wrong. But hang on; Johnny Cash must have had to ride in an elevator *some* time, so the boy looked again. He nudged his little brother, 'Curtis: I think it's Johnny Cash.' Maybe the man heard him, maybe not. But he bent low and smiled a warm, wide smile and said, 'Hellllllllo boys.'

The child was star-struck and cannot remember if he said hello back; little brother was possibly unmoved, being too young and green to comprehend that Johnny Cash was not to be seen riding in an elevator with you any day of the week. Cash was, like him, a Southern man. Little links kind of went in deep: faith and difficulty and broken things and joy. And riding in that elevator. Alison noticed that Dixie Delicious would listen and feel at home; saw that Cash was flawed, powerful and weak. He had struggled with addiction and the darkest of insecurities; had gone on a journey from the Arkansas mud to a meeting with a luminary or a President. Cash had faith that was angry and brave and music that haunted even when it jangled. So our boy shared and, for a quiet moment, he picked 'Down there by the train' with its invocation to meet him if you had travelled the low road; if, broken and sinning, you had passed the same way.

'Could that be so? That my friends and I don't have to do this alone?'

There are some times when the puzzles and the headaches just drift away: the meeting of the man, the thought of the young Dixie Delicious and the notion that now the man who was *THE ONE—who could not be otherwise—*had a faith that was flawed and wanting and made sense, now that was like moisture on Alison's parched and callow soul and for a while it washed away her feeling of the absurdity and booted those who created it out of the door. It was temporary, but it was beautiful while it lasted: *it was utterly beautiful*, and she had the tiniest of notions that one day it would come back. One fine day when golden light breaks through the mist and, as in the song, Judas Iscariot, betrayer of Jesus, carries John Wilkes Booth, assassin of Abraham Lincoln; when rifts are healed and the person who hated you forgives you.

Tear-drops fell like summer tempests and Alison, glimpsing the world through another's eyes, (sometime while listening to Johnny Cash) sensed possibility and found it both gorgeous and painful. But we must carry on, hankie applied, and tell you that when Dixie Delicious followed Alison there was much wailing and gnashing of teeth from both families once everyone began to understand that he might be staying. For issuing from tomorrow, come today and other people, when time is no longer away.

Dead Santa Maria was there, inviting them all out, smilingly, winningly, 'Come and see my bitch daughter. Look what she's done *now*.'

One of the neighbours came out from her house with Dead Santa Maria and shrieked, 'What the fuck are you doing marrying your holiday romance?' and there was stony silence from all members of both families, probably for the same reason. The words *shotgun wedding* hung heavy in the air and over in Georgia the furiously Anglophile family of Dixie Delicious went off 'yonder' a bit. Alison dutifully tried to win over them, despite her *not* being a good church-going girl from below the Mason-Dixon Line. She might by now have been Oxbridge and able to read Greek and Latin, but she was still a liability of big emotions, with a tendency to curse, an untidy Anglo-Cymric background, two dead parents and a Brother who Might as Well have been Dead. In normal families, older siblings didn't usually leave the younger ones out in a dark and shadowy wood to be eaten by wolves, and normal people didn't discuss violent and splashing death over tea. Did they?

'It's okay,' laughed Dixie Delicious. 'My family is entirely dysfunctional, too.'

'What about the way the dead are present all the time? That there's little distinction between who's dead and who's not? In my case, who's real and who's not? Santa Maria is now Dead Santa Maria, but it hasn't made any difference!'

'Ah, maybe not that bit, although my mother insists that being dead is no excuse, but that's because she's a steel magnolia.'

Up went the stone of Sisyphus and down it rolled again. Sisyphus started again, along the way he gathered faux pas, wrong manners and trod heftily on some nuances while pushing uphill. Dixie Delicious said, 'Don't invest too much,' but that was hard because Alison would always cast around for a parental figure who didn't wish for the bucket. Someone to call her *Dear Child*; who couldn't even *think* something like that. It was a thirst that did not let go. Alison continued with a scruffy litter of errors and up came the black thought: 'It's always you, isn't it Alison? First your mother and father, all those pointy people along the way, your brother and the mother you are looking for. Doesn't matter whether you're Alison or try to be Hapless. It won't work. Look, there's

Mary, throwing a coprolite—or a boy on a bridge throwing a snowball. Or Sardonic Steve saying, "Hey bitch! Long time, no see: I could lay you out. I could have you begging for mercy on the floor if I wanted that. And maybe it's what I'll do." '

On the darkest days, there are so many people to point.

'You you you: YOU did it. You killed the pretty little girl. You said, "fuck" to Heroic Alice and her mother and "fuck" before that by the ballerinas outside the village hall. You killed your parents and you ruined Christmas and God laughed, though He was Dead if He ever Existed.'

If you were Baby in the Bucket and everyone saw and everyone nodded assent, where exactly would you go from there? At best, times of relief, those miniature times when you come up and see the stars through the aperture; when you can navigate the pretty gaps between trinkets on the colour table, are only days, hours, even, of respite. When you are a child *and* when you are a big girl.

In the end, through a pathetic haze of tears and the fear that she was about to kill someone else and dance on the grave of another mother, Alison went to the library in desperation to find the Dorothy Rowe books once recommended by Helga the German psychologist with whom she had had some putative therapy. She discovered the utterly shocking exploration of how rejection is not necessarily about the rejected person, but could be about the rejecter: Alison read it and almost fell backwards and asked herself, aloud, 'Fuck me. Is that something everybody knows? Is that possible?'

Dead Santa Maria was hanging around by the handicrafts

section; she was glowering, for it was a bit of a knock-back for her. Could it be that Alison had—drum-roll—acquired a little insight? Certainly, she had been asked to leave the library if she talked aloud again and was reminded that normal bibliophiles do not use inappropriate expletives, but the telling off was worth it. For if you have insight, there is less that others can do to you. And maybe, if you got in, you can get out?

'Remember, Alison, that "depression is a prison where you are both the suffering prisoner and the cruel jailer." '

'Oh, God Bless you, Dorothy Rowe,' said Alison, showering her with kisses.

'That is just fine and dandy. Shoulders back and chin up—and do remove your dead mother from the library! She's a real child frightener.'

It was a glimpse, but it did not last yet. *Not yet.*

For, in a semi-rustic setting in the provinces, all was not well. Dixie Delicious had come for a visit (which was very good) but everyone was muttering. There was a considerable deal of curtain twitching before Sardonic Steve came into play, lugging Dead Santa Maria with him. Alison had made him puce with anger; for that we must not nod at her approvingly. He appeared below the bathroom window one night, dressed in a hoodie and shouting at Dixie Delicious to, 'get out of my town.' Dixie Delicious was surprised to find himself on the set of a Western (especially as he was from Georgia). He wanted to say, 'You gonna shoot me?' but remained silent. In the end, Alison's doting elderly neighbour dug out a bike chain from his shed, slung it over his shoulder and went off to sort out Sardonic Steve. '*Like a father I might have had. Keep you safe, baby girl. Don't worry, baby girl: I've got you.*' After that, apart from a break-in, through the first floor windows using a ladder and a work-shy but otherwise strong arm, he restricted himself to notes shoved through the back door. One said, 'Send your Flag Waver to MacDonald's for the day. I want my things from the shed.' So that was nice but a shame that this was his view of Americans: there's nothing wrong with bunting and ticker tape, after all.

There came another.

The Words.

'*We're back, bitch.*'

'I could lay you out with the words I have kept just for you. Did I mention Dead Santa Maria is with me? She really is a saint now, you know. And she's a star in Dante's firmament.'

'You read Dante?'

'Yes. There was fun to be had. That day, *I was Charon*: scowling at you as you stepped into my boat and when you fainted, I was laughing because, if you want to die or you want to live, you're going to have to pay for it. You are no Beatrice! Dante and Virgil hate you and spit in your face and you will be left in the nasty dark and shadowy wood to be eaten by wolves and again I will laugh. Murderer; bitch; remember me.'

Alison faced the loss of the house she had bought, her job had fallen through and then as the day fell she would lie down, unemployed and cash strapped, on the bed and just breathe through the panic and the threats, hoping the wolves in the dark and shadowy wood could not trace her. There was less time to let thoughts of Baby in the Bucket rattle around in her head: this time, it was all about keeping a roof and dodging the bullets.

She began to think, with a kind of desperate logic, 'If I could bring each moment to its crisis, would I stop getting depressed? If I burned everything down, would things be so bad that I could not be sad, that the embolus of fear would die and shrivel and the fresh air at rock bottom would suffocate the nasty, itchy, scratchy, dark thought in the palm? I could sit at ease and wear smart summer-white trousers, walk along the beach and be daring enough to eat a peach while I was doing it.'

She looked this one up: it didn't mention the misquotation of T.S. Eliot, but the fast and desperate, almost happy logic came tidily under hypomania in the *DSM*, the *Diagnostic and Statistical Manual of Mental Disorders*.

'Am I bipolar? Flights of creative ideas? What's wrong with me, exactly?'

Quite reasonably, she told Dixie Delicious that he was misguided if he ever thought of marrying her: 'Look, I'm Baby in the Bucket. Maggot and wart. I'm Weird Kid and Should not be Here. I have a history of making people unhappy, my exes end up hating me, my brother has dumped me and I've tried to kill myself twice. And when I'm thinking, all screwy, I even bastardise T.S. Eliot. And I just looked myself up in the *DSM* and I'm potentially bipolar, a depressive, with several anxiety conditions, a personality disorder, psychoses—so many head friends—possibly obsessive compulsive and definitely with an attachment disorder…and what about dissociative identity disorder? I mean, it seems all under control; I *think* I put all my friends there,' Alison tapped her temples, '…but then what about Hapless Ally—because she even tries to go the pub independently of me…'

She trailed off. Dixie Delicious had raised his finger to his lips to still her.

There was an awkward silence. He'd told her he loved her. That definitely meant he was about to fuck off and, anyway, Dead Santa Maria was outside the window—up a ladder; it was on the first floor: dead people can climb quickly because they are less frightened of falling. And Alison was about to be annihilated. Who was this, holding the hand of Dead Santa Maria and carrying the bucket where Alison should have been left? It was someone who had her face, her gesture, her shade, only the someone was prettier and bouncier and made you want to laugh. It was Hapless Ally.

'Dixie, there's someone you have to look at. Look outside the window. It's me: it's *other* me, who's taken on a life of her own. How did that ever happen? She's supposed to be, more or less, under my control. And it's Dead Santa Maria: it's Mummy—and she even likes you. She's saying, "Don't do this. Pick again. You just don't know how misguided you are, son."'

But Dixie Delicious went down on one knee, held out a bright diamond engagement ring and said, 'Well how's *this* for misguided?'

And the figures outside the window were going down the

ladder, down, down and in the firmament a star now danced as the glittering ring slipped on the finger and the wolves howled at an unquiet distance: so let us release some binding words from the gentle hands of Professor Pobble and say that 'Time was away', because just sometimes the minute holds you. So *it's okay, baby girl.*

And isn't that just romantic? Proposing even though there were threats outside the bathroom window, your fiancée had a second personality which, apparently, had just been made flesh, your mother was going to be gravely disappointed, your father wouldn't understand *why* when there were plenty of hot women in Georgia and half of Wales (most specifically the uncles—for *always* there were uncles: have a look at Dylan Thomas's *A Child's Christmas in Wales*) was going to interrogate you and say, *in loco parentis* and in a properly scary-like Valleys' baritone, 'Now, what exactly are your intentions towards my niece, boyo?'—and a very dead mother-in-law had climbed up a ladder to spit disapproval at her bitch daughter, but liked the look of you. Now, what did all that foretell? It didn't have a cat in hell's chance, did it?

Now, that depends whether, when in hell, you have a guide.

From elsewhere, Dante and Virgil smiled.

8

Honeymooning in a psychiatric unit

Now, we couldn't say the wedding day was the happiest day of Alison's life but at least it was undeniably funny—in retrospect. They both cried through most of it, two of her burliest cousins acted as security in case Sardonic Steve showed up and told them to get the hell out of his town and stop hanging out with the vicar he thought was a bastard anyway and the youngest bridesmaid pitched (as they say in the South) a *conniption fit* and shouted, 'I never wanted to be a bridesmaid' and screeched, 'I hate Alison!' through all of the vicar's address (such that to this day no-one knew what was actually said or at what point they were actually married). Dead Santa Maria was shuffling about somewhere, Brother who Might as Well have been Dead and Vaguely Dead Dad didn't even give it the time of day. But, miraculously, Alison did not trip and cut a hole in her train or say the wrong name during the marriage vows; she could, however, sense the glares exchanged by the groom's spectacularly-divorced parents, and chanced a look: they were sitting there, rictus smiles on and stiff backed, with the groom's stepmother wearing a discernibly different corsage from the rest of the most intimate core of the wedding party. Dixie Delicious's mother had stated, 'I am not making a corsage for that woman—that hill of white trash,' and so that was that. Dead Santa Maria stood beside her as she said it. Hapless Ally was there, too, looking prettier than the bride: she had detached while the host was distracted.

Alison thought, 'Not here; not now on my wedding day. Let me not be Baby in the Bucket today,' but had no-one to say it to. Then, after the service, as they stood blinking into the summer light, down the stairs from the bell tower came a hulking lump of a fellow; Alison realised with some horror that it was the bell-ringer she had once pleasured after Evensong, having been a bit strung out on dry cider. And now he had rung a peal for her wedding. The man scowled at her and looked her up and down, growling, 'Nice fairy costume.'

'Thanks.'

'Yes,' said the bell-ringer with flagrant sarcasm, 'that was what I forgot to say to you. *Thanks.*'

Alison tried earnestly to control a terrible gripping panic: sneering folk and screaming bridesmaids/dead and undead relatives/snarling in-laws/insatiate bell ringer/mocking alter ego. Not so festive a line-up. But there followed a strange sensation: it was the same wash of tenderness for her parents she had felt, unexpectedly, in France that time and what it came down to, standing there in her bridal gown being roundly told off for getting it wrong was, 'I want my mum. I *want* her.'

How could that be? *Mum. What?* Dead Santa Maria's cold, shiny shark-eye looked at her from the darkened nave. She didn't advance to comfort her daughter.

'Oh—she was a jagged, pointing monster, *but she belonged to me.* And maybe in a way she thought that I was her and she was me and that was why she hated me: because she loved me and didn't want to. Perhaps she really truly loved me against her will and loathed me for it? How unhappy must she have been? And I loved her and I loved her and she will never let go of me and I killed her and I want her back and maybe I have to kill her again!'

You're not supposed to be thinking dark confused things like this on your wedding day. Thinking dark confused things isn't mentioned in the guides and the bright magazines and the wedding journals—*Pollyana fuck again.* But perhaps the point was this: for Alison, things were broken and striated and yet it—this day of coupling—couldn't be taken away from her. And it couldn't be taken away from Dixie Delicious. There had been moments of significant beauty and comedy, when her uncle Bert, recently widowed, had promised to walk up the aisle with her in a gold lamé suit (an unusual suggestion for a Welsh hill farmer). He settled on a gentle tweed with slightly grubby trousers in the end. Dixie Delicious had, he intoned, met with his approval on sight because, 'You're not a bloody Englishman.' Also, during the hymns, the beautiful Welsh baritone of Uncle Howell had reverberated over the flags of the church floor. These fine Welsh waves echoed unnoticed under Southern feet as the groom's spectacularly-divorced parents exchanged cursory glances; one had the beginnings of a snarl around the corners of the mouth. It was incendiary: dark and light in one nave. The flowers were very 'Country Living'; the pollarding of the lime trees had, as Uncle Howell said, 'brought the lime trees on lovely' for her procession in and out of the church. Yet, against the soft, pretty foliage, there were strange simmering resentments afoot, a potential satin-gloved bitch fight between two Southern Ladies of different ilk, between what Southerners might call *country* and the fine steel magnolia.

It is like life and it is not one thing.

Dark and light in one nave.

There stood, in the aisle, the possibility of grievous bodily harm—Sardonic Steve versus The Flag Waver—and yet onward went bride and groom and all was well, even when the wedding cake was so intransigent, it had to be attacked with items from a mechanic's toolkit and, when that didn't work, with a hacksaw that was found, incongruously, under the optics on the bar.

A little-seen uncle bore down on Alison with the words, 'Oh and your mother was such a wonderful woman, but...well, then there was *you*; yes well...' Neighbours clucked at the wrong length of the dress and, in tears, Alison, temporarily floored and unable to find the comedy, snuck to the house of her friend Calypso Caroline next door and they sat in the kitchen with the papers—newspapers: on your wedding day!—a fag and a big mug of tea. Then, after she washed the bride's tired tired feet in their bath, Calypso massaged them and said, 'This will be funny in a few years' time and, really, some of the people at your wedding are wankers' and thus Alison and Dixie Delicious slunk back in, without anyone apparently noticing that they'd been missing. Alison pondered that if next time ever arose, it was definitely an elopement or a Pamela Anderson and Tommy Lee-style Miami number on a beach, in a bikini and with plenty of tequila.

And yet,

It is like life and it is not one thing.

Dark and light in one nave.

At least there was no honeymoon in a Fucking Caravan: they had three glorious days in Catford visiting family, including a visit to the psychiatric unit of a nearby hospital to visit a cousin unable to come to the wedding owing to a sectioning incident, during which they played hangman and did crosswords with everyone in the day room. This preceded five days in Carmarthenshire cleaning, de-fleaing and liberally applying WD40 to the stuck windows in her uncle's house instead. The experience was graced by extended phone calls to bank managers and mortgage advisors because Sardonic Steve wanted his cash. She was sad she had made him unhappy. But, of course, that was a commonplace feeling for Alison. St Lucia was out, as our newly-weds garnered resources for Sardonic Steve's legal suit against her and pursuit of the home he didn't actually own, but on which he had done some work on the days when he got out of bed before eleven.

What it boiled down to was this: Alison, befuddled by life, could not always read the words on the wall.

'The writing was on the wall: did you not see it? Could you not read the words?' she had asked herself. 'Maybe you *are* Baby in the Bucket!'

'Words are what you are made of; words are what make you live: the substance and shift of you. Do not fail to read them' came a voice: it was Helen's. 'You remember that painting we once looked at? Perhaps you were too young to understand at first?'

In Rembrandt's painting, 'Belshazzar's Feast', the painting she had first glanced at with Helen on Tyneside, the subject, as he serves his forbidden wine, looks over his shoulder at the words from *The Book of Daniel* now inscribed on the wall and reads, 'You have been weighed in the balance and found wanting.' Now it is too late: he has chosen to pour the proscribed wine and to continue pouring; he has heard already the stern words of command and now he sees these frightening words of judgement illuminated on the wall at his feast. Does he not fully understand? Not comprehend, because the artist mis-transcribed and set down the Hebrew in columns, rather than in the right to left script as we should read and write it? Alison thought of that painting now, the day she and Helen looked at it before the days of morphine and 'Countdown' and wondered what else she had failed to read and what the consequence of that might yet be.

That very night Belshazzar was slain.

'What will come next? Will Dixie turn out to be like them? Is the writing on the wall again and I can't see it?'

Again, not so festive.

It's probably not often that Babylon is cited as a conduit to Catford, but anyway, when you really look at Catford—I mean *really* look at it—try to read its words and symbols—you see that all sorts of things release their latent value and their own kind of beauty: arches; signs; gardens; parks; day rooms for psychiatric wards. There just aren't any white sands or indigenous tropical fish. One cannot complain. Words—wherever they are said, what they state and what they connote—are no less beautiful further from the equator. Thus, it was Alison's considered opinion that the perfect day wedding and the honeymoon-in-St-Lucia are, like family, a flexible construct.

'Does it really matter,' Alison asked herself some years later, 'if that is how it is?'

There, at its heart, is something private and knowing and which cannot be taken away even if it should end or if much of its beginning is stoked by painful loss, if you will forgive the paradox of that statement. After all, if you have love, can't time be away?

Shortly after the marriage, Catford and Carmarthenshire, Alison spat out the embolus of fear so it was right in front of her, growing; mutating. The shadowy thought pressed against the palm scratched, itched and would not fade to wisps of silver and gold; instead, it darkened and would not leave. Alison was packed off back to Helga, the twinkly-eyed German therapist she had first seen, poleaxed by muddling grief, anger and also ugly, guilty relief after the death of her parents within a year of one another. Many of those memories came flooding back, again and again they came: with her new mother-in-law's clear disappointment and anger at her as a pretty little toccata, the fugue was of her father choking and rambling and cursing and articulating in staccato, '*You Have Let Me Down*' and her mother was angrily dead in an armchair during *Neighbours* (the indignity) and found by a neighbour who had popped by to borrow the lawnmower.

'I should have been there, looking after her even though she didn't want me there' was a refrain that lived with, '*Selfish selfish selfish stupid dirty fuck off Alison!*'

The growing embolus of fear waited to dissect and kill.

'Who to tell? Everyone knows what you're like!'

The chant of Santa Maria and Dead Santa Maria could not be shared and thus scratched away or dissipated with the cheery Frida again because the crawl space was all burned up by the landscaping of its new owner and Frida had long gone back to Sweden permanently and was seeing a new man who wasn't a pop star after the love went tits up (which is *way* funnier in a Swedish accent) with Benny. Unfortunately, looking to Camus was not overly productive because he was a bit hard-arsed on guilt and berating of the self and poor old Sylvia was deader than ever and was just waiting to be played by Gwyneth Paltrow, with Daniel Craig doing a 'Just for Men Hair Club' Ted.

Thus, Alison conceived a new idea; didn't even share this with Helga, in case Helga thought it a shade too far. Alison needed a new Frida and a new kind of crawl space. She didn't quite need someone for intense erotic adventure or to teach her fellatio (Camus) or a delicate and passionate soul (JK), and quite clearly attempts at making up with Mary Anning were not going to be fruitful because, after a sort of falling out and separation from Miss Philpot, the latter's attachment with Mary was deeper than ever. There was no way Alison could play beach gooseberry with them. So what she wanted—and fast, because she could feel herself going under—were some new female icons who looked as if they couldn't care less.

Who could say to Dead Santa Maria, 'Get out!'

Who could say to Hapless Ally, 'Get gone!'

Alison took Helga's drugs, (some whizzy SSRIs to begin with) cast the net wide and stumbled upon two new friends in one afternoon; really, she should have noticed them before, but that was probably all to the good because they would not have got on with Frida. Frida was a gentle, cheery soul but Alison knew that, when roused—especially by other women—she might be pretty tricky. Radio 2 had been on in the background and the girl had heard them: two divas—one from Tiger Bay (as was) and one from the Smoky Mountains: Shirley Bassey and Dolly Parton. Shirley was stored in Alison's head in the box which was marked, '*This is something that could be useful later*', which box was next to another labelled, '*Randomly acquired information which isn't needed at*

the moment, but could be on some future occasion'. There was
another box, of course: the one that Dead Santa Maria had
said was inside the nasty little girl for all to see. The one
marked *THE WAGES OF SIN ARE DEATH,* in angry
upper case.

Dolly was placed in the forefront straight away—a
stunning little white bird with big feathers and shiny
rhinestones. She was tiny, but she was powerful. And she
could be heard properly as she was, in Alison's head, because
she was Southern like Dixie Delicious. And, with Alison
sitting snivelling in the house, alone apart from the ancient
cat, it went like this....

'Dolly, what should I do because my neck is in knots and
I am scared? It feels like they are coming for me. I can't
go out because what will happen if I run into one of Dead
Santa Maria's friends and they give me *the look?* The look that
says, "Oh everyone knows what you are like." What if I see
Brother who Might as Well have been Dead out and about
in town because this is where his financial consultant is—just
down the hill there—he goes there to count his money
because there's too much of it to do it on his own—oh, that's a
horrible thing to think and say, isn't it? That's why I'm Baby
in the Bucket. What if I see someone who just knows I have
caused harm? I might fall on the floor! Oh that's a terrible
thing to think: so self-indulgent. I don't matter. You would
have left me in a bucket. Yes, you too...'

A little hand with long shiny red nails was placed firmly
on her arm. It was small, but mighty and Alison knew that
Dolly was the big sister she had always wanted and also

possibly that maybe she was a lunatic to be a twenty eight year-old, newly-married woman, sitting in the front room talking to a pretty little white bird with pneumatic lips, big hair, fabulously enormous breasts and the tiniest of waists. Who wasn't actually there. But Dolly told her stories of shiny things, joy, being poor and happy; how she had personally built Dollywood and all her projects brick by brick with her child-hands and she rose up through the flames like a funny little ivory phoenix and said to Alison's sadness, 'Don't sass your momma.'

Alison watched her doing all that and realised that, for as long as she could remember, she had been singing along to Dolly and humming her songs; the first one she could remember was 'Coat of Many Colours' where Dolly, fierce and proud and happy, sang about her upbringing, dirt poor, in Tennessee. Alison wished that she could learn something from Dolly: about understanding riches, being happy, moving on or loving your momma, because of how she felt about her own mother—about the burden of being born to her, about Dead Santa Maria's near-lifetime of maladies and about her rage at her daughter for the illness, near lunacy with the ghastly dynamism of metastasis and the choking death on the bathroom floor of Alison's father. Well, it wasn't exactly tidy or comfortable or proud. It was a bitter and complex creature and its sinister images were forever skittering about in her mind.

There was her father now spitting, guttering and dying—shrieking once again about Jesus and pointing at her with a trembling arm to state, 'You did this!'

There was Dead Santa Maria at his side, Mummy and Daddy, and she joined in the shrieking: 'Didn't you know he was dying? He is a good man and you are the same selfish little bitch you always were!'

Big bad pictures, but there was the warm little talon-tipped hand on the arm again saying, 'Boo! Run along now. You hear me?'

And, 'Ah think you should have some hot tea.'

Alison brewed tea and Dolly admired the cornbread Alison had made; it had been baked in a cast iron pan with moulds the shape of corn ears, sent recently from Georgia, and they ate it warmed with butter and everyone felt a little bit better. Dolly talked about acrylic nails and where to get reinforced bras and how to make your lips shine. And she sang to Alison about how you could be rich even though you were poor if love had been sewn into your motley coat by the mother who adored you so.

With another snatch of song, Alison felt ashamed that her coat had not been made of rags stitched together; that she had had new clothes and plenty of *stuff* and that she should not be there crying. But Dolly did not judge. Sure, she had been a second mother to her younger siblings, for, 'Ah was one of twelve, the fourth eldest, and that was trouble enough. But honey, we had love.' And her father had paid the doctor who delivered her with a bag of oatmeal. Things were tough in a one-room cabin in Locust Ridge in The Smoky Mountains. Yet, Dolly told her not to be ashamed of feeling blue and sitting there nursing the bad black images—and she delivered a megawatt smile with her expensive teeth and Alison realised what it was that made her ogle at Dolly and want to be her friend and keep counsel and be kin with her: she radiated a kind of joy; a sort of confidence. Not arrogance, but a gentle knowledge that you're kicking about and doing your best and singing about 'Jolene' with a loud clear voice. Dolly stood up.

She had a fringe on her white leather coat and she flicked it assertively in the face of the trouble that stood all around Alison, announcing, 'Oh Ah can see your trouble stood up there. Just because Ah'm always smiling, don't mean Ah'm never sad.'

Alison was amazed—and even more so by what happened next: Dolly pulled herself up as tall as she would go, reapplied her lipstick, readjusted her breasts (her 'girls'; her 'puppies') and puffed up her hair a little. Then she rubbed her hands together and looked the dark thought in the palm up and down from her golden eye and prodded a finger into the embolus of fear, which was fervently trying to bleed darkness into the room; to paralyse its owner—and she said, 'You know what? It's so hard to be a diamond in this ol' rhinestone world but let's both of us sparkle!' and she kicked the terrible things across the room and went off to catch the flight for the first leg of her world tour with the husband who had adored her quietly and out of the limelight for fifty years. Alison put on her Dolly Parton album and felt a bit better, although she was still scared about what would happen when the terrible things slunk back, bruised, into the room. She ate a little more cornbread and butter as a salve.

The next day, Helga the German therapist was in

forthright mood and told her she reckoned Alison had been through quite enough but Alison reckoned she hadn't been guilty long enough and so the two, neither budging, were at loggerheads on the matter. Plus, she had let Dolly down now that she was wallowing and stewing overnight in guilt: she was all in black, apologetic, not a feathery, glittery girl-woman. Could she get *nothing* right? The fear came back and gloated. Alison had so hoped that Dolly had properly broken it up so that it couldn't manifest, but no such luck: back it had slunk, and Helga said of the fear, 'You must, my funny funny little friend Alison, develop some belief in yourself. Start to believe that this terrible thing is not always about to come and fell you.'

Of course, the question of the patient was, 'But how do you know?'

And the answer, 'You are being a difficult patient so shh,' in her firm Germanic style.

But there was something about Helga's intelligence; about her maverick sense of stating opinion rather than the more traditional therapeutic route of allowing answers to emerge. Alison adored her. Could it be said that to make the sick well, you need a certain amount of bluff? Where confidence is alive in your words, transmuting into the shape of the letters—giving itself to the listener? It went something like that. Later, Helga saw Alison in the waiting room as the latter clock-watched until surgery started, when Dr Krank-Werden the GP could reassess the medicines because the SSRIs weren't stopping the flappy hands and the night terrors.

She galumphed over saying, 'Ooooh *sehr gut*! Is this him?' to Dixie Delicious.

In the next appointment she roundly told her patient that Dixie Delicious was dishy indeed and that she should not allow other people or bad memories or the disabling sense of past mistakes made 'to crap in your den' but to, 'Use this time to be at it like bunnies with your new husband. Bunnies have fun. They don't keep taking crap from dead mother bunnies. They don't worry about being some other rabbit, like in a kind of theory of Platonic bunny forms. There is no ideal rabbit. You need more fun and more bunny.'

Be more bunny. That actually made sense.

Helga did not have further time for Alison.

'There are many more out there. I do not have time enough as there are many madder than you. (Alison raised her eyebrows because those in therapeutic support roles are not supposed to use the word 'mad'). 'Yes, I know: I don't fanny about. Crazy things need sorting out elsewhere and I do not think anything more terrible will happen to you, but if it does, come straight back and we will sort out mad. And in the meantime, remember the bunnies.'

More putative therapy, for surely there were much more pressing cases; people who were incapacitated, in a place beyond words, and thus it is with mental health budgets and the walking wounded and thus followed a year or so of puttering around, waiting for something appalling to happen and with occasional tremors when she thought of whether Sardonic Steve would reappear any time soon; he had after all promised her that he could lay her out, any time he wanted, with the things he could say. He wouldn't have to do anything; he just knew what to say and even a look could see her on the floor, incapacitated, finished maybe. Finished by *the words*. Without Helga to help her.

Oh bitch, I know what you are like. Everybody knows what you are like. You are the most selfish person I have ever met and I want the missing years of my life back, bitch.

Those words, playing again, as they did, to the familiar tune in Alison's head, would rattle around. The embolus of fear could be there in the long grass, rolling to her feet on a balmy summer's day; sometimes in her head; sometimes in the shiny eye of a stranger or the face of dead mother. They were a trinity: Dead Santa Maria; Brother who Might as Well have been Dead; Sardonic Steve. How could they not all be right? And thus came another collapse, sitting there at table thinking about what to do: how to annihilate yourself, before someone else did—with knife or drug. The thing was, Alison clearly wasn't very good at doing the dying: it hadn't worked twice. It was almost funny.

Alison's kindly GP put her on some further kindly medication—trazodone, because the sertraline kept making her giddy; a little diazepam for bedtime: all the tablets to be kept secret and apart, for risk of overdose, by Dixie Delicious—and the sessions with funny Helga took up again, now that Alison had ticked a few more in-need boxes, until gradually, timorously, an infinitely small, infinitely delicate thing came forth: calm; a little bit of happiness; some time off. Dixie Delicious, with his broken and beautiful faith and his reading aloud to her was a not insignificant factor in this. He couldn't see the terrible things; he never saw an embolus of fear or felt the itching in the palm where the black thought pressed in and from where it threw out shoots, but he was getting to know where to look and also angry that their happiness should be blistered by past hurts and wrong-doings, even if they had, truly, been administered by his wife.

'I'll be buggered,' he said, showing an admirable grasp of English idiom for a Flag Waver.

He was just a man she met, going the other way, on a street, in a monsoon flood. Shit like that doesn't happen; doesn't work.

Does it?

9

Studying genetics; becoming a mother

Now, the next shenanigans in the life of Alison were originally called *The Having of the Babies*. However, that sounded rather as if they'd been eaten, ordered or bought in—so we shall settle on *Becoming a Mother*. It is a bit convoluted, so are you sitting comfortably? Alison always loved a gerund, though; she'd be sorry to see one go.

If you are a mother, or currently aiming at that target, you will doubtless be familiar with all the paraphernalia that goes with the pregnancy, birthing and trying to get there in the first place stuff.

People spout forth, 'Oh do let me tell you the story of my friend who had twenty-eight miscarriages and then a healthy quad! Do let me share the story of the baby that looked fine but was a goner from birth/the child who had the cord wrapped round his neck/the mother who died three times during labour and had to be resuscitated/the giant baby who ruptured his mother's cervix and she always walked with a stick and weed uncontrollably after that and so of course her husband didn't want her any more. Also, this poor woman never went on a trampoline, laughed or coughed again. Ever.'

Please note that this tale recounts this kind of commentary not as if it were true—but because it *was* true; just, you know, standard tip of the iceberg labour-day tales that people tell. The correct response to the unsolicited horror story is an unsolicited, 'Fuck off!' It's particularly good because people don't expect a pregnant bird to swear, unless, of course, the pregnant bird is also a pontificating benefits cheat, airing on *The Jeremy Kyle Show*.

So, Alison found herself expecting a miraculous birth shortly after the decision to be expecting had been made. It was unexpectedly quick. What she could never have imagined would be the story that followed next, even though she also thought it couldn't last: for how could Baby in the Bucket have a baby? And getting onto the bus one day, having so far escaped the nausea so common to pregnant women, she bled profusely and so began her long relationship with what is often known as an EPAC unit in hospitals. It's where you go in early pregnancy if there's a problem you knew about or which has been foisted, frighteningly, onto you. In those days Alison and Dixie Delicious knew next to nothing. The scan—in the darkened room into which you have blundered, snivelling—shows nothing or that there has been something: a sad little empty *something* that didn't make it and is *elsewhere*. Not because 'Time was away', but because time was there and time killed. And this is where they were, blood after blood, not understanding why but with the nasty ruminating thought in Alison's mind that she did not deserve to be a mother; that she was being shown such a thing by God or whatever God meant—and that is a hard thing to let go of. Especially if you have a hecatomb of a mind, full of dark tunnels you go down and from which you may not emerge to see stars through a beautiful aperture. Or an alter ego who is often you, but who periodically splits because she's the better part of you and gets to have more fun.

And of course, the comments: they began with miscarriage number one and carried on to number five.

'Come and babysit for my children instead.'

'Do you think it's your, you know, *mental* problems?'

'You could always adopt!'

'It's because of your, you know, *anxiety*.'

But, most helpfully, a Helga-style Doctor who said, 'Grit your teeth and carry on.'

But three no baby was just about okay, whereas five no baby looked like time to stop. Then something funny happened and unravelled a lot of strange and mysterious thoughts in the curious mind of Alison. She got a picture of her chromosomes and met the most marvellous person called Patricia Queen the Clinical Genetic Nurse, hereafter known as PQ. Her name was fitting, for p is the short arm on the top of your chromosome; p stands for petit, while q is the long arm but its letter doesn't stand for anything—it's just the next letter in the alphabet: PQ taught Alison that in their many long Q and A HA and PQ OEDs. Now, wouldn't you

ANNA VAUGHT

like to hear the story of the tiny but powerful woman who could drip genetic formulae like honey and also learn how Alison got to be a mummy—three times, but with a litter (the vocabulary here becomes strained) of the eleven who didn't make it?

Being pregnant and then, abruptly, *not* being, is a strange and dislocating experience; in the beginning you know nothing, then suddenly you know way too much. You know every little twinge of your body, every little sensation; you are a word-hoard of facts and a little book of statistics, all about pregnancy loss and hows and whys and suddenly, aided and abetted by the plangent horror stories well-meaning onlookers tell you, staying pregnant and birthing a live child appear to be impossible. Something peculiar happens to your rational mind and you become of the opinion that reproduction has everything stacked against it. You could give up at this stage; people do. And this is where you need a cunning person like PQ. Also, if you've been inclined to mental health adventures, it's an idea to stay in touch with *the team*, if you have one, because the risk is that a conspiracy theory takes hold, where dead shouty mothers and undead siblings halloo at the windows of hope and properly besmirch them: you can't see out, then, to a different day.

You think, 'I can't be anyone's mother. No baby wants me. They don't stay. It's because I had low mood, did self-harming, had depression query anxiety disorder, query obsessive compulsive disorder, query bipolar, query mood disorder, query and *all those voices*, but no, it doesn't fit schizophrenia, schizo-affective disorder or—although we could be proved wrong—brief psychotic disorder. But so many queries: what comes next? Perhaps my instability explains it all?'

Alison had rather a lot of blood tests after miscarriage number four and discovered something very interesting: she had a thing called a balanced translocation, where one part of a chromosome pair swaps places with another part of a chromosome pair. Should you want to know in more specific detail, part of the long arm of a chromosome number six had stuck itself on a short arm of chromosome seventeen; chromosome seventeen had reciprocated (not that genes are sentient, exactly), so that bits of it were stuck on chromosome six. This time, it was the numbers that were wrong, not the words; they came, for Alison, with a sense that she *should have known*—the *numbers were on the wall*: that night Belshazzar was slain. She should have seen.

'I am innumerate as well as illiterate. I am a lot of things and none of those things are good. I have been weighed in the balance and found wanting and the words and numbers were on the wall, weren't they?'

Alison's thought was this was just bloody typical Alison (which, funnily enough was what one of her neighbours said, but she's dead now so that's bloody typical of people *who can't help but make comments*). Her second thought was to hold the hand of Dixie Delicious and have a cry: but then a third thought came on the wing—a funny, detached little thing, all its own self—and it said, 'Now that *is* interesting.' For a moment, Alison was able to step back and spectate;

to look for that interest. The gynaecologist took up the last part of the narrative, for what was more (again *typical*), the translocation was not in all of her cells, but only in some: it was called a mosaic. Her fourth thought was, 'That's almost pretty,' because she couldn't help but visualise all her muddled chromosomes like the colourful beads, coalescing into a random pattern, in a child's kaleidoscope. Like gem-words trying to find sense. Equations compelling us to solve them. Writing on the wall.

Alison sat at the kitchen table and pored over the pictures: slides of her broken up chromosomes.

Normal karotype. Something about her had been defined as *normal*.

Cell showing balanced translocation.

The chromosomes were partly from Dead Santa Maria.

Gifting.

'She is me and I am her. She gave these to me and lots of them were broken. She can't have done it on purpose, but say her spite was so big, even at that time, that something fractured. *Something to stop more of me.* Yes—say that something stepped in: like the cells knew somehow. They were sentient—trying *to stop more of me.* Or maybe it was her. She cursed me: Maleficent Mother, and nobody knew her secret. Somehow she did it. Did she invent Hapless Ally, as well? Was she born with me? There in the cells and the roots of what I am?'

'You are rambling. This has to stop,' said Dixie Delicious, whose heart was breaking, too.

Alison and Dixie Delicious hunkered down at home to potter and ponder. Alison knew she might be taking a chance. If Dead Santa Maria had been right, was procreation okay? Had God who was Dead if He ever Existed given her a very big hint. *It stops with you?*

'Irrational,' said Dixie Delicious. Because, like PQ, he revelled in logic and not in the whipped-up illogical mind. Sometimes she thought he was cold, but he wasn't: he just made more sense than her and, for the emotionally labile, that's a tricky thing to admit to. You get to see clearly what a screw-up you are.

It was Christmas and felt very lonely. They hadn't talked ps and qs with PQ yet, Dixie Delicious's parents couldn't bring themselves to understand so Alison focused instead on teaching her mother-in-law to make Christmas pudding, brandy butter, bread sauce, all the tastes of the season and none of which you generally encountered in Georgia. Another Christmas that sucked. Even the snow fell as grey slush. It felt like nothing gave a fuck; not even the weather.

They watched the 'Indiana Jones' film again and Alison thought what she might write this time.

'Dear Mr Ford, you know I asked you when I was a kid about whether you'd had a shit Christmas, cooked the giblets in the bird and put too much tinsel on the tree? Can I ask you now, when you cracked your whip and wore your hat rakishly, were you also thinking, "I suck. I was that Boy-in-a-Bucket"? No, of course not. I'm sorry and I hope you get the grail, but remember to close your

eyes. Did you have to do the Harrison-Comparison thing or was it all okay? Do you know what translocations are?'

The hospital had said she should write to Brother who Might as Well have been Dead, to tell him about the funny genes in case he wanted to have children too. Alison whispered, 'There's no point. He was Number One Son. He wasn't made of the same things. He was *The expensive delicate ship*. His chromosomes could only ever have been perfect.'

The doctor said, 'I'm not sure I follow you.'

The nurse said, 'Did you just quote Auden? "About suffering they were never wrong/The old masters?" '

For poetry is eponymous. Even if you can't read, like Grandfather back at The Hill. And words are magic, even if a bad person said them.

Brother who Might as Well have been Dead wrote back on a scrap that, 'what does not concern me doesn't interest me,' or it might have been the other way round, which was nice. Also that he wasn't interested in genetics or children, because he didn't trust quacks or the nature of the beast and you couldn't trust anyone and it wasn't like anyone cared and children were bastards, so why would you? It was an unnecessary missive anyway, because Alison's genetic twist was pronounced to be spontaneous in her. It just bloody would be, wouldn't it? A neighbour commented, '*A rarer form of something? Well that's just bloody typical of you, isn't it?'* (But then her house blew up in mysterious circumstances so that's just typical, again, of people who can't help but make comments: they also leave the gas on.)

But days shift and maybe it's just easier to say that someone habitually acts like a tosser. And thus jog on. Folk make comment. Siblings don't care or notice. Mothers hate you, even when dead; fathers have acquiesced while their wives leave a hairball from the child on the carpet, as a warning. And thus, again, with the New Year came PQ, who told them to believe what the textbook says.

'Balanced translocations are rare but people with them can and do have healthy babies.'

Dixie Delicious, like PQ, told her to stay away from the internet, but there she was, looking at memorial gardens and baby angel poems and pictures of babies with profound disabilities; at children never released from the ward because what PQ could not, of course, promise them was the birth of a healthy child. It is the recipe where the cake did not rise because its ingredients were wrong. Alison spent a long time trawling; becoming obsessed with knowing all there was to know and obsessed with the picture of her cells: looking for a message in the short and long arms. She found that babies had been born with a bit of extra six and a bit of seventeen missing, but that the obverse was thought to be 'incompatible with life.' That chilling medical word. Not *viable*. The horns of a dilemma: 'What do you do?' thought Alison.

'Say I was never viable in the first place. This is the sign of that: the writing on the wall. Do I carry on, knowing that I may have a baby that is dreadfully sick and will not live long? And would the terrible things come up at the same time and properly fell us both: sick infant; sick mother. So it begins again.'

Alison reflected that these questions had no tidy answer, but she was one tenacious little bugger—couldn't help it sometimes—and wasn't going to give up just yet, either way. Grit your teeth: it is the impulse to survive, perhaps strongest in those told that they should *not* survive and that they *cannot* because they are Baby in the Bucket.

PQ could offer no particular reassurance, but was hugely reassuring anyway; she was funny and giggly and as small as a borrower and as wise as an owl. Alison learned that the 'outcome' can never be certain. Translocations are not all made the same and even one which appears to be a match with yours, does not necessarily tell that the same genes are affected because the break may not be exactly in the same place. It's both fiendishly complicated and terribly, painfully simple.

Alison told her aunt, a nurse. And funnily enough what she said really helped: 'Oh I expect you got that when you got a cold as a child. You were always getting colds. Don't you worry about that, now.'

Obviously one does need to set to one side any concern about the confusion, as a nurse, she entertained between the common cold and profound genetic change to the blastocyst during cell mitosis. Yet saying confidently 'Don't you worry about that now' elicited a surprisingly confident reply: 'All right,' said Alison, 'I won't.' Because that's the thing about reassurance or about nudges towards comfort and optimism: it's not all in the words, but in the sentiment behind them: it is distraction; someone else's sanguine attitude. An invitation, however misguided, to hope. *Set that down, someone. Set that down*—in the annals of mental health and possibilities of present and future. You don't need to be fully understood to be loved.

But it was frightening—the scans; the first view of a punchy little embryo (and the obstetrician's Marian comment: 'A papal blessing! I see a heartbeat! Did you pray to Mary?'); later, the amniocentesis with PQ sitting there, willing her charge on silently, as the fabulously glamorous and glossy Dr Ching rubbed on the anaesthetic, then got to work with the giant needle. Alison watched the steady hand at first and then closed her eyes to it all. Social obligation after trauma saw Alison fainting and falling on the floor afterwards, having tried a little too hard to be an extra big and bouncy Hapless Ally and coping ever so well. Coping especially well because there was an inconsolable woman in the waiting room, keening and swaying. Alison—as the alter ego faded away, for Hapless Ally totally lacked empathy—wanted desperately to help the woman and found it intolerable to see someone so sad. She was looking around for the nearest kettle to make tea and suddenly she swooned and fell on the floor. Tiny PQ—with a 'tsk tsk'—shifted her with a pair of man hands onto a gurney. Alison is glad, now, to introduce others to PQ, Borrower nurse and geneticist. If you are unfamiliar with the NHS, you need to know that it may have been scourged and stripped of funding and resource, but it is still a thing of rare beauty, because it contains the Mental Health Rescue Squad, Helga, Dr Krank-Werden and PQ.

Alison experienced the wait for results as the cell culture

is grown as the strangest of times; one of stasis: you cannot remember a life before it or grasp a life after it. They went out walking, feeling a wash of exhaustion; she brushed her fingers along the comfrey leaves as they walked. A red kite circled overhead and Alison sat down hard, next to the footpath: it was home to rest, but there came a call on ps and qs from PQ. 'All is well. Normal chromosomes and would you like to know—would you? Well…it's a boy! And congratulations to you, 46, xx, E (6;17) (p21.3; q25)/46, xx—which is you, Alison, expressed as a genetic karotype. Look: there is only *one* of you. Isn't it beautiful?'

'There is only one of me.

There is only one of me.'

When baby Noah was born, Alison was scared to look at him, or touch him. Eventually, she held him with a surprising confidence to her breast, but struggled to soothe him with words or use the word 'son'. She felt he couldn't stay with her; that it couldn't last. Dead Santa Maria would get at her somehow, or perhaps by mouthing her love aloud, Alison would invoke divine nemesis from God who was Dead if He ever Existed.

Dixie Delicious would sit with her and make her say things like, 'This is Noah, my son. This is my baby. This is my son. This is my child.'

It was hard for her to do because she felt frightened that she could not manage or do it properly, that she did not deserve him and that he would be taken away. And this,

Dixie Delicious, with clear sight of this complicating subtlety, attempted to fix. In the end, the words, they won. And the good sums and done-right equations did, too, because Alison, although the sadness would not go, went into a chemist, baby in sling and said, in faltering voice, 'I'd like some colic medicine for the baby. For. For. My son.'

But from here, the story may disappoint, because after a tale of the magic of children and the saving graces of the simple telling, we must return to rocky times because Alison gets bitten, then mauled and it all goes, shall we say, tits up. Children, however much they are a blessing, are not a salvation and were not put in this world to fix their mothers' broken minds.

Not long after, Alison had acquired, as if by genetic stealth, two strapping boys. Two magical boys, Noah and Asa, who might one day grow up to create worlds in the margins of their pages or castles in words; they are boys to tell stories and build bold landscapes, if they have confidence enough. Alison thought recklessly of having a large brood, but, what with all the adventures at EPAC, the long pointy needles and the empty scans, it was time for a rest after that. And she could not be sure about staying sane, which is not a little matter however hard you have learned to laugh. Strapping boy number three will propel himself forward into the narrative a little later on, once you hear of how Alison learned a thing or two.

The night that Noah was born (*my son; my Number One Son*), after PQ had popped by, Alison sat alone in the maternity ward and felt a horrid slump; the lead weight falling down. There were all the gentle coos and all the caterwauls of the newborns and, a little way off, a labouring woman made a long 'Moooooo!' like a heifer bearing down and later that night another was screaming, 'No No Fuck! Fuck! Fuck!' as Alison had a school dinner tea of faggots, those perfect-breast municipal mashed potatoes and a sweetcorn, pea and tiny carrot mélange, Angel Delight and oceans of tears. Noah the baby next to her—with his funny little whooping cry, his breath holding and his extraordinary shock of hair with an Elvis Presley quiff—one of the midwives had said, 'That baby looks like a used car salesman!'—well, *she didn't know him.*

It is an extraordinary thing: you are alone, in charge of a baby: he has sent his things on ahead, with baby grows bunched in drawers and tiny non-slip socks (why *do* babies need non-slip socks when they cannot walk?) and padded suits because he's a December boy. You are expected to know every inch of this child; to know exactly what he would look like and how he would be. But you do not know him and he does not know you, and yet when you thought you would never have him you could visualise him exactly. And it made Alison cry. It was partly the expectation and partly the keen sense of being alone and being a failure: of not knowing how to do this, in the midst of a gang of mummies who are glowing and doing and up and about and to be intricately connected with their babies already. A message every day; a ruminating thought: *He is not for you.* The hollow laughter of Dead Santa Maria. Perhaps it was not that way for you;

perhaps it was different for you, but this is how it was for Alison.

These days require company: for Alison, it took a couple of particularly sequinned imaginary friends, because she didn't know how to make—well not *real*, because real is subjective; and not *substantial* because how can we say something is insubstantial if it isn't there but provides support and solace all the days of a life?—but *conventional* friendships, in the way most people might understand them. When Alison felt most alone in the child-rearing days, she would imagine Shirley—passion and pouting; raising and twisting her arms as she sang and filling—*absolutely filling*—the room. She had no doubt Shirley could have kicked Dead Santa Maria a storm as she sashayed in in her red spangled gown. Alison was having less luck, because while she sat on the sofa, much wanted infant at her breast, the itchy scratchy thought in the palm was now awake and active and she was aware of the dark thought, the embolus of fear and the stone falling down, down, in the heart. Shirley would not have stood for that nonsense.

'Shut up bad things. Let's dance instead!'

'I can't. I just can't. And I can't still the chatter in my head.'

'But *I* am in your head. So let me help you sugar?'

10

Helter skelter with a baby

When Alison started going to mummy groups the familiar, dark old feeling came with her. There were moments of joy, but their familiar was the plummeting sensation. She made, in the end, friends for lifetimes; women to laugh darkly, to drink and holler and act like naughty schoolgirls: women who were madonnas, sexy and funny. She met others who were arrogant, obsessive, snobbish and whose intellect and sense of comic value after birth and during child rearing had, as another friend put it, gone south with their tits and pelvic floors. Alison was afraid to even articulate this thought in her head to begin with, having been raised as a low-life or maggot. But in later years, watching the unpleasant spectacle of nice but evilly competitive mothers, with their cupcakes and pigs in blankets, well she wasn't so much any more. Wonderful mothers; smiling bitches to other mummies. There. She said it. Shirley told her to.

'Shirley, they don't like me. And their tits are on straight like Heroic Alice; their lip-gloss is smooth; their babies aren't fretful and if they are, I don't think it's their fault.'

'Ah, think of something else, my girl. Puff your hair up big; wear bright lipstick.'

'My heart sinks. Their cakes; their sex; their everything: it's all trimmed up better than mine.'

'Let's have a cigar. Va va voom!'

In the early days, after tea and home-made cakes and all that jazz, there was a squalling baby to be settled in the car and tears as she sensed Dead Santa Maria trying to get to her; whether with love or loathing or a mixture of the two, it wasn't always entirely clear. Tempting fate, after seeing the mummies swept off by the grandmothers, sweet children dandled and dimpled happiness, Alison would try to talk to Dead Santa Maria. She would say, 'Is this how it goes? I am no good. My baby is perfect. But I should have been left in the Bucket. Little bitch podding broad beans, cuss by the bonfire and fuck-wit on the coast path with Daddy. Or is it—is it—am I doing—am I *acceptable* at this?'

But Dead Santa Maria scoffed, and Vaguely Dead Dad whispered, from the coast path of the past, 'Be quiet, you little fuck-wit: the cormorants are more interesting than you!' and the dialogue came to an abrupt end.

Then once, driving home in indigo twilight, she was terribly afraid, imagining what Shirley would do should she ever feel as Alison felt now. As a mother—as a human being. It wasn't that Shirley was perfect; she had had, after all, a few children from relationships and marriages that had hit the rocks; the papers had once said that she had married a gay man and had a well-publicised affair with someone else's man. But oh—she had spirit; she had confidence and you couldn't keep her down, gliding from pillar to post, from Hall of Fame to Hall of Fame. Alison sang songs from Bond films in the car. And Shirley boomed, 'Focus your mind on *Goldfinger*. Hear me swoop; hear me roar!'

Alison tried, but couldn't muster up the élan and vivacity of Shirley in sequins at the Royal Albert Hall. She imagined her being born, in a dusty little house on Tiger Bay in the days before redevelopment, Ikea, spendy hotels and penthouses with a view of Steep Holm and Flat Holm. Even then, Shirley had pizazz and knew she was going somewhere, even if she didn't know where she was going was just yet.

'I want to scream out loud! I want to say that I am angry and lonely and that I do not know what I'm doing,' said Alison to Shirley.

And Shirley bellowed, 'Sing and shout girl! Go show the world what you are and what you can do. You shouldn't have been left in a bucket. I would have told them a thing or two, my girl. Do you hear me apologising when I hold them in the palm of my hand—my captive audience?'

And, most audaciously, '*Go tell your dead mother NO! That's it. Tidy.* Now, don't be a fool! Do I have to ask you, whose coat is that jacket?'

'Apologising,' thought Alison, aloud. 'It's like with my baby I am little again and apologising for being alive. *Saying sorry for having Christmas presents.* Feeling like a clown and not knowing how to give to my baby what he needs. And Shirley, what do I do about Hapless Ally? She's me—a better version of me; the one I summon up so I'm not jeered at. But she isn't just me—she sometimes goes out on her own. To the pub, to hang out with Dead Santa Maria: to laugh at me from around corners!'

Shirley laughed: 'You have to find a way to tease her out, pen her up and stop her breathing. And maybe one day *all* your friends can help with that?'

Alison knew the stirrings of panic: Shirley's spirited words and their promise of hope and help couldn't quite reach her—she sensed that something very big and nasty was about to happen and stopped the car for a few moments because she was crying so hard. The cry was harder because everyone else, all the other mummies—pretty mummies; alpha mummies every one—had stayed on for tea, beaming and happy and tired and chuckling about sore breasts and wincing and laughing at tales of episiotomies. Alison was alone, even in company.

Starting the car again, she let out a thin, dry voice: 'Help me. Help me please, Shirley. Will you help me?'

And Shirley started singing and telling tales in between snatches of song. In her rich voice, she was telling Alison to wear glitter, to get her hair done big and stand up straight and she was telling her her story: 'Everyone told me to shut up. Even in the school choir, the teacher kept telling me to back off until I was singing in the corridor and I didn't care and the whole school could hear me and I sang for joy!'

Alison wondered how it would be to keep on singing and

talking and going in a direction that you had set yourself. Could you do that if you couldn't get all the voices and the smackings with a hairbrush and mutterings about buckets out of your head? Shirley just laughed at that and said they'd called her a darkie; said she'd never get anywhere—well maybe get to be running about on the Cardiff Bay mud with a boy if she was lucky. Or maybe singing in a smoky club with no chance of advancement beyond that. She went to Penarth once, but they were all posh there and thought, as the old joke goes (say it aloud), that *sex was what you carried coal in.* But Shirley had always felt she could rise up and fill a room, even if everyone said she couldn't; she had always known and the others, well they could all go to hell, couldn't they? Nobody ever put her in the shade.

'Lose this fear, my girl. Let some of my stardust rub off on you. Do it differently! And sugar, you should see what I would make of anyone who tried to put me in a bucket!'

Va va voom!

It was mid-December and Alison was driving home, having this conversation with Shirley, past the Westbury White Horse and the soft slopes around it. Shirley had told her that there was not enough space in the room for her and for Dolly, so Alison suppressed 'Jolene' as it came up on her lips while she felt the tremors inside.

The darkness began to settle on her and, while Shirley rested a while with a Martini and a cigarillo and Dolly whisked her fringed jacket, jacked up her puppies and swished off, rolling her eyes at Shirley, comic-cross. Alison wound down the window and heard, above the grumblings of the tiny child, the winter song of the robin: the exquisite, plaintive winter song. Above her, the beginnings of the plain rose; the hard furrows were struck across the earth and the white horse was gleaming. She felt it would have been more beautiful in chalk rather than the immaculate white-painted concrete which it now had become, but she also knew that it had been vandalised and they had had to preserve it thus. But the functional sheen lowered her spirits further. Imagining the furrows and falls of the chalk, instead, Alison could hear that Noah had fallen asleep and his breathing was deep and even. Shirley was quiet for now and in the darkling quiet, Alison heard again the winter song of the robin and felt the hard beat of her heart—its rate rising uncomfortably, as it did, when she became suddenly aware that she had forgotten the dark thought in the palm, the embolus and even Hapless Ally just for a little while. Then she remembered what the little, dark nuzzling thought in the palm—the familiar, loved and hated little thought—had said all those years ago in the orchard. The voice had come up, 'Can you remember when you were just Alison? And you understand the name I gave you, don't you? You feel it, don't you? It is coming, Alison. *Coming*. And *she* is coming for you, Alison and you are going to have to decide and one of you is going to have to win.'

'You mean I have to fight her? Kill her, even? But how? And do you mean I will cease to exist?'

But now no voice rose up to answer her. Instead, she became aware that she was no longer driving but was still and lost to the fear. Would the self (our rather selves) she was begin to dissect? Who was who and could she even tell any more between plain old Alison or Hapless Ally? Were they now always indivisible? Had her defence become her annihilator? Alison hadn't seen Hapless for a while, but she also believed that Hapless had been out on her own; developed autonomy beyond her host when she really willed it—and people appeared to like her.

Thoughts came tumbling in and in and out and out as Alison tried to steady herself. All the words were in a rush, but if they could have been disentangled, they would have said, in different strains, 'Shirley, are you still there?'

'Dolly, what would you do?'

'Camus, Albert, do you still want me?'

'Mary, be my friend again.'

'JK, write me a poem. Write me anything, I don't mind even an indulgent or demanding letter!'

'Sylvia, write something dazzling! Illuminate this twilight with your words like axes! Frida: are you free? The crawl space is gone but could we meet now? Somewhere else? Can you come?'

And mixed in with this, as there must always be a tumble of ingredients with foolish, clumsy Alison, another figure appeared; someone who had been in this very spot. She looked up at the horse and remembered with the brutal, weird, busy mind, the description of the sapper, Kirpal Singh, coming to Bratton, (the village from where Alison had just come), to learn about defusing bombs, in Michael Ondaatje's *The English Patient*. It was just *typical* of Alison—so *bizarre; so WEIRD KID and eldritch-child*—to populate any landscape with literary figures and subsequently feel compelled to watch what they did. She quickly made a busy peopled landscape: *that* made each place all the lonelier. Here was someone animating the landscape. Kirpal Singh stood where the saddle of the white horse would have been and began to make his way down across the vast shape cut into the chalk hill.

A soldier. A sapper. Was there anything *he* could say? Alison looked at the horse and imagined Kirpal Singh's feet raking gently through the chalk, but something was wrong: he could not walk there now, the chalk had been covered over by shiny white-painted concrete. He would slide down, damaged, from the saddle, the darkness of the skin and the khaki uniform tumbling in contrast against the still brilliant white. He was strong and able; entirely focused, but even he would end. Still, figures ran down gleefully behind him, admiring his khaki, bedazzling him. Dead Santa Maria was there, hand in hand with Hapless Ally: both were strong and pretty. One was dead; the other a creation of a febrile imagination, with the talking, nuzzling dark thought parcelled in the palm and the dark embolus of fear rolling behind her—reaching target. Alison's thoughts shifted again: the tea party back in the village; the sure confident mothers and the reassuring attendant grandmothers. Alison had little to offer her son. *Useless.* Still the heart raced, thump against the tumbling of Kirpal Singh, who was falling now, flailing on the slippery bank, against the deep breathing of the infant, the thoughts of beautifully crafted cakes back in the village, the plaintive beautiful winter song of Robin Redbreast and the smirks of robust but Dead or Not Really There Santa Maria and Hapless Ally.

Alison could have been sitting there minutes or hours as the thoughts rattled helter skelter. It became like a horrible game of word association and went something like this—all odd and painful memories and curious associations glimpsed in a flash: from a slap at a fair—'You! You! You! Nasty, hateful little girl'—in a heartbeat to a poet who died in fifteen twenty nine.

So on it went: 'Helter skelter. Ha ha Hapless Ally. Helter Skelter—John Skelton-Skeletonics—Helter Skelter John-helter skelter at the fair. I was banned from the fair and the helter skelter at the fair with Santa Maria and she is still here as Dead Santa Maria. *Slap.* And she said then and she says now, "You are a little bitch and so you will never go to a fair again and you will never have a goldfish, little bitch!" "But Mummy what about the other children and the grinning red-haired boy with a fish in a bag? Was he really really bad, too?" *Slap.* "I was right all along! You should have been left in a bucket and also your babies will come to hate you!" Helter Skelter John—skeltonics—John Skelton at the funeral of Edward IV: "Where is now my conquest and victory?/Where is my riches and my royal array?" And again he comes, worrying: "Humbly beseeching thee, God, of thy grace!/O ye courteous commons, your hearts unbrace." And again, "*Et ecce, nunc in pulvere dormio!*" *Slap.* Why do I remember all these bloody quotations and I have no-one to tell?And Kirpal Singh is standing in the chalk-white, where the saddle of the horse would have been—and I am so lonely and I am so wrong. The ways, the roads, the littoral and the mountain and on the chalky downs are so deep and the weather is so harsh and the concrete white horse does not rear and run and now Kirpal Singh is striding down across the huge animal that looks like a child's paper cut-out and he will fall and he will be hurt—and now I am falling on the helter skelter and I cannot control this speed—And the old white horse wants to gallop away into a sweet meadow but he cannot: he is mired in shiny white concrete...'

And the baby woke up and the surprise and sudden tender shock of it made the word association stop for now. She took him from the back seat and cradled him in her arms, fed him and settled him and began driving home: a terrible, important moment. Rounding a corner nearer to their house, the sulphurous-yellow light of the Co-op supermarket hurt her eyes after the darkness, with the trees bent low over the country road. It was just one of a series of yellow lights punched into the black, with a pattern continuing until they met the lane to the house. Home, Alison held her baby tightly; he was asleep again. She sat down heavily in an armchair, exhausted by the helter skelter moments and the depressing, jarring movements from dark to ugly yellow light on the journey, and rang Dixie Delicious: 'Come for me. I am losing my mind,' and she was still sitting there two hours later when Dixie Delicious came bowling in.

He had to mop up a lot: Alison had been badly fissured by the itchy, scratchy thought in the palm; the embolus of fear had dissected, done its work, and fitted back together as a jigsaw. Delicious lost his temper and beat all the things he could not see with the umbrella he always carried in the inclement British weather.

Alison was, thus, put on some new medicines the following morning.

'We must weigh this one up,' said Dr Krank-Werden. Books were rustled. 'Paroxetine it is, okay?'

'What are possible side effects this time, Doctor Krank-Werden? I'm likely to get all of them.'

Dr Krank-Werden drew a deep breath and said, pat, 'Well, paroxetine hydrochloride is used to treat a variety of mental health problems. It is thought that paroxetine hydrochloride increases the activity and levels of certain chemicals in the brain. This can improve symptoms such as depression and anxiety. Some people who take paroxetine hydrochloride may find that it intensifies depression and suicidal feelings in the early stages of treatment. These people have an increased risk of self-harm or suicide in the early stages of taking paroxetine hydrochloride. As paroxetine hydrochloride starts to work these risks decrease. If you are taking paroxetine hydrochloride, or you care for someone who is taking paroxetine hydrochloride, you need to look out for changes in behaviour that could be linked to self-harm or suicide. If you notice any of these changes or are worried about how paroxetine hydrochloride is affecting you or someone you care for, you should contact your prescriber, a mental health professional or call 999 as soon as possible.'

Dr Krank-Werden drew another deep breath and sat back in her chair.

'That was a lot of repetition, Dr Krank-Werden.'

'Oh God, I know. I'm turning into a leaflet. Or a textbook.' She paused. 'We've known each other for donkeys' years, haven't we?' she said.

'But I don't know anything about you, Dr Krank-Werden.'

'I have only a little story to tell,' sighed the doctor, possibly the most loved general practitioner in Albion. 'I am not a very interesting person.'

'But look. You're lovely. You wear colourful shoes and giggle and you've got a picture of the Annapurna range because you went there.'

'That was another me, I think.'

From the back of the room came a sardonic voice: 'Oh poor doctor: lost her colour, has she? *And her.* I don't believe in any of it: it's weak; it's pathetic. Depression? Racing and ruminating thoughts? Mental illness? Ha! I was always strong and resolute, could always keep my head straight, but look at bitch-daughter!'

Dr Krank-Werden turned suddenly in her chair, her eyes now aflame and looking straight at Dead Santa Maria: 'Have you ever heard of the Hippocratic Oath? To do no harm? You might glance at it.'

'You can see her?'

'I can't see her. She's not really there. *But I can see you. I am learning really to see you.*'

And,

'Shall I wear my colourful shoes again tomorrow?'

'I think you're getting your mojo back already, Dr Krank-Werden.'

The doctor, with a promise of turquoise for Thursday and fuchsia for Friday, held Alison's hand firmly and despatched her into the waiting room, with a further promise of a referral to a specialist, a psychotherapist this time, from the big hospital. Helga was unavailable, back with the incarcerated and bound over and the practitioner was to be a new diversion for Alison. Our girl had been truly fond of Maverick Helga and felt relief that Dr Krank-Werden had spoken to the voice she knew her patient heard. She had met some good people and felt grateful and guilty for taking up time and space: it felt like it should go somewhere else. Once, a nice lady from 'Cruse', the bereavement support group, had come to the house after both parents had shuffled off within inches of one another (and whom Alison had mourned with confusion, anger and grief, but now wished would just fuck off and leave her alone, none of which she told the nice lady, because it was all too shameful to state). Some days—the help—it worked: but it only worked for a while. Some days, like with the lady from 'Cruse', Alison had to say things that weren't true, for fear of causing offence or startling anyone. But Dr Krank-Werden was enthused by this new specialist; this lady was high powered, good at fixing the stubborn hangers-on, not easily startled and inhabited that bit of the hospital psychiatric wing which you can visit without clearance: just an appointment. She was called Dr Anchluss and later she breathily worked on, 'Yaaa, *The Process*'—of which Alison was entirely sceptical.

So, in a sort of gala day for mental health intervention the CPN—that's a community psychiatric nurse, for those of you who aren't one and haven't gone bonkers or been caring for someone who is—visited her in the morning, just to get the stock rolling. Alison was was managing to be particularly Hapless Ally at her best and larger than life; trying to impress and look like a competent mother: she was feeding porridge to her nicely attired child when the CPN arrived and, with the knock at the door, back came the thin dry voice from the samplers at her grandmother's house: 'Thou shalt not!'

And back came the words of Dead Santa Maria in the waiting room: '*I* don't believe in any of this. It's weak; it's pathetic. Mental illness—ha!—*I* was always strong and resolute, but look at bitch-daughter! Only weak little saplings that fall in the mud have such pathetic things and give them labels. Depression! Anxiety! Pitiful, *pitiful* people. They should be *euthanised*!

The CPN was unaware of the disturbances and the company in the room. She chimed, 'You make porridge for your baby? I never did anything like that!' So Alison—taking 'cheery' and 'jolly' down a peg and sending Hapless Ally astray—made her a cup of tea and told her that she really shouldn't be worrying about that and they talked about nothing in particular because it was a short visit and how on earth could she explain the helter skelter episode beneath Westbury White horse? Also, she was worried about whether the CPN was feeling unsettled, perhaps worrying about her own parenting skills because she'd been doling out Ready Brek, or sugar on the Frosties for her squalling offspring: Alison certainly didn't want to burden her.

Next, another CPN appeared. Well, perhaps he was a

CPN: it wasn't entirely clear. Perhaps he was a door-to-door trader, a Jehovah's Witness or someone from MORI who'd just wandered in—easily done, as Alison frequently left the doors open.

He said, 'I'm from The Team and I've come to do a carer's assessment.' He was jaded and a bit sad-eyed.

Alison trundled off to make him tea while he assessed Dixie Delicious to see if he was unhinged or with a peculiar anxiety disorder (is that what she had?) too. By their second chocolate digestive, Dixie Delicious and the man from The Team had come to an understanding. The man, Colin, was here to assess what Dixie Delicious needed as the carer of Alison.

Dixie Delicious had little to say other than, 'A mallet? A hypnotic to knock her out?'

Colin looked startled at first, before he settled into the jokes and embraced Dixie Delicious's comments on how marvellous it was that you could get these things around here, when it would cost an arm and a leg on your insurance if you lived in America and, if they moved to America now, America would decide not to even cover Alison for help because she had a pre-existing health condition. So he would be adrift with an unhinged wife. Colin had been to Florida on holiday once, so they had a chat about that too. Alison sat in the other room, listening in, and felt guilty for sucking up NHS resources.

Colin referred to resources for carers and, as memory serves, to a carer's package—which is maybe like the 'Bounty' pack that 'Mumsnet' had mounted a campaign against: wherein a cheery lady comes to the delivery ward and offers

you photographs with your new-born and you get the
package of nappies, miniature Sudocremes and sachets of
highly-perfumed washing detergent. What would it have in
it? Vouchers for dinner out? Days off coupons? Vodka, or
perhaps an afternoon with a particularly athletic whore for
the jaded male carer? They never did find out, but Colin
wrote a lot of things down on his clipboard, then sat
discussing with Dixie Delicious and Alison (baby at breast;
Alison, not Colin) how he too would love to live in an
old house like theirs; how he'd always wanted a place with
history, lovely old stone and an inglenook fireplace, but was
never going to be able to manage it. His divorce and
subsequent sourness had sucked him dry; any leisurely
stonework or carpentry was over for him.

'Lots of things are over for me these days. My house has got
no character. It's a soulless box, really. Maybe I'm a soulless
box, too. But there we are.'

So Alison offered him another cup of tea and mollified him
by saying that old houses took a fair amount of upkeep and
were prone to things falling off and dust and he shouldn't feel
sad but just concentrate on making his home cosy.

Colin said, with a weary sigh, 'I don't know who needs the
help and who's best at giving it here. I really don't...oh dear.'

Thus it was that Alison reassured him that she was actually,
albeit creatively, the patient and tended to rely on a host of
imaginary friends, but that last night Dr Krank-Werden had
given her some diazepam so she was in a medicated calm.
And also that, in adventures of Alison—and attendant Hapless
Ally—when mad, once you had spent your worst moment,

there was a short time of calm and passion purged, when you might make trifle or build a retaining wall. That was how she been able to shop for biscuits for Colin. So she got out the custard creams now and fancied that his eyes lit up.

Dixie Delicious and Alison never saw Colin or the first CPN again and very much hoped they were okay. Particularly Colin, because he had looked a bit tired—a bit feverish, almost. The carer's report never ensued, when Colin went back to his soulless box. But Dr Krank-Werden was in touch with her plan for the exotic with Dr Anchluss. None of this *bit of CBT where we examine your core values malarkey,* but a whole year visiting a hospital for probing therapeutic support. And psychotherapy with 'Yaaa…' Dr Anchluss. And would Alison get to see some properly, interestingly insane people at this venue? Was she amongst them? That wasn't a normal fascination to have, now was it? Was it unkind? Was she mad herself? Are you allowed to use the word 'mad'? And were there any responsibilities Alison could properly shirk if found to be that word?

11

Meeting another Good Doctor

Dr Anchluss worked in the bit of the hospital psychiatric wing you could visit readily. Alison always wondered what lay behind the doors that one couldn't go through, but which closed with a swoosh when someone did. She didn't understand whether she was actually mad or could be defined as mentally ill, but thought probably not to the former because she could get tea on the table and the baby fed. And probably yes to the latter. Her sensations felt heightened, so that lights hurt her and noise assailed her; household smells were, by turns, exquisite and a torture. The petals of a rose in the winter garden caressed as the softest velvet, then scratched like sandpaper. Bacon in the fridge would make sandwiches, but while she grilled it, Alison thought of death, looking at the household implements with thought of annihilation, not of cooking. Is it possible to kill yourself with a spatula and a balloon whisk? Was it possible she had psychotic episodes, all full of messy fast-firing thoughts? Episodes all dirty and unstoppable and full of quotations and characters come to life in the vicinity?

In psychiatric terms (Alison had had her pen and notebook out as she read and researched) psychosis connotes (*connotes* being a favourite word of Dr Anchluss along with *yaaa*) that the patient does not have a firm grip on reality or is delusional and she was wondering whether that fitted her. Was she psychotic? Sardonic Steve had thought so. Alison wanted, above all, some sort of working definition by this point. The NHS information website defines the key areas of psychosis as:

'*Hallucinations

*Delusions

*Confused and disturbed thoughts

*Lack of insight and self-awareness

Before Alison trundled off to Dr Anchluss, she had looked it up. She had also looked at puerperal psychosis (or postnatal psychosis) which, according to the NHS website, featured,

*A high mood (mania), for example, talking and thinking too much or too quickly

*A low mood, for example, depression, lack of energy, loss of appetite and trouble sleeping.'

Now, Alison had travelled from a slide at a fair and not winning a goldfish, to an early Renaissance poet in the blinking of an eye; she had skipped without pause from a nearly glimpsed figure of a fictional Sikh sapper skittering down the chalk/concrete at Westbury White horse to Shirley Bassey roaring across Tiger Bay. And back again. She spent more time with head friends than room friends; couldn't really draw a clear line between real and imaginary; between quick and dead—or undead and Might as Well have been Dead—or Dead if He ever Existed. Did she have lack of insight, delusions, hallucinations? Wasn't her thought best fit for 'thinking too quickly?' Or, 'confused and disturbed'? And yet she had also fed a baby, driven home the right way and, the following morning, thought to get the custard creams in for Colin the anxious nurse. Did that follow? And what about mania? There was—admitted to painfully and shamefully—just a tiny thrill within the anxiety of jerking from image to image, line to line, quotation to quotation, helter skelter at the fair to John Skelton, the poet, and his merry rhythmic 'skeltonics'. Was that mania? Mania with some perverse deliberate edge? Alison had looked up manic depression, or rather bipolar depression, and found:

'If you have bipolar disorder, you will have periods or episodes of:

*Depression—where you feel very low and lethargic

*Mania—where you feel very high and over-active (less severe mania is known as hypomania).'

Alison thought that she might have all three illnesses, but perhaps inconsistently—and she wondered if Dr Anchluss could enlighten. Dr Krank-Werden had said Dr Anchluss was an expert on inter-relational, inter-personal issues and, looking that up, Alison discovered an area of psychotherapy known as IPT—interpersonal psychotherapy. Was that Dr Anchluss's job? Alison sensed they were going to be spending a long time talking about Dead Santa Maria. And if they did that, Dead Santa Maria would find a way into the room.

Outside the psychiatric wing, there was a depressing, scrubby garden. It was, as she came to call it, The Viburnum Jungle. Just as her dead father had loathed lilies, Alison found viburnum a loathsome plant. It is a pointless municipal parks and gardens plant; its leaves invite you to take no joy in their texture; its flowers are assertive, but never pretty—it is a means to an end: a plant of no beauty. It was here in abundance before the psychiatric wing and, worse, it was smothering some rock roses planted near it, swooping down and killing them with shade and ugliness. Shiny emerald leaves, curling brown at the edges; clouds of white flowers with a dull sepia tone to their edges. Below the viburnums, with the dying rock roses, were the yellowed leaves of daffodils that must have flowered once but gave up, gasping, sandy soil, cigarette butts and a Twix wrapper. Alison went in and introduced herself to the lady reading 'OK' magazine, with its strapline, 'Look: a royal princess wears the same outfit twice!' She sat down, having been ticked off on today's roster. The smell of the place reminded her, vaguely, of the funeral parlour with her father laid out, but with a lacing of tobacco on top. It was different in that way because dead men and even the more irreverent class of undertaker do not smoke. She had a terrible urge to laugh; it felt also like a cremation service she had once been to and that awkward waiting bit where the coffin starts moving. A cousin from The Hill, dead but how she didn't know, bid the angels howl as the coffin slid along its track, the purple velvet curtains parted unevenly and the coffin went through them then, suddenly, 'SNAP' as the curtains were pulled back into place and Alison, inappropriately, listened hard for the whine and roar of the inferno beyond, but was disappointed in this. Her laugh had been excruciatingly stifled; her body shook with it and she faked a cough so that she could go outside.

The swallowed laugh now, with The Viburnum Jungle, the no-smell, the fags and the sense that there might be lunatics shuffling nearby, well it was just as inappropriate and its stimulus just as darkly, horribly funny.

And here was Dr Anchluss. She was dressed in expensive casual, but she had rubber-soled pumps, a bit like the soles of a surgeon. Perhaps that was because she was trying, with her quiet walk, not to startle the mad people, which possibly included Alison. During the adventures with pointy sticks at the same hospital, as the fabulously glamorous Dr Ching administered amniocentesis, Alison had been dazzled by the glitz and surety: all in black Gucci and with sharp kitten heels and dressed to kill. The steadiest of hands.

'Holy fuck. What a gorgeous, competent woman. I want to be her and I bet she doesn't need an alter ego.'

This was probably not quite a normal thought as you lie, pregnant, on the bench, waiting for the big needle to penetrate your abdomen and when it does you are amazed it hasn't killed you. Now, Dr Anchluss was all soft edges and quiet shoes; a different creature, if clothes maketh the man. Alison, mind wheeling, wondered if it was really the other way round: was Dr Anchluss a kind of power monger in the psychiatric world, whereas Dr Ching had struggled to be noticed and dressed, with desperate calculated ambition, to create effect? This turn of thought was getting nowhere and Alison realised that she was not concentrating properly on the little vomit-coloured room in which she was now sitting, not even having noticed herself entering the room and finding a chair.

Dr Anchluss said hello and greeted her with a limp handshake: Alison was instantly suspicious, for Dead Santa Maria had always told her to beware of a limp handshake as it signified a lack of vigour or commitment.

'If someone doesn't shake hands like a man, don't do business with them.'

Dead Santa Maria had also told her to beware of people with thin lips because thin lips, so people know, *connote meanness*. Alison looked carefully at the doctor: Dr Anchluss had a fine, wide and full mouth and rather exquisite cheekbones to boot. Not for the first time, the girl wondered how many of her late mother's presentiments had been taken for gospel by her daughter; perhaps that was part of the problem and part of the inter-relational get-out was to disentangle the two.

Alison now had time to scrutinise the room because Dr Anchluss was not saying anything, but rather looking at her in an enquiring way. It was embarrassing. But here were a weeping fig, a single hibernating hyacinth in a pot on the window ledge, lots of empty shelves and a big box of tissues on a yellow pine table. The room smelled of pine disinfectant; from outside came the siren of an ambulance and now Alison was off on another journey, recalling the festive honeymoon visit to the psychiatric unit to visit her cousin. She remembered talking to a cheery man called Jim: he was larded with tattoos and the cuts and slashes of the chronic self-harmer. His eyes were deep set, tired and far-away sad. Alison was always looking to see if other people were thriving or withering and always looking for the signs of self-harming because she nursed the scars on her upper thighs and a few much fainter ones on her arms. Some months after their marriage, Alison and Dixie Delicious had visited Istanbul and, in a café by the Aya Sofia, and as a dervish whirled while they ate their fine *patlicani*, she had noticed a couple at the next table, holding hands and looking into each other's eyes. She had sensed unsteadiness somewhere at that table and looked at the arms of the pretty woman: they were deeply lacerated at regular intervals. Some self-harmers might, for all Alison knew, tend to cross hatch, but she recognised the marks on the woman's arms as the deep gouging, slow and steady, of someone attempting to regulate their pain and offset a bizarre and hideous mental confusion against effulgence of blood and an almost rhythmic cutting of the flesh. Alison had wanted to go over and say something. But *what?* She thought about that as she sat in Dr Anchluss's room waiting for someone to say something. She thought also of the time that her dear friend, Luscious Lizbeth, had glimpsed the jagged lines and enquired. Alison said, 'I was in a briar patch. You know, like Brer Rabbit?'

She thought, also, about Jim in the Catford psychiatric ward: 'Never really been to school but I can do *The Times* crossword; the cryptic one, not the one for retards. There are lots of fucking retards in here.'

Was he still alive? As the fifteen people in the smoky day room had pressed upon Dixie Delicious and Alison, congratulating them roundly on the nuptials two days previously, Jim had said, 'And you fucking came here for your honeymoon? That is the funniest thing I ever heard!' And also, 'I hope you come again but I'll probably have jumped in front of a tube train by then.'

And suddenly Dr Anchluss spoke. Very. Deliberately. And softly. And quietly. She had a melted chocolate voice cooing, 'Now, why do you think you are here?'

Alison did the only thing she could think of and burst into tears and Dr Anchluss pushed the big box of tissues towards her. It was a big and nasty cry and she was fearful that the itchy scratchy thought in the palm and the horrid embolus of fear would take up and find suitable home in the small vomit-coloured room.

Dr Anchluss looked at her in a cool and inquisitive way and Alison thought only that what she wanted right now was a very hot man and a very big ice cream to lick. Also, she became aware that her breasts were pulsing in that curious new mummy way; it wasn't the thought of the hot man that did it, but the fact she had left her three month-old breastfed baby with a friend and had timed the feeds a bit wrong, so the knockers were complaining. Alison took a few more tissues from the box, folded them into a wad and stuffed them in her bra. Sure enough, the other breast joined in so she grabbed more tissues and made another wad to keep the rebellious right knocker quiet. She should have had some breast pads with her to staunch such a flow, but they had used the last two for coasters the previous night as she and Dixie Delicious ruminated, over cosy-time tea, on how this therapy was going to work with a new baby in tow. Now Alison's mobile rang: reflexively, she answered it. It turned out to be GCSE Gina from the school where Alison had been a member of the English department until maternity leave: GCSE said, in her most strident teacher-voice, 'When are you coming back as we are really struggling with the exam classes?'

'It's not a good time right now.'

'Well, when is a good time? You've left us in the lurch and colleagues and parents aren't very happy about it. We feel it is *just typical of you*. Ha! Goodbye your brilliant career and what a shame for the GCSEs. Everyone will know what you have done.'

So panic about this; letting everyone down; the colleague's voice all testy and GCSE-deadline-irritable and instantly like Vaguely Dead Dad or Dead Santa Maria—*You. Have. Let. Us. Down.* And in the room was an inflated pair of knockers with milk dropping softly down from the tissue wads and across her abdomen. And she was sitting with a silent psychotherapist, with another ambulance siren wailing and calling nearby. So she answered Dr Anchluss.

'I am here because everything I have ever done has been a mess. I have ruined lives, I am scared I have brought on other people's deaths to the point where some of them aren't dead any more, Brother who Might as Well have been Dead hates me and doesn't want to see the baby. I have let people down—my parents; the students at the school; *their* parents; my baby deserves better—I have even written him a goodbye note—it's folded up inside a copy of *The Collected Poems of Louis MacNeice*; I can't keep my thoughts in a straight line—they are just racing from point to point and concept to concept; I've been a failure at everything and don't say it's not true because I've been told so many times that it is and…when I was five I pushed a girl…and I try to be another…to be Hapless Ally—palatable me—but sometimes even she hates me—and she detaches and goes off and has fun somewhere and…'

Dr Anchluss slowly raised her hand and said, 'Yaaa. One thing at a time.'

The doctor's face was inscrutable. She said nothing more and, because her patient found the ensuing silence embarrassing, Alison thought she should take a deep breath and change tack. So she came up with, 'I read an article about therapeutic architecture in hospitals and wondered what you thought about the idea of therapeutic gardens, places that might be curative? You know, in a place like this? Outside, there's The Viburnum Jungle, all hard shiny parks and gardens leaves; there's a Twix wrapper and a packet of Rothmans. Is there something I could do to get some planting together? For, umm, visitors?'

Dr Anchluss laughed softly. Oh my: this was *excruciating*. Her breasts set off again. Pulse; drip.

Past caring, Alison asked, 'What do you think about what I said? Not about the viburnum, but about feeling shit for so much of my life? For feeling'—there was no holding back—'like someone who should have been euthanised, scraped away like excrement from a shoe' (which revolting image upset her as it lurched from her mouth) 'or left in a bucket?'

'Well, yaaa. What do *you* think about it? That is the more important question.'

Fuck: this was not going to be easy and Alison had the ungenerous thought that it might even be pointless, but Dr Anchluss now smiled warmly at her and Alison felt a little unkind and wondered if the psychotherapist was just a bit shy. At the next appointment, her friend let her down and Alison had to take Noah with her. This time, there were no leaking breasts, but instead the baby bit her on the nipple which startled her from the dark reverie in which she had been considering why there was what appeared to be a tall chimney at the hospital. Once, as a child when she and her friend Samantha Stokes (the perky knowing one from much earlier on whose parents had a porn collection, and whose mother carried on with Mr Gibbs the wicker-work man in clear sight of others) had attended the veruca clinic together at this hospital, Samantha told her that the chimney belched out people smoke: the building below it was where they burned the dead people who no-one claimed, she said, dark eyes gleaming. But the bitten nipple brought Alison back to the room and Dr Anchluss asking, 'What would you like to talk about today?'

'I don't know. My mother?'

Alison groaned inwardly as she began tales of the

imaginary friends, the slashing and hacking and head banging, the sneering of Heroic Alice and the spoilt little girls at ballet, and Dead Santa Maria. Curiously enough, Dr Anchluss never said a word about the imaginary friends, although it occurred to the patient that this must be a germane area for the psychoanalyst. Instead, Dr Anchluss wished to expound on theories of attachment and the Freudian notion of memories locked away but nonetheless conditioning what we are, what we do and what we have done. The Doctor had a way in: it came down to not being bonded to the mother in the days before she could remember. Alison, ever the practical sort, knew a bit about Freud but could not see how this helped. Certainly, at Addenbrooke's Hospital she had been lying on the bed, brushed by the tentacular memories, *the memories before I could remember.* But how did any theory now rid her of the obstacles, the bastard black embolus of fear and the searing anxiety and sick-making panic?

She had two questions.

'One: how is knowing or accepting that I am shaped by my unconscious memory going to help me? Theories of attachment are all very well, but it's not as if I can re-attach.'

There was a face at the window, behind the pretty head of the psychotherapist. It was Dead Santa Maria, called up by her name and having a hollow laugh about attachment.

Answer: 'Well, yaaa. We must TRUST THE PROCESS.' (Laugh. Fingering of hair and attendant waft of L'Air Du Temps perfume.)

Further laugh from outside.

'Two: please could you sum up what I am or what I have got? I know there is something wrong with me, but it is a strange amorphous shape and I want to tidy it up. And I want a label; a definition.'

Answer: 'Well, definitions are not always helpful. But we could say that what you have experienced is COMPLEX TRAUMA. Yaaa; what you have described connotes COMPLEX TRAUMA.'

'But I didn't experience trauma. I just had a shit time; still do.'

Silence.

There were many weeks more, sitting in the vomit-coloured room, connoting until no more could possibly be connoted and the room had spun into its own, strange little crepuscular world. From outside there came a puff of smoke from the hospital chimney; a siren; from somewhere inside, the occasional loud yell or scream, which might have been laughter. Alison tried to liven up the proceedings by writing an essay on her experiences; she wanted Dr Anchluss to mark it and write, 'Yaa, well done', but the essay never came back: maybe it had been sent to Colin the CPN and hopefully brightened his day. After appointments, Alison would get out of the sicky room and The Viburnum Jungle and feel a big solid lump of cry overtaking her: was this getting better—TRUSTING THE PROCESS? And what she learned after a year was this: she learned something about Dr Anchluss's beliefs, she had a few definitions of *stuff* but mostly she felt terrifically guilty because it was her considered opinion that someone else should have benefited from Dr

Anchluss. To Alison, things would, after all, have gone along better with the hot man and the licking of an ice cream. And even now, that feels like a spoilt and appalling admission and that Aneurin Bevan would be turning in his grave at such ungratefulness at the help laid on. One day, there were no further appointments; it didn't really matter. They hadn't even tackled the Hapless Ally bit yet. No matter, because, after all, Alison now knew she had suffered from (yaaa), 'COMPLEX TRAUMA and attachment issues although I wouldn't go so far as to label these an attachment disorder.'

One evening, she sat in a deep bath full of Crabtree and Evelyn lavender bubbles and thought again about what it meant to TRUST THE PROCESS. She thought hard about being knocked down, about not being held and when touched, in the wrong places; in a way that *must* have been wrong, but because it was Alison, it was tolerable; allowable: about being told she was disgusting and that everyone knew. All that returned was the same nauseating feeling from childhood.

'I am a maggot. Everyone knows: Brother who Might as Well have been Dead, Dead Santa Maria and Dad: they tell everyone, don't they? Mother's doyennes of the town council, the nasty, smiling porcelain doll-faced women, they passed it along too. The girl with the bad head who died? Yep: that was me, too. Mum and Vaguely Dead Dad: yep, I finished them off, while I was at it. Even awful Miss Hamm, stifled by a pickled egg at the piano—yes, me. I can't possibly be wrong because there is, has always been, too much evidence against me.'

Alison, still sitting there in her bubble bath, remembered trying desperately to atone for her mother's death at the graveside. Then, she had stepped forward and knelt down by the dark space. The brass plaque on the coffin was very shiny; she could smell earth and something sweet; furniture polish—an abhorrent vanilla-scented one. She was a maggoty-worm-bucket girl, praying in the mud while everyone walked away.

'*Fake praying.* It must have looked like *fake praying* and that's why they did not walk with me. That and the fact I must have killed her.'

Life was over; she had just wanted to say sorry and, like a child, expected a tirade of blame afterwards at the funeral tea. Instead, they had stew and trifle: it had turned into a strange, dark tea—as if at Terry and Helen's house, and life sat next to her, not in her: attired from birth in its funeral weeds. No-one said anything. What do you do when the host has blood on her hands when she serves up the trifle with tinned slug-strawberries and squirty cream? Few came from The Hill. Mad but Nice Andrea was there, tartan blanket over her knees. She twitched and shook and her pale blue eyes were watery and vague; Alison assumed she had been sedated to lessen the trauma of getting out of bed and driving thirty miles. But it had been a brave thing to do. Alison wanted to say, to the watery eyes, just as she had as a child, 'Auntie Mad but Nice, I really don't mind about the madness. But will you just hold me and tell me I'm okay?'

Evil Plant Emily and Pugnacious Pete (Alison's father older brother) had started out from The Hill but got lost on the way. Brother who Might as Well have been Dead (but Quick, for this special occasion) ignored her, but gave her a quick, rigid hug (as they were in public) as he left for his gated community off the M25. He was looking forward, he said, to stays at his provincial residence: his dead mother's house was to be kept up, just so, for his visits. So she was to be cook and housekeeper, there at the shrine to Dead Santa Maria in thrall to Dead and Might as Well have been, with both of them yelling at her.

Next to leave were Mad but Nice Andrea and Uncle John, the vet. Mad but Nice Andrea was shaking into her tartan; terrified by the world. She said, 'We won't be seeing you again' and was helped into the car by John, her animal-frightening husband. Could Alison detect antiseptic and the tang of chloroform? Alison watched them drive off, with Mad but Nice Andrea clawing and banging at the car windows, because being in a car frightened her. They were good people: they were land-locked, trapped and emptied out by The Hill—but they had tried. How she wished for a last attempt at conversation.

That evening she had been alone in the house and saw that on the shelf of Dead Santa Maria's bedroom there were some Christmas presents still to be wrapped: her mother had died after a festive trip on the bus and a jaunt to Habitat and Laura Ashley. Alison scooped them all up for the charity shop and down, from childhood and The Hill, came a thin dry voice of, 'Thou shalt not' and, 'Look at you, selfish little bitch. You can't even be bothered to wrap them up.'

'But I don't know who they're for.'

'Not for you. No, they are not for you. Nothing is for you and nobody will come.'

Alison still sat in the lukewarm bathwater, remembering her father's funeral. It had been a blistering July day. She had found herself in a separate pew from her mother and brother; they had gone in ahead of her and stood, three rows in front, leaning on each other. The vicar was addressing them directly in their sorrow and Alison could not think of a clearer telling of what she was and had been, so separate on the end of the different pew. At the end of the service, the vicar shook hands with all the mourners and Alison filed out with them.

When he got to her, the vicar said, 'I am sorry for your loss. Have you come far today?'

And she said, 'I am still a long way away. But he was my father.'

The man looked perplexed and Alison felt sorry for him, but to explain would have taken too long. Now, sitting in the water with the dying bubbles, Alison thought that TRUSTING THE PROCESS just meant constantly flaying off your skin to feel the hurts again. It would have been more useful at this stage for Dr Anchluss to say, 'Yaa. If I were you, I'd find a new crawl space.' Up came a big bubble. It was in *her*. And Alison retched into the bath. It was a bit of a waste of that nice Crabtree and Evelyn, whose lavender could not soothe her.

12

Beginning

After Dr Anchluss had wordlessly terminated their acquaintance, Alison just carried on, as you do, ashamed to go out and embarrassed in company, but forced to participate and to keep counsel because of the children. It was a heavy load, though—the leaden feeling in heart and stomach. Eventually, Alison's nerve failed again. It's not that it hadn't in the meantime, but there hadn't been quite the inability to corral thoughts; to stop banging your head or scratching your arms. This time, she sensed, there was to be a fulfilment of the chilling childhood prophecy: by this time she had Asa and baby Josiah to care for as well as Noah, yet the voice said, 'It is coming Alison. *Coming.*'

The writing was on the wall.

In earthquake terms, it was The Big One. But what about the children? What would it do to them and where was shelter? It was a Friday morning and she sat shaking, having been awake all night, rigid as Dixie Delicious and the children slept. The children were in the moment, cocooned by darkness; Dixie Delicious, by and large, parked yesterday *then* and tomorrow *not yet.* But Alison lay there and was unable to pin down her thoughts as, once again, they played helter skelter, shouting louder and louder and winging out into the room.

The cacophony went something like this: 'I killed a girl! My mother said her parents could have thought it was me when she died—and I didn't push her but everyone thought I did. It doesn't matter that I was five: I am intrinsically the monster now that I was as a child. I do not deserve to have the babies and I'm going to be found out and Sardonic Steve was right and my brother was right to do what he did, looking at me in disgust; touching me like sin and rot. I am a maggot. Abhorrent. I have killed people and Sardonic Steve said I was an evil bitch and that he could have me on the floor and he's right: I would have deserved that. Dead Santa Maria said I would dance on her grave but I didn't: I prayed alone in the December mud at her grave—but maybe I was really thinking about dancing? I ruined Professor Pobble's happiness: three universities and I was a fraud! One for clerical error and two because of Professor Pobble who was so brilliant—and he loved me and wanted it all for me. I let my Vaguely Dead Dad down and shouldn't have touched The Fucking Caravan and it isn't possible that it could have been a mistake! I should have known that the lump on his leg meant he was dying—and it was my fault because of the sufferance and because cancer is passion repressed which is what Dead Santa

Maria said—and once when he was a shrivelled-up man stuck in the bath I could hear him crying and I pushed the door in to try and help him and he was crying for Jesus and Saint Jude and I thought he would be glad to see me so I could help him and he said, "No—not you: get out" and I remembered when he was stung by the bee of Apollyion in France and I had done the wrong thing again and he said, "You have let me down you little fuck-wit!" and I ran, but the wishing tree and the crawl space were locked in the past where I could not reach them—and even my genes are snapped off and translocated and…but…so…if we all go to heaven what will happen there?'

It was four in the morning and Alison trembled and made her way downstairs, going through the slow, rhythmic movements of making a cup of tea in a favourite mug. Then she sat down in a sitting room armchair with a blanket. By six thirty when the baby and Dixie Delicious woke up, she was in the foetal position and drenched in tears, trying to think of what Albert Camus would do in the face of despair.

'Alison, imagine that Sisyphus is happy as he rolls his stone every day.'

'I can't, Albert. I can't do it any more. I am over.'

'Roll the stone up the hill, but if it should roll down again, you must resume your labour. That, my Alison, is to live authentically.'

'I can't. I don't have the strength this time.'

In this violet-tinted early morning she felt too far away from Albert for it to be of help. The phrase of Patrick Kavanagh's—'The millstone has become a star'—started speaking to her. Professor Pobble had once said it to her to lift her up and shift her perspective. Would it be possible now to displace then transfigure this nasty, intractable knot of sadness so that it was a blessing? A guiding light: 'The millstone has become a star'. *No*, none of this felt possible now and all too late, and she hated the books for bouncing up at her with many an apposite turn of phrase.

Heavenward, came Yeats.

'I must lie down where all the ladders start
In the foul rag and bone shop of the heart.'

'No!' cried Alison, 'Don't remind me of Helen, only pure and good and too special for that godforsaken house. She told me these words. She told me always to read the words. But it's as if I cannot read. And I can't do what she told me to. How could I? My heart is too foul. How could it be a start?'

Alison did not want to lie down; she didn't care to go foraging for understanding in her heart's dirt and waste. Instead, she wanted quiet and an exculpation: for someone to prove *it was not her: she did not do it all*—to convey publicly that she was not the nemesis of the friend or the parent or the poor girl. She wanted quiet and for the violet-tinted morning to turn blue and less frightening. Breastfeeding the baby helped to still her; the child was dependent on her. Dixie Delicious was torn in two. He did not have anybody understanding at work so there was no choice but to leave and, for now, to let the exigencies of motherhood force Alison to cope. But today, everything was back to front and the wrong colours; clothes were in the incorrect place; there were two packed lunches in one bag and she was crying and her knees were buckling as she came apart. It is a testament to these children that they went off and out, knowing that they were loved. And knowing you are loved is all, perhaps. Not feeling guilty; dirty; too responsible too soon, or with a head full of macabre images and angels howling.

'Bye Mum.'

The boys' eyes were like saucers.

That day was long: it ran into many others, with torrents of tears and admissions of guilt and incessant cries to be rubbed out, not to exist, never to have existed. Of being almost force fed water and tea with sugar, of retching emptiness, crying on the floor and banging her head against the flagstones and door-jamb. Alison could not stand up without falling down. But one by one they arrived: Sunlight Susan with a lemon drizzle cake pushed through the slightly open window; Frangipane Angie and Crossword Katie with a plan of what to do; Jedi Jesmary who got a GP appointment even though there were none and marched in with her; Luscious Lisbeth who rolled up her sleeves and got cooking, grabbed the baby, said, 'I'll feed him' (possibly from her own breast) and started assembling sandwiches in preparation for the long haul. It was as if they were preparing for an expedition. And finally, Wordsworth William brought his laptop, got to work and took up residence and Beverly Bluebottle hung a home-made lavender bag from the door and said, 'Smell this, rather than thinking, just yet.'

It was an extraordinary thing. Alison couldn't see it at the time, the room friends, not head friends. Well, she could see it, but the thought ran that it was not personal to her but just good people, too good to be *her* friends, making sure that a mother of three was not squished or skewered, like Grandpa's comically extinguished brothers at The Hill.

Dr Krank-Werden whispered, 'Oh, *not again,*' with her eyes dancing and, possibly under the influence of Jedi Jesmary, started writing a letter to Pink Pantiles House, the house where reside all the folk who administer to those who are unsteady, but not actually incarcerated or bound over: MHRS: Mental Health Rescue Service (although 'Squad' sounds much racier than 'Service'). And three days later, with Dr Krank-Werden clearly having seen this as an emergency (or possibly having been unknowingly induced to by Jedi Jesmary's powers of conviction), Alison found herself in a funny municipal room. It did indeed have a flip chart on a stand in the corner (with the word 'Signposts' underlined by a confident squiggle); it had hateful little glass vases of single artificial flowers in that strange clear substance which pretends to be water. It smelled like school dinners. More specifically, it smelled like Terry and Helen's house when Mammy had been boiling sprouts for four hours. There were boxes of tissues and tables at Hobbit-height and fawn carpet and the room belonged to no-one in particular.

Its inhabitant, CBT CPN Carole, introduced herself and they were off, discussing core values with a chart and a handout. Cognitive behavioural therapy: where one challenges unhelpful thought patterns, bringing cognitions to bear on actions. Alison had done this many times before; it had worked for approximately twenty minutes before the creeping thoughts came back and sat on the CBT thoughts.

CBT CPN Carole started filling things in as Alison, by rote, dictated what her core value was and how she could replace it with some other thought.

Carole said, 'You are doing this very well.'

Alison responded, 'Well, yeah: I know how to do it' and Carole looked disappointed.

They filled in a lot of *challenge the unhelpful thought* stuff. Alison was fairly rattling through it, between bouts of crying and hand wringing and worrying about the children. And so it went on.

'Oh yes, you are doing very, very well,' said CBT CPN Carole again, as she spelt *they're* wrong and put in a further errant apostrophe on the pie charts they were working with, making Alison immediately uncomfortable; moreover, making her think she was an unkind soul for being adversely influenced by punctuation and homophone spelling errors.

Alison and CBT CPN Carole, who was a kind lady with a pretty and open face, were not the best of matches. It was too easy and Alison knew it was not going to work. After an hour and a half, Alison was overcome with worksheet fatigue and asked to stop. In the silence, words bubbled up: 'Carole, I'm really sorry. But I've done all this before. It's nice, but it doesn't work on me.'

'This is what is open to you.'

'Can't you stick me on the ward and give me something a bit hard-core and some drugs?'

Carole's mouth fell open and she looked shocked, then crestfallen, then became defensive and clearly cross. Alison felt guilty and so she said, 'That's a really pretty dress you are wearing,' which disjointed comment wrong-footed CBT CPN Carole, who looked like she was thinking, 'Shit: this one's a proper nutter. And she's a gobby one, too.'

'Sorry and sorry again, Carole. And sorry also that someone else is here, although she's usually part of me or me instead of me.'

'I beg your pardon?'

'Hapless Ally. She's sitting next to you, silent at the moment. But she's agreeing with you and at the same time, the dark look in her eye is telling me you're wasting your time because I'm a fuck-wit and Baby in the Bucket. She's saying, "Suck it up maggot" and somewhere out there and in my head, Carole, is Dead Santa Maria and she's baking the most beautiful cakes, but in the marzipan, the butter icing, the detail on the finest Simnel cake you ever saw, there is venom. And her eyes are coffin-cold as she carefully applies the decorations to her dainty creations and she says, "Happy Birthday" or, "Happy Easter, my darling and these are all just for you..." '

'Errrr...'

'Santa Maria (well, now Dead Santa Maria) is my mother, the blessed pillar of the community; you know, the one who lives and bakes a storm in that risible hinterland of socially lauded but cruelly dysfunctional families? Yes, that kind of thing. Hapless Ally is the more palatable version of me. The bouncy, funny, bull in a china shop one created to thrive and dive and be loved. She's me and she's not me, but to complicate matters she quite happily goes off on her own because I'm no fun and also I think she really hates me too.'

'Ummm.'

'To be fair to you, Carole, I don't really think CBT is going to manage this effectively.'

Silence; there came a whine from the fridge in the corner of the room, coughs and shuffles from elsewhere.

'I can see from your notes that you saw Helga and also Dr Anchluss. You have hopefully learned a lot from them and can put it all into practice with some work with me. We know that CBT is very effective.'

'And I know it can be for some people. But I can't challenge my core values if I don't know what my core is. Carole, I was not any farther forward after a year with Dr Anchluss, and Helga was great, but the wards were full and then she retired or possibly just dissolved and I couldn't see her for long enough anyway because she was so popular. I am really sorry, but the sheets are not going to work on me. Setting aside the fact that I've got a detachable alter ego, don't generally distinguish well between dead or alive people and have a host of imaginary friends. I also *know* what the answers are for your worksheets. They are easy to infer. It's not exactly (thinking of Jim in the Catford psychiatric unit) the cryptic crossword is it? (Had he been here, Jim would have said it was "a crossword for retards.") I can see what the answers are, but I cannot test them on my pulse or see them in clear images—cannot make them into things which are real and work and do helpful things.'

'I'm sorry. I don't understand.'

'I know, I'm sorry and I feel I'm ruining your day. But, okay, let's try the first question you asked me. "Someone you know doesn't reply when you say hello in the street. You feel upset and that you must have done something wrong and this affects your mood. What, however, might be a more helpful or realistic way to think of things?" I know the answer you are looking for is that maybe they didn't see you; that they were lost in their own thoughts—or that they were myopic. But what if they were just a plain rude bitch and, yet again, you had chosen badly with your friends and acquaintances? That would feel like a slight; like loss; depressing. You had poor judgement. Alternatively, say they ignored you because, as has frequently happened in my upbringing, they thought *you* were a bitch? Evil? That you should have been left in a bucket at birth? That you were a dreadful let-down to your parents? That you did harm? What if they had got wised up to who and what you were? When my mother and her friends talked about giving me to the gypsies, they didn't smile. I thought they were serious: I was right. My mother's dead now and she's still at it; she just says less, obviously. Look—the curse in someone's no-hello would be believable to me then and now and CBT wouldn't exactly touch it because the anxieties are packed down so tightly in my personality: they are now part of who I am and, frankly, I have often been right in thinking these things.'

Silence.

'I am really sorry I am being difficult. And, honestly, I feel desperately miserable and jumpy and sad. I feel as if I am coming apart at the seams. I cannot bear the thought of tomorrow and I want only to sleep. A challenge and lucidity are my weapons. Please don't take them from me. I mean accidentally.'

Silence.

'Well maybe you could look over these worksheets on core values and try to replace them with some more helpful thoughts and practise doing it? We know that CBT is very effective in treating depression.'

'Carole, we—and when I say "we" you must see that there are more than two in this room—are going to have to agree to disagree. And I read articles in three papers which said that the government's multi-million investment in CBT was misplaced because its effects were too often unreliable and short-lived.'

'I am sorry you feel that way.'

CBT Carole and Alison did not part on good terms. Alison had been an awful patient and there was to be no sticker. Hapless Ally and Dead Santa Maria stayed behind to bitch about her, though.

The next day Dixie Delicious took a call from Dr Krank-Werden which announced awareness of Alison's falling out with CBT CPN Carole and a year's programme at MHRS of something called CAT, which is to say cognitive analytical (or analytic) therapy. It involved diaries and letters and appealed straight away because it had homework which got read and marked. But there was a week to get through before an initial meeting, so Dr Krank-Werden proposed another bout of anti-depressant: this time, mirtazapine—'Ooh, another tetracyclic antidepressant, Dr Krank-Werden!' said Alison—and, once more, a spot of diazepam in case of emergency. Real room friends passed by. Luscious Lizbeth came over every day, with her sleeves rolled up, rooting through the fridge and sorting out the children and the shopping with Crossword Katie, who had helpfully devised a rota alongside Frangipane Angie, who showered her with kind images and pastel colours from her garden. Somebody, possibly Sunlight Susan again, thinking how important it was to have an extra cake on hand, shoved another lemon drizzle confection through the cat flap and she saw the shapely arm of Juicy Lucy thrusting a big bunch of flowers through the half-open window. Alison could notice the cake and the flowers, but she couldn't really *see* them or experience them. *Not yet.* The state she was in had transmuted from one in which the nerve endings had been on fire with curses ringing round her head, to one in which she didn't really feel anything; as if the nerve endings had been cauterised, perhaps. It was the aftermath of the crisis and a consequence of the drugs. She could only see things slowed down and tired, hardly at all, or through a glass darkly.

In the first CAT session, Alison felt obliged to perform. It took her little time to realise that the person she was with, Dr Crook, was hugely skilled and had seen through such a performance straight away and raised a hand to stop it. Her patient sat back in her seat, caught in the act and embarrassed.

'You do not have to put on a show for me.' Dr Crook wrinkled her nose and her eyes twinkled like Santa's, should he ever be a knowing and insightful clinical psychologist.

'I'm sorry. It's like I was being Hapless Ally, not Alison. I felt compelled to perform because it was all a bit awkward.'

'Ah yes, CBT CPN Carole mentioned that Hapless had not been so helpful.'

'She believed me?'

'She must have believed she was real to you, so Hapless Ally has to be considered. But slough her off now. As I said, you do not have to put on a show for me.'

'But that's what I'm used to doing. I put her on, if she'll do my will. I know it doesn't really work, but it always seems a better chance of being accepted—of not being laughed at or convicted of the most awful crimes. Yes, I know: a ruminating thought. All the terrible things I've done. But Hapless Ally: sometimes she goes out on her own because I repel her, so I think, "What must I be that even my created alter ego had to develop autonomy so she could get some time to herself?"'

'Now, *that* is a new concept for me,' said Dr Crook, twinkly eyed and interested.

'See, I told you, I'll be worse than anyone who comes through these doors. I feel sorry for you, Dr Crook.'

'I said, "new", I didn't say, "worse". Listen carefully to my words. I give them to you with no subtext and only an interest to know how I can help.'

The words again. The words. *Listen carefully to my words.*

Alison drifted off into a dark and shadowy wood of sorts as Dr Crook scribbled on her pad; she was remembering many things and the itchy scratchy thought parcelled in the palm and the sinister embolus of fear made her heart rate skitter and her fingers twitch.

'But who am I? Who am I, really?'

Once, when Alison was at university, she took up a relationship with Tom the Brilliant Cellist. Alison was surrounded by brilliant people; brilliant people who were also brilliant at other stuff. She tried to be Hapless Ally—the better me—when she thought of the bucket and also of how she couldn't even please her father with washing The Fucking Caravan. To Dr Crook that was an unhelpful and repetitively intrusive thought. We all have intrusive thoughts, of course, but if our whole life is predicated on our preservation of them and our whole self is compounded of others' opinions, then we do quite clearly feel, well, like shit. Alison often did; sometimes it really was no-one's fault, but the thoughts came in an instant, disabling her: the pulse raced, the heart fibrillated and the stomach lurched. Fuck: there it is again. It's me and me and me all over again.

Tom the Brilliant Cellist was brilliant at most things; he was beautiful, fantastically, carelessly stylish, had read everything and he was looking at *her*. He got her into bed very quickly and a lot. A *lot*. He wasn't as incendiary as Albert, but he was close. But there was a man—another man—with a Coutts account, exquisite jaw, trust fund and an eponymous brilliance. And he loved Tom the Brilliant Cellist.

The eponymously brilliant man jeered at her, 'Ohhhh Alison—this great big personality—but who are you?' His beautiful eyes were on fire and his cruel mouth terrifying.

'I'm sorry—I just don't know. A sort of…crazy multitude. I contradict myself. I contain a multitude,' she said, borrowing Whitman when her own words failed.

It was an exposure, really: of the big bouncy Hapless Ally she had created. He could see it, sophisticate that he was, and it repelled him.

Alison went back to her room feeling a fraud. If the eponymously brilliant man could see it, then maybe so could everyone. Either way, it confirmed things to her: she was a maggot. A weird welding together of two discrete personalities that irritated and disgusted. She went off walking in the rain. Next day, Tom the Brilliant Cellist dumped her, frowned like thunder and went away. He spat, 'You repel me. I am not in love with you. I was just using you. Because I could. Because that's all you're good for.'

Later, she saw him laughing with the eponymously brilliant man. Maybe they were lovers. The day after that she saw Tom walking along the banks of the Cam with a beautiful girl who wore the bold vintage clothing Alison had always wanted to wear but didn't have the confidence to try. The girl smiled at her. Tom sneered. Perhaps it was a threesome. A foursome: there was Dead Santa Maria waving from a punt. A fivesome: she was sharing champagne with Hapless Ally. Alison thought about drowning herself in the Cam, but the thought flickered in her mind of choking on the plentiful waterweed. It would be beyond terrifying. She ran back to her room wondering whether she could stifle Hapless and just be Alison. Would that be more acceptable? But she was not sure if she could even prise them apart now. Instead, she cut her arms and upper legs, slowly and methodically, and went to bed, crying for hours. She thought, 'I can't hurt myself enough. *Because that's all you're good for.*'

Alison brooded on all this now; it rattled around her head with the comments of Sardonic Steve and his majestic, epic scorn and derision: 'Selfish bitch!' and, 'I *despise* you.'

Dr Crook pushed the tissues forward and Alison looked at her: Dr Crook's eyes were doing the Santa twinkling, the corners of her mouth were turned down almost comically and she had cocked her head to one side. She was looking intently at her charge and with a powerful sympathy.

'I am so sorry you feel so sad. Shall we interrupt that chain of thought and perhaps you can tell me what it was about?'

See, that's the skill isn't it? It's all in the delicate lexical placing of 'Shall' and 'perhaps'. The direction is clear enough, but it is issued like an invitation not an imperative and the 'perhaps' sows seeds not of doubt, but of possibility. Alison was awestruck by this fine woman and immensely comforted because Dr Crook thought Alison had been right, in her own case, to question the use of the few weeks of CBT.

'I was right?'

'Of course; you would have run rings around it and annoyed everyone, frankly.'

'I assent.'

So they were off. There is little in what Alison said to Dr Crook that you will not have heard in the pages of this book. But it was clear certain themes were going to come back again and again. There were buckets, lilies on dead fathers, mothers dead in armchairs, giant tits on a wall and terrible dreams for years and years. There were Fucking Caravans and rough sex and shame and the embolus of fear and horrid dreams of hands and arms being on her where they should not have been. There were people who laughed, people who spat and people who pointed; The Hill with its sepulchral cold and damp and frightening eyeball pickles; Nativity Baby Jesus and Crucifixion Jesus, one of whom was screaming and the other of whom was yelling but both of whom were insistent in what they communicated: 'Go away, Alison. We are for others, we are not for *you*, oh dirty girl, rot, maggot! Fuck fuck fuck-wit, fuck off!'

Also there were the People of God who spoke in tongues and the people of church who rightly saw the nasty blot of the true sinner: the child murderer, parent murderer, bad mother, poor wife fuck-up. It was ugly and raw and exhausting.

Sometimes she was so lethargic, sentences came laboriously and missing a subject, object or predicate; sometimes she was all flapping hands and extreme—almost joyous nervous energy.

'Just stay with me. We will look at potential causes, the thoughts that follow, the feelings that follow those. When we have done that, we will look at how to challenge the thoughts and thus evolve some new responses. Then you can bed those in.'

'Is that actually possible?'

'Of course.'

'I mean, do feelings follow thoughts?'

'Well, where did you think feelings came from? They're not always clearly divisible, but it's a good start.'

Alison was stunned at someone suggesting such a thing. It was like the Dorothy Rowe in the library moment, but rather more expansive: like gold, beaten thin. And what was more, embracing the theory and practice was to be collaborative.

*Pollyanna **not-fuck**!*

Alison met the psychiatrist, Dr Mirror-Neuron, who advised her that she was not bipolar, which she had queried before, although, he said, to be really sure he would need to see her during or just after an episode. Alison said, inappropriately, 'Are you asking me out?' and he looked at her askance, possibly checked where the door was. No-one laughed. It was deeply awkward.

Alison muttered, 'I'll get my coat, shall I?'

And he replied, 'No, because we haven't finished our appointment yet.'

He was definitely not asking her out.

Dr Mirror-Neuron had a rusty brown briefcase, stuffed with paper. It was cracking like an egg; ready to spill. How she wanted to look through those tumbling papers, always tempted by the exotic notion of lunacy. She had so many questions for Dr Mirror-Neuron, but they were not about her. She wanted to know how he would define mental health; what was his definition of madness? Were labels and clear diagnoses essential? Did he think sociopathy was not a mental illness but a fundamental failure of the amygdala to light up and fire? She had been reading about the work of Bob Hare, an expert on psychopaths, because obviously that's what you do when in the throes of a major depressive episode. Dr Crook didn't know about Bob Hare and his test, but that was because Dr Crook didn't get time with the really dangerous bonkers people, or at least that was what she had appeared to say, euphemistically. There was so much of interest, Alison had forgotten about herself. Surely a good thing? Did Dr Mirror-Neuron get to see, diagnose and possibly prescribe for psychopaths? And what kinds of things did people do in psychotic episodes? Why did he think more cases of schizophrenia in the young were being diagnosed? Alison chastised herself for her prurient interest, but she was truly, *utterly* fascinated by what he did in his day.

Dr Mirror-Neuron had sad eyes. He might have been seventy, but he could have been fifty. He was an attractive man because he was a clever man. But he had a bit of his dinner down his front and Alison contemplated, again inappropriately, that maybe he had not had a shag for a very long time. Perhaps he, too, struggled with images of macabre things and angels howling because of what he had seen in his working life? That gave him a a louche Albert-appeal.

She said to him, 'I feel I am taking up so much of everyone's time. I mean, I do cope most of the time. There must be others who need all your time and help so much more?'

He looked at her sternly over the tops of his glasses and pronounced (she remembered it word for word), 'In this line of work, we do not talk about deserving.'

Alison was not sure if that was a pointed comment. Did he mean, 'Yes, I entirely agree with you and you are getting on my nerves, I might add'? That pondering was her fault for not sticking with CBT CPN Carole's 'replace the negative thought with something more helpful' worksheets.

Alison ventured, 'Well what about schizophrenia because I looked up all the symptoms and I've got quite a list of head friends, and there's my alter ego and Dead Santa Maria and could I have a personality disorder because it doesn't sound good when I say it out loud, does it? And what of dissociative identity disorder?'

'No. And no. And no again.'

'A mood disorder.'

'Unlikely.'

'And are we going to monitor for bipolar?'

'No.'

She left Dr Mirror-Neuron, who was busily rifling now through his giant pile of papers. As she left, another woman came towards the door and knocked. The next patient. The knock was small; near inaudible. The woman's movements were extraordinarily quiet. Was she embarrassed to be taking up space in the world? Did she think, 'I am a ghost, slipping silently along the wall. Is that all that I am?'

Alison found the creeping, apologetic movements of the woman unutterably moving.

'I want to hold you and make you leave a mark on the world and a firm knock on the door. Because even when you're a ghost, you're people, too.'

It was hard not to talk to her or reach out to touch the ghostly hand, for you could never be sure if a person had no-one: no-one at all. Alison was a lucky girl. *Because she was not someone who had no-one.* Because she had friends who made rotas to protect her from too much addling involvement; friends who made lemon drizzle cakes and spare lemon drizzle cakes, reassured the children and kept her alive. And head friends were their own privilege, because where else could Mary Anning, Dolly Parton, John Keats, Sylvia Plath, Shirley Bassey, Albert Camus and Frida (the brunette one) from Abba be sitting on a Dorset beach together, straddling skeins of time and skimming stones across the soft, fudgy lias to a friendly sea? And now Alison also had a particularly excellent (if she could ever be a judge) clinical psychologist in her gang.

Dr Crook was then and is now, like Santa, the bringer of gifts, for it was the year with her that stopped the stone at the bottom of the hill. Or perhaps stuck it at the top, where it couldn't roll down again to a tired Alison. They met most weeks and Alison later became acquainted with Dr Hook, new GP still on rotation and, as Dr Crook had it, particularly insightful of, err... 'Nutters?' interjected the patient. Both appeared to their patient to be able to see the world clearly. Dr Hook was giggly and quite outspoken and when questioned, 'How do you know?' by Alison, she would look her squarely in the eye and say, 'Because I just know.' Alison never doubted her. Both Dr Hook and Dr Crook had the gift of careful placing of words. Words matter, and so does knowing how to *do* things with words. They issued invitations and Alison accepted. And the reason Alison did not doubt the kindly therapeutic team was because they had the quiet, smiling confidence of the clever and generous: for the patient it was a winner; a panacea; a cure.

Over the year of CAT, Alison learned really useful things in her lessons from Dr Crook. She learned about Traps: the *striving trap*; *the trying to keep things in perfect order trap*; the trying *to be a certain way around others trap*. Alison had spent a lifetime (so far) trying to impose some order on her messy and precarious world, from the rules of the room and the miniature books onward. It was truly helpful to unpick some of these and find that the sky had not fallen in.

'I want to do so many things.'

'Why do you want to do them, though?'

'I want to do them so others can see me doing them.'

'But I could say, that if we do things only so others can see them, so we are viewed and applauded publicly—that we are reliant on others for our self-worth. You are not a composite of others' approvals.'

'But no-one approves of me, really.'

'I do.'

'You *would* say that.'

'Dr Hook approves of you.'

'She *would* say that.'

'CBT CPN Carole approves of you.'

'No she doesn't.'

'Okay, that was stretching it a bit. But how about Dixie Delicious?'

'He just hasn't found me out yet.'

'He doesn't sound like a slouch to me.'

'Well…'

'Shall I let you think about what you're saying to me?'

Once, when Alison returned home from a vigorous session

at Pink Pantiles House, some words of Dr Hook reverberated in her head—in the car, out through the window and into the world around.

She had asked, 'How do I know I haven't damaged my children with my ups and downs and my instability?'

Dr Hook wrinkled her brow and told Alison that, despite her wobbles and the mad bowling match in her head, a doctor would have no doubt that her children would have the best chance to be happy and healthy individuals.

'But you can't know that. You haven't seen me with them. And Dr Crook said you were a trainee…I'm sorry; I didn't mean that quite the way it came out.'

'Oh, I *do* just know that. I see many, many people. So I know. And don't you be so saucy.'

It didn't sound very scientific, but she was firm and it looked like she must have compelling evidence from somewhere. Perhaps they both had a kind of psych-cam in Alison's house. And Dr Crook and Dr Hook did something else. They both assured her, this time with bookish proper scientific evidence and a firm look—despite the screaming and blue murder that was coming out of her mouth and the blood on her palms as they did it—that she had not and could not have killed a girl, however wrong her actions age five.

'It's that thought: it never goes away. If it doesn't, must it not be true? It goes, "Am I, was I or will I be a murderer?" and it has made me reckless and periodically unhinged for thirty years and never let go. As a child, as grown-up me, it's being scared that the police will come to the door; that I shall be roundly caught in the street and charged by children and parents. You would call it a ruminating thought. I am terrified to be me and only me.'

But Dr Hook said, 'Let the thought flood your head and feel what it does to your body. You know how that panic feels—the stone you tell us about—the stone which drops down, down. You feel a surge of your flight or fight chemicals. Let them flood you as you think the thought and feel the feeling.'

'But the sky could fall in!'

'I think not. Now notice that nothing else has happened—has *ever* happened. This way, you will retrain yourself and the fear will diminish. It is groundless. Just because you think or feel something does not mean it is true.'

That liberating statement!

Dr Hook mouthed it so confidently; gave such flight to it—imbuing the words with such possibility, but still Alison brushed past too quickly, deciding that that this would, indeed, be marvellous; that she could give up the permeating anxiety about arranging and rearranging things and reciting the first lines of *The Secret Garden* four times. That she could go out other than apologetically or in disguise. But how was *that* going to happen? No no no: not possible. She thought of buckets and the day everyone said, '*You did it! You hurt the lovely little girl!*' And she said to Dr Hook, 'How do you know? How can you tell? You weren't there.'

And there, as I told you earlier, was a rambling, bumbling idiot in the room who was spitting out—in a desperate and horrible rush for expressions and to purge the long held evidence against her in a big rude yell.

'When I was five, I was playing with a girl and she fell and cracked her head open. Everyone said I pushed her. But I didn't. I just **didn't**. She died when we were teenagers. It was her head. Something awful wrong with her head. Dead Santa Maria said her parents might have thought it was my fault. So I couldn't write them a card. They might come for me and she would understand why. Just typical. I have had nightmares about it all my life. It is like the Sylvia Plath story called 'Superman and Paula Brown's New Snowsuit', where everyone rounds on the girl who didn't do it, who didn't ruin the beautiful clothes of the popular girl, and the more the clumsy unpopular girl tells the truth the more everyone's faces say, "Yes of course you didn't but you must ring that nice Mr and Mrs Brown and apologise and write a letter to nice Paula". And they all know and everything, everyone and the world have changed—and her parents are so disappointed. And anyway everybody knows what she is like. Damn Sylvia Plath: no, damn Paula Brown! Damn Santa Maria! And fuck fuck fuck nasty evil me!'

Her screams were building to a crescendo and there was a little blood on her palms where she had dug in her nails. Gradually, diminuendo washed in as Dr Hook continued to meet her gaze, unwavering and determined. When the noise stopped, there was a long pause. Dr Hook left the room at a gentle pace and came back with Dr Crook and she said, looking intently and sternly into Alison's eyes, while Dr Crook put the gentlest of pressure on their patient's hand.

'You did not do this. You never did this. It is not real.'

It was the most frightening moment of Alison's life. A dreadful confession of what she had been and quite clearly what she must still be: the ensuing silence was bitter and cold. Someone spoke. The fragmenting words came from her own mouth, again: 'But how do you know? How? But...You weren't there?'

And when Alison raised her head, she thought she saw Hapless Ally out of the corner of her eye. Previously, the latter had been smirking, waiting to adhere and improve on the little murderer, or waiting for a day trip out on her own, when she could stand Alison no more; now she sat slumped in the corner, muttering quietly as the patient was stripped back to a core.

And what she muttered was this: 'Bitch. You little bitch. You can't ever be just you now. The words of the good doctors can't help you now. It is too late. Ha ha ha.'

'Dr Crook. Dr Hook. It's *her*. It's Hapless Ally. Can't you see her? Can't you? I have to have her and she has to stay because if I don't and she doesn't, what will happen to me?'

Dr Hook said, 'You are being a difficult patient. Shh now. Let her go. Be laid bare for the first time. Could I shove her out of the window? It's a way down and that might finish her off. I'm not saying I can see her, but if she's here, she's here. I'm sorry; is this a bit like looking for the monsters under the bed to reassure the small child before sleep—only in the process we confirm to the scared child that there are really *are* monsters?'

'Not quite. She's real to me and, I think, to herself. And

anyway, no-one ever reassured me that there weren't monsters under the bed. Dead Santa Maria would have assured me there *were*.'

And as for the startling suggestion—to shove Hapless out of the fourth floor window? The good doctor smiled, from a place beyond words.

'I'm not ready to open the window just yet,' whispered Alison.

'Why so? This is a timely death, isn't it? And couldn't a killing in the right context, of course, be good?'

'Can we do it next week? I want some time alone with her first. I can't really explain it. She is me, well, part of me and yet she's learned to live separately. I hate her, but that's partly because I love her and don't want to. And I think she both loves me against her will and hates me because the love is more powerful than the intent. I bet none of that makes any sense at all, does it?'

Dr Crook said, slowly and sweetly, 'Oh we hear some interesting things within these walls.'

There was a long pause. Hapless Ally was nowhere to be seen now but suddenly, like a fine shaft of light across a hoary sky, Alison heard the words of Dr Hook again: 'Listen to my words: again, just because you think or feel something doesn't mean...it's true.'

And Alison said, 'I'm sorry, but WHAT?'

Alison needed to hear it again, for she had never, in a lifetime, thought of such a thing or the glorious implications of knowing it. And back at the library, the great Dorothy Rowe was laughing about Alison's tardiness and flicking

Dead Santa Maria with one of her fine books and yelling, 'Get out!'

And another thing, painful in its sweetness, took place as Dr Crook added that Alison was a model patient, engaging and grappling as she did with what was laid on. That they both thought she was lovely: an avalanche of compliments, where Alison was both delighted and mortified. She could only look down and shake her head. But there was more.

'It's my—our—opinion that for every hundred people I might see who have a similar pattern of life experience and difficulty, maybe three or four would be off the ward. You are a fully functional human being. You're able to be out there—being and doing. You just need to know that.'

'I am not functional.'

'But you *are*. I'll grant you that not everyone has a gallery of imaginary friends, a colour table wherein your whole world is miniaturised and envisioned, a set of tiny rules and an alter ego, not to mention one who has learned to detach. Not everyone I meet has a dead mother shuffling behind them, I suppose...'

'What about the genes? The translocation? That I'm born broken, even on a cellular level.'

'That is the silliest thing you have said so far because from where we're standing, your chromosomes have done a pretty good job. Time to open that window?'

'Almost. When I do, she'll bring a friend: Dead Santa Maria. I think they'll team up. But...say...I'll summon up some of my own company, too?'

'You do that. It could almost be fun. It will be a red letter day.'

And Alison sat looking at The Recovery Squad and crying and shaking and saying, 'Oh it could, it could... Icouldreallydothisnowcouldn'tI... thank you, thank you for the compliments and are you sure thankyouthankyouthankyou but are you sure and no not now—but can we open the window next week and I'll definitely bring those friends?'

'Room friends or head friends?' asked Dr Crook.

'You be my room friends, I'll do the rest.'

Dr Hook met her insistent, questioning look with her dark velvet eyes. 'It has been our pleasure and yes, next week, if you are sure you need a little more time.'

Alison sat in her car outside Pink Pantiles House; there was much to think about. A sense of liberty brushed against her back and tenderly against her hand. Combustible but beautiful change—transformation—was, for the first time, a possibility. Letting her thoughts take shape, she also recalled a conversation with a midwife when her youngest child, now seven months old, was born. Alison had been startled when the midwife had said, 'I want to take a picture of you for our Baby Wall. We were all looking at you on the intercom camera when you came in for the baby's weigh-in. You make it look so natural. It's just beautiful.'

And she took Alison's new baby, whirled him around and said to her colleagues and another visiting mother, 'Look, this is our (she said '*our*', which brought forth tears for the thrill of being part of something) Josiah. Isn't he lovely?'

Alison, then as now, had been overcome to hear something like that. She had always felt that she didn't have much idea how to be a mother and was scared that she would pass on to her children the strange internal inscape and the chants and the helter skelter images. That Dead Santa Maria would pop up, somehow, intoning, 'That baby should be Baby in the Bucket too if *you're* his mother. And oh oh oh, say look! Check out the snapped chromosomes.'

The effect of the midwife's comments had not lasted until morning, but had now revived; with a cheerful wave from Dr Crook at an upper window, a pretty scrapbook was assembling in her head now: it was almost too beautiful to tolerate.

'I would move mountains for you,' had said Dixie Delicious. Now, she wondered if she could move them for him.

At home, Alison sobbed as she prepared tea for the three children; she was peeling carrots.

And this is what happened at the sink, because it had to.

'I hate you but I love you, Hapless Ally. You're part of me but you're also not me, are you? We've been together since I was a tiny girl on that day in the orchard with the face of the celandines turned to the sun. The first time I felt the itchy scratchy dark thought in the palm and I knew that inside me was the nasty embolus. So can you speak to me? I know, right now, I'm truly being me. It's no oil painting, but it's lighter.'

'You'll never be free of me, Alison. I am you, always there, you know that you become me—and I love you and hate you.'

'We cannot do this any more. I'd like to think of it as Ariel being released to the elements, but I am no magician: it has to be more brutal—there is no other way.'

'You cannot be free, it is too late.'

'I will miss you, but this is timely. I have to write your name on the paper. I have to set down in words what I'm going to do. Here: "Goodbye Hapless Ally." '

'Cross it out.'

'I will not. I want a star, not a millstone.'

'Forget your silly poetry: you can't do this.'

'I can. We don't need any more dialogue,' said Alison with a startling conviction. She looked closely at the name on the scrap of paper, then scratched at it with the chopping knife. It was fractured—bleeding black.

There were vegetable peelings to go in the garden composter and with them Alison placed the little jag of paper; for a moment she watched the ink run under the scraps. She could hear the nearby crying of the intangible person who was losing her name, losing her life, but she walked back into the house and did not turn around.

13

Letters to Dead and Undead

Alison was sitting in the car outside Pink Pantiles House. She had been there for half an hour at least. A man walked past wearing a red jacket. His jacket was very red; his bag very blue. Even if its effect should turn out to be temporary, to have this time, now, seeing things as they are—maybe as they always were—and vibrant and freshly imagined, like the innocent, shimmering Christmas bauble at the beginning of this story, was world enough.

Compliments aside, however, Dr Crook was not going to let Alison off the hook just yet, and part of this therapy, this cognitive analytical therapy, was that she wrote letters to dead people or people who might as well have been. Alison decided to dive straight in and say a few things, as she had not previously had the chance. There was an enormous job of work to be done; letter writing and a mighty killing and the killing was already underway; moreover, during some very hard thoughts and much talking aloud, Alison had invited the whole cabaret of imaginary friends to be there at the latter event. If the killing were to happen, witnesses would be needed to make sure the timely event had been carried out effectively.

But first the letters: they were to be to Dead Santa Maria and Brother who Might as Well have been Dead. And they went like this:

'*Mummy/Santa Maria/Dead Santa Maria,*

Why did you…

Pull my hair so hard and hit me with a hairbrush and tell me I deserved it or worse or nothing less? Why pull my ears, push me over and kick me in my side when I was on the ground and tell me I deserved worse? Why did you always tell me I was the most selfish person around? That I had no ambition or determination unlike the lovely daughters of some of your friends, like Heroic Alice: star pupil; star child—or the mimsy scarf girls at ballet; the smug little bastard who belonged to the dentist? Why always intone that all the family knew exactly what I was like? That they too agreed with the bucket: nothing wrong with that. I still, as a very big girl now, find it hard to relax because I learned others could see into my soul, like you could, when you glimpsed the box with THE WAGES OF SIN ARE DEATH daubed on, inside me, your ugly, translucent octopus-ugly baby. You would always say that other people knew what a problem I was because you told them and anyway, your porcelain doll-faced friends could see it all for themselves couldn't they? Yes, of course: I was translucent. You laughed about me and said all this with your harpy friends in tow, except that I thought that they, like you, were exemplary women; pillars of the community; well respected, so it had to me, didn't it?

You said that I was so horrible I was looking forward to dancing on your grave. It came out with force when we were folding laundry once, standing in the bloody airing cupboard, for heaven's sake and so I have grown up trying to shrug off difficult associations with buckets, emergency services, coast paths and airing cupboards. Not to mention cabbage and pickles and plug-in air fresheners and the smell of vanilla, although admittedly those weren't all entirely your fault. You would always tell me that I was very hard on other people, always disappointed in my family and particularly in my brother, which caused him—your sweet, special, expensive delicate ship—a lot of pain. Oh! Did it fuck. Because, looked at another way, maybe you both sucked and so I wasn't the spawn of the devil if I was disappointed. Now, I'm not so scared to say that aloud in case of invoking divine nemesis, because I'm beginning to believe in God. Dixie Delicious says He is alive, and not Dead if He Ever Existed but also that He doesn't approve of my swearing.

You would say, I think it was daily, that you, Vaguely Dead Dad and Brother who Might as Well have been Dead would spit in the face of my ungratefulness. I was ashamed and I would run for my crawl space and wail to Frida, "They hate me! It's because I'm all wrong! I'm evil!" and she would hug me and we'd do the harmony bits in 'Fernando' to calm me down. You told me, when Dad was dying, that I didn't appreciate him and was as thoughtless as ever and Dad knew that too and I'd let him down and his cancer was all the sufferance and passion repressed and I made him sick.

And he screamed in my face, "Don't you know that I am at the point of death" and reminded me I couldn't even remember to put the bins out or swat the bee of 'The Book of Revelation'. You. Have. Let. Me. Down. He was on the point of death for years, but this time he really meant it, gurgling and incontinent and cursing me. I thought that maybe I had brought this on. Sat in assembly thinking, "I killed the girl, I probably killed Grandma and muffled up poor Mfanwy, I should have been put in the bucket and none of this would have happened." And the teacher said, "Pay attention, pay attention, girl!"

I remember you shrieking at me, shrieking that I didn't understand Dad was dying, but it took me a long time to realise that you hadn't told me how or why. Even Dad just pulled over in a lay-by and said, "I've got a lump on my leg," which was a little euphemistic, don't you think, looking back? Getting to Cambridge: well, ooh at last you did something right and how this was echoed by the family. Really hollow praise. And I was the interloper in the quad anyway; stuck out like a sore thumb: dirty girl: thumb stump. And Brother who Might as Well have been Dead: to add to this, you told me they were dying more quickly and more would die because of me and now you don't speak to me at all and in my darkest moments sometimes I wonder if I killed them and will kill others by being born. Did you spread a dark lie? Was I the darkness? This was my earliest fear, hidden in the miniature books and told to Frida and now to the nice Doctors Crook and Hook. Was I always no good; a burden; poison to all; with you under *sufferance? But I showed clever eventually, didn't I? It was show and tell at that pretty point, wasn't it?*

Those teachers at school: "Oh what a trial to your poor parents, you must be. A wet flimsy thing: look at you. A crying shame." Once, I came in late and Miss Crumble said, "Oh again a burden to your wonderful parents, to your mother, father and brother, oh a fine triumvirate they are" and she was looking at me with her gleaming sardonic blue eye. I said, "I couldn't wash my school uniform" rather than, "She kicked me in the side and in the head and drove off and so I had to walk four miles to school with not enough time and I was sick four times into the foxgloves by the path" because, after all, I'd been asking for it, hadn't I? And my head was so sore. Sufferance, for sure.

Why, when I took an overdose, all the paracetamol I could stockpile, did you not try to help or hold me but just told me I was a selfish little she-devil? And how was it that I've never given myself permission to feel that I wasn't all bad? Why didn't you make me feel I was ever a joy to you? I remember being all dressed up as a teenager; somewhere to get to; boys to chase (not that they actually wanted Hapless Ally because they were pelting after Heroic Alice) and you said, spitting a curse while you shelled the broad beans, "Ha! I've got a slut for a daughter. Look at her, the dirty little slut." Now, I try to tell my boys they are a joy however revolting they are, and believe me, they can be pretty revolting. Why did you never hug me or kiss me? I have no memory of this, although I know now from a photograph, silly that I almost needed proof, that you held me when I was a baby and at my first glance you look happy in that moment, posing sweetly for the porcelain doll-faced friends. But you weren't happy to me after that. And now I look again at the photograph and see that your arm is stiff and your grin is strained. And I know it was different with Helen.

I used to hear you talking to Dad at night and you'd say what a brat I was and screech blame at him and say that he'd given me too much, probably down to the idiocy inbred at The Hill. You said, "I never wanted her anyway." And so, thinking of your little chinwag, this is to you, oh Daddy Daddy, my daddy: why did you never redress the balance; why did you acquiesce and not stop Mum when she was pulling my hair or calling me a slut? You just shuffled in the woodpile, stoking the fire. I still remember on our coast walks you didn't really talk to me and one time I plucked up the courage to ask you if you enjoyed being with me. I expected a slap. Instead you actually said you would rather be with your son because, well lots of reasons, so just because. "Be quiet. Fuck-wit. Just not be. Fuck-wit. I'm watching the fucking cormorants drying their wings on the rocks." I remember the exact words and I feel like digging my nails into my hands now. On the bus back, St David's, Solva, Pencym, I held the side of my face hard against the window, steadying myself. These were such formative memories, weren't they? On holiday, I couldn't pelt for a crawl space and have Frida there to comfort me and sing to me, Keats was poor on inter-relational stuff, it must be said, and Camus wasn't there yet. So I swallowed it and sat there trying to find a friend in my head and wondering if I could rush for Stack Rocks and tumble into the sea. Perhaps I could well and truly make a spectacle of myself and go head first down the cleft cliff and through the roof of the chapel in the rocks at St Govan's. Ha! **Now** you're looking at me. "Never crush a child's spirit" you told generations of parents with your big headmaster hat on. What about me, Daddy? Dirty-maggot-bucket-child?

Is it right that I spent childhood and teenage years gripped by guilt, headaches, self-harming, pulling out my own hair while you told me, Oh Santa Maria, how much you did for me? To Brother who Might as well have been Dead and the porcelain doll-faced friends of Dead Santa Maria: why did you tell me that I was lucky I hadn't been aborted, that Dad didn't speak to Mum when he heard she was pregnant and that she sat in a very hot bath and drank proscribed gin. I didn't immediately understand this, but I surely do now. I survived, dammit. Tenacious little bugger, as it turned out: she hated me for that, my first act of rebellion.

I guess that pretty much wraps it up. I know you did your duty by me and I thank you, but Lord did you let me know it. You made the most beautiful cakes my friends had ever seen. Birthday cakes. Ice cream cakes, with chocolate Siamese cats adorning their sides. I can't have known you fully. You made me beautiful cakes. And you were my jagged, pointing monster, but I loved you, Mummy, I loved you. I couldn't help it. I still love you and I want you and I miss you. I think of you every day and I will never stop. Yet I know this: I have three boys of my own now. Sometimes the eldest two worry about me and they talk about heaven and how, if I ever die, it's okay because they'll see me again. And I'm going to verbalise something that feels wrong AND right here, which is that, *in all honesty, the thought of seeing you and Vaguely Dead Dad again does not comfort me. I try to believe and try not to believe in heaven. I have to say goodbye and confine you to my past. I **have** to. Brutally, maybe. As with Hapless Ally, it's you or it's me. I'm also going to give myself permission to do something else: when family and your friends or pupils you taught, speak about how kind or brilliant or marvellous you were and strike up with, "Oooooh, your poor mother," I'm not going to feel sick and think I caused you not to be so with me: I am so tired of scurrying back to rules of rooms, the beginning of The Secret Garden, miniature books and rituals and the navigable spaces between the pretty objects on the colour table. I want to be Alison, not funny, ridiculous, and easier for everyone to tolerate Hapless Ally. So, instead, I'm going to think another compassionate thought: "She WAS all that, but she wasn't your mother and you don't know: you just think you do." I feel lighter just saying it. Maybe the glittering Christmas bauble on the tree in our house now can be just that: a pretty little trinket which I can look at and see as if it were for the first time—without its being laden down by enervating and painful nostalgia. Not that you'll get to see it now. Oh—we have such a beautiful Christmas tree.*

I wish that things could have been different but I hope I will find salvation and comfort in what I can do for my children as they grow and go out complete into the chilly old world.'

Dr Crook insisted on a letter to Brother who Might as Well have been Dead, which had Alison reeling and saying, 'Noooooo!' But the doctor said, 'Oh, now I think you're running away from it, aren't you?' and Alison remembered the elderly lady at the bus stop and thought of *running to*, and wrote this:

'*Here goes. When I was a child I idolised you. You were like a more fun version of a dad and I would sit on your lap and watch telly or just chat. You spoiled me with sweeties, long walks, playing badminton. And when you, suddenly changed and cold stony-faced, took me to the wood as daylight slipped away and left me there to be eaten by wolves, I would always forgive you and try to forget. I would say to myself, "This is a grown-up joke I don't understand yet," and when the worst of the fear was over I would say, "The wolves never came, after dusk. Maybe the wishing tree wished them away?" You would joke with my friends and always come to help entertain my friends at birthday parties. You could juggle; make things with balloons: that's why I didn't dare rail or retaliate when you encouraged my friends to laugh at me, smirking in victory as you did it. The maestro! And I was scared of something, but I didn't know or couldn't articulate what, exactly. It came from the corner of your yellow eye. I know that when I was about ten, something changed, or maybe it was always there but I didn't see it until I became more, shall we say, sentient, my newly knowing state coinciding with the time you, all so publicly, went off me. I remember what I willed myself to think of as happy visits; day trips. But they were punctuated by anger, weren't they? You said I was the apple of your eye and that I would always be your precious "little sis". But there would be the sudden wild anger; exuberance followed by angry tears, and I didn't understand. Were you so sad, too? One day, you made the peculiar statement*

I didn't know whether to admire or run from. You stopped in the street and said, "I enjoy being a bit of a bastard and kicking people when they are down" and you were all swagger and brilliance. You said, "People are all shit. It is the nature of the beast. You can't trust anyone and no-one will care for you" and you smiled knowingly as you said it. Gifting.

That night I discovered the huge porn collection under your bed and couldn't take my eyes off what I saw. Above your bed was a huge photo of a naked woman, breasts on show, all shiny tabloid and emerging from the sea, her lips parted expectantly. I stayed in that room with you, sleeping at the end of the bed with the giant tits looking on and the porn humming under the bed, easily within reach. I read it, learning its language, its forms and shapes and I clung to The Wind in the Willows, incongruous in your bedroom. Tits. Being a bastard is fun. Readers' wives. Cunts. The clit. Look, it is the nature of the beast. No-one will care for you. Fanny. All people are bastards. Bestial. It is the nature of the beast. Hard-on. "None of this cares for you. Oh my precious, precious sister. Raaarrrrrr! Who would believe you? No-one will come!"

And holding the hand of a boy in a field of daisies was dead.

For some time in my teens you stayed away. When you visited I remember you on edge; aggressive; I was nervous around you; you used strange language around me and shaming memories erupt: you would lean closer to me, looking from the corner of your yellow eye, and say, "How are your periods?" or, "Have you got a fat fanny?" or, "Look at your breasts. Your silly little breasts." That might have been funny from kin close in age, but when I was thirteen, you were old enough to be my father and you shuddered in disgust when you saw me and it mortified me and made me ashamed of my changing body all through my adolescence and I would look at myself and be sick and so it was really only my adventures with Albert Camus and jaunt with Denis the Lusty Blacksmith that made me consider the possibility that I wasn't some kind of, I don't know, physical outcast: dirty girl: my sex repelling all those around me—but Albert and Denis the Lusty Blacksmith thought I was hot, hot, hot. Of course, the boys in school thought I was persona non grata: eccentricity, oddity and trying too hard tend to have that effect on people. It had to be me, didn't it? I would have shrivelled up without the hot blacksmith and my imaginary existentialist. Vive La France*!*

And the nightmares I have had about you? I do not know whether they were true, but I know that the night was heavy and that it took me twenty-five years to be able to name the sexual parts of the body because there laid fear and loathing. For me, it's hard, because my waking and dreaming and my real and imagined encounters are historically a little blurred, but I definitely do not cry to dream again when I dream of you; instead, I wake and cry not to and I'm a lucky girl now because I reach for the hand of Dixie Delicious and what can you do to me now?

I remember your drinking and exuberant dancing and wild unexpected swearing and the sense that our parents gave me, expressed quite calmly and not in the white heat of anger, that they preferred you. Oh yeah: I got kind of used to being under sufferance and with a muddled sense that I was shit and you were Shinola.

I never felt cross; I just felt sad and dug my nails into the palms of my hands and scratched, scratched, scratched at my skin. It was things such as this, I think, that made a place for the self-harming to start. I felt rage and frustration; they held hands with disgust at my own body: emerging breasts and all. I recall being thirteen and accidentally bumping a drawer on the wall of a bedroom in your house: it made a mark. You were incandescent with rage: you and Mum called me a selfish little bitch, throwing curses into the starry night and I ran out into the street, somewhere, anywhere and when our parents left, you said, "Quickly, take her, take that, THAT THING, with you." I hadn't meant to cause harm or damage. "You marked his wall. You marked it. It was you, you, you. And you are marked, too!" Mum and Dad just told me again how selfish I was and, well, everyone knew that. I felt kind of desperate and just wanted to know if anyone thought differently: it sounds so pathetic! I said, "But his next door neighbours said I was lovely" and Mum barked out a laugh and spat, "That's because they don't really know you." I cried silently for the two hundred miles home. Santa Maria threw a carton of orange juice, a Club biscuit and a bag of crisps into the back seat at some point. Like a bone to the nasty little dog. They did not turn round.

I feel that there's a kind of spitefulness in you as there was in my mother. And what, as a child I must have, inchoately, begun to think of as true and eternal simply wasn't. What you said: about us always being together; about you and me having adventures together; taking on the world, well I thought it was possible. I thought that with your thoughts and words you could make a star dance or melt its heart; really your words were hollow, beating on a raggedy old drum. The emptiest heart spilling over into the fullest metaphor: I just didn't know it yet, or I tried not to know it. And what you conjured yourself to be was just a layer covering up resentments, wounds and imagined slights; misogyny, pornography, the self-denial of a functioning alcoholic; a repressed and angry son. Look at me: I have morphed into a cod psychologist: isn't that just typical of Baby in the Bucket Alison—ha ha ha? I can't not be your sister, but if you're Brother who Might as Well have been Dead, I hardly expect to look on you again—and I will survive: with my most excellent bazookas, much beloved of my husband. They're a double D! I just had them measured up. And they weren't covered in shame! Yet, say I do see you, expert on pulling the wool, on subterfuge, on being the out in the cold injured one, turning up to caress a hearse or wear your mourning weeds with gravitas as you breathe excitedly on the coffin plate, well I won't see you. When, in moments I wish would not come, a picture of you arrives in my head and you sit, like Jaggers, in his "deadly black horsehair chair", nails all around it "like a coffin", I must try to unseat you—chase you away. You must not inhabit my head while you continue to take from me and snarl at me. I've said this much, but I wish you only happiness, no harm. You just have to go now. So Brother who Might as Well have been Dead, Mummy/Santa Maria/Dead Santa Maria and Daddy Daddy/Vaguely Dead Dad, you cormorant and caravan-fancying man of mine and man I loved, well, at last, I'm through. There is no more to say.'

And Alison finally got a 'Well done' on her essay. And

the sky did not fall in, as Chicken Licken feared it would. A thunderbolt did not strike for shame.

'I will get you a drink of water,' said Dr Crook, 'after which Dr Hook will be popping in because, as you promised, it's time.'

This was going a bit too quickly.

'No time like the present, Alison.'

'So soon. I can't, can I? This is a kind of hospital. How can I kill someone here?'

'You already started, Alison. With the conversation you had with her, the name dripping ink in the composter. Finish the job. Euthanise her, or she will kill you.'

Alison was terrified, but there was no escaping the fire. Slowly, she pressed her hands on the side of her head and said, 'Out you come, everyone: roll up. Come and see.'

Into the room, following Dr Crook with a glass of water, came Sylvia. This time, happy, pleased with a poem; there followed a beaming JK, with flowers for a favourite pupil and friend. They were lilies, so they had to go—but it was a thoughtful touch. And who was this on his arm? It was Miss Fanny Brawne, bright star, because, in this story, it worked. He survived and they were together: the letter he wrote—'I wish that I was either in your arms, or that a thunderbolt should strike me'—she treasured it, his health came back to him and now he and Fanny were in the same world, conversing and enjoying delicate pleasures, for ever: because, in *this* story, it could happen.

Next came Mary Anning, with her eyes to the ground, as ever: looking, looking. She brought a picky hammer with a ribbon on it as a gift and was saying, 'I'm sorry I said you were Haaapless, Alison' while a thunderbolt and a flash of lightning struck behind her, missing Keats and Fanny, but eliciting a wry smile from both.

Now came Frida (the brunette one), resplendent in platforms and with a silver beret over her luscious hair; it still hadn't worked out with Benny, but she called across that now she was dabbling in Norwegians again and, 'Man, they are hotter, baby girl.'

An expectant pause and so, *Ooh la la!* Enter Albert, gitane in hand, notebook in another and football kit in a bag which swung in a louche fashion from his arm: he was so very much alive—for in this story he survived to be an old man, won the Nobel prize for literature (twice: they made an exception for him) and was kept on as goalie for his Algiers team until his seventies because he stayed such a fine figure of a man. Behind him lay a noticeable gap, when, from the corridor outside, the playful shrieks struck up the song: 'Ah'm the star!' and, 'No sugar, I am: Va va voom! And don't cross a girl from Tiger Bay!' And thus Dolly and Shirley tumbled into the room, settled down reluctantly, on fire with beauty and charisma. And they hugged, because they were friends and knew there was room enough for more than one diva.

If you had cared to look outside, to a parallel window on the fourth floor, you could have seen Virgil, Dante, Whitman, William Empson, possibly even Louis MacNeice with his elbow resting rakishly on the shoulder of someone who might have been Professor Pobble. They looked on, gently; faithfully all, this time.

'Quite a gathering?' asked Dr Crook.

'Oh yes.'

Now, Alison screwed up her eyes, thought of Dead Santa Maria, drew her hand across her diaphragm and across her palm and took up the black embolus of fear and the itchy, scratchy thought parcelled in the palm. This time, in the commanding presence of the good doctors, they dislodged and became separate; no longer a teratoma on their host and she handed one each to Doctors Crook and Hook, saying, 'Do as you will.'

Dr Crook pushed an elegant thumbnail into the embolus and bled it dead.

Dr Hook held the itchy, scratchy, dark thought in the palm until its life and vigour were extinguished.

Both the dark things lay as dust, now. The spectators approved.

And heads turned. Dead Santa Maria was at the window scratching and mouthing about Baby in the Bucket. She must have come up the fire escape for, as you know from the day of the wedding proposal, dead people can climb fast. And, so, into the room came Hapless Ally, less substantial since her name began to suppurate in the composter, but still far too confident just at the moment of her annihilation.

'Roll up, my peanut-crunching crowd: Killing Hapless Ally!' announced Alison.

'Oh get you. I've just been out with Dead Santa Maria. She really is quite the girl and wishes I had been her daughter,' laughed Hapless Ally.

'Yes, I bet. But you know, I'm not sure I care anymore. And I want to say this:

'YOU DO NOT EXIST

YOU DO NOT EXIST

YOU DO NOT EXIST'

'Yes, Alison. That is it!' shouted Albert joyously: 'Existence precedes essence. But it is your existence, and while you live, she cannot; and while you live, you are free to decide who or what you are.'

'Oh, Albert.'

And Alison took his hand and, even though Alison was married now, he held her against the wall and kissed her with some certain passion and said, '*Voila!* The scenery collapses!'

And, hand in hand with Albert, Alison took a firm hold of she who had been Hapless Ally and shot a firm goodbye look at Dead Santa Maria and she wrestled both of them to the window and threw them with her own certain passion down, down, down. Hapless Ally was dead before she fell, of course; and Dead Santa Maria was dead before Hapless Ally fell on her, of course. And the crowd in the room hugged and roared and screamed and were gone.

Alison was on the floor, cataleptic with relief and the joy of being single and indivisible, should such a thing be possible.

There was an eternal pause.

'I think you're alone, now,' said Dr Crook.

Alison hugged the good doctors goodbye and scurried off down the fawn carpet, past the flip charts and the efflorescence of artificial dahlias in fake water. She had to get out before she started crying or panicked that she would not be able to do the next bit on her own. The waiting room was busy today. Everyone looked down at their feet. She wanted to help and fix whatever was broken. But she was spent for today. A quick glance in the rear-view mirror at Pink Pantiles House and she was gone.

14

A Wall of Yay

Life is a funny old thing; we all know that. It is certainly
curious, you know, how things fall out. How things fall apart
when the centre cannot hold. How they are fixed. Books
fall open on the right pages, and here are serendipitous gifts,
waiting for you to cup them in your hands.

Dixie Delicious.

Noah.

Asa.

Josiah.

One man found on a street and three sons gifted by God
and all things that are good.

'The millstone has become a star.'

And Frida, Albert, Sylvia, JK, Dolly, Shirley, Mary Anning:
it is an unusual list of playmates, but in some lives, fantasy and
fact mingle and they certainly did for Alison. And one learns,
with some difficulty, that it is acceptable to be different; to be

the odd one out. To be Baby in the Bucket and change that dynamic: one need not wear one's awareness of self and past with a heavy self-consciousness.

While Alison sat, ruminating, in bounded a boy, a friend of one of her sons.

'Whatcha doing?'

'I'm reading. *You* know me. I'm always reading.'

The boy was a cheerful soul. One who stopped at beauty—and he said, 'I've been adding to my Wall of Yay!'

'A Wall of Yay!' A happy scrapbook of a wall, which contained pictures he liked, memories, photos of things he'd done that he was proud of: isn't that an entrancing notion? Something jubilant and life-giving. The boy's mother, Crossword Katie, suggested that Alison might make one for herself—but while our subject was entranced by the healthy and happy attitude of the boy child, she did not see how *she* could possibly make such a wall. Yet gradually, remembering the diligent attentions of the good doctors, she dared to say to herself again that it was possible to unpick some of the most frightening things in her head and so, for the first time, Alison came to look properly and closely at pictures of herself as a child. There she was, giant bottom in the air, bending down to kiss a donkey that was either dead or asleep; there she was, again, a happy if rather porcine little girl with a doll and a towel after a bath—all dark hair and giant brown eyes and, even as a tot, the deep dimples that Dixie Delicious had always particularly liked. She didn't look like she should have been left in a bucket or in a dark and shadowy wood to be eaten by wolves, or an exacting, tiring burden for a mother to bear. She just looked like an ordinary kid.

'How can that be?'

Silence.

'Let me write this down—it can go on "The Wall of Yay!" too: "The millstone has become a star." '

Alison put the pictures in a pile and found some things from Dixie Delicious and the children: there was a collage from her oldest son, Noah, of assorted heavy metal groups and the legend, repeated, 'Mum: you rock.' There was a little paper heart from her second son, Asa, saying, 'I love you' and a hand-print painting from her youngest son, Josiah, which, in its own way, said the same. With these she put a quotation from her husband: it was scriptural, *Proverbs* 31:10, and her husband had chosen it for their wedding. The dark thoughts, the depression and confusion had meant Alison could *look*, but she could not *read*. Today, she read this, from her husband's fine sloping hand, 'She brings him good, not harm, all the days of her life. She is far more precious than jewels and her value is far above rubies and pearls.'

It was, in particular, the bit about bringing *good, not harm* that steadied her nerve and comforted; in truth, she hardly noticed the detail of the gemstones: *harm* was what she had brought about all her life, she had thought. *Under sufferance. Dancing on your mother's grave. You pushed that lovely little girl. Look what you did to Heroic Alice.* But of course, there would be no room for that on a Wall of Yay—which, because, there wasn't a suitable wall, and just because it might make her look like a show-off arse to anyone who didn't understand the context, grew into life on the back of a cupboard door, by the kitchen roll holder and fire extinguisher (she had inherited her father's talent for setting fire to stuff).

Alison wished that there were a place for the pocketful of things which her eldest son had brought home for her when she had been properly mad that time—all the things he had found in the roots of the holly tree at school: a red ribbon, a bead, gold thread, a pretty stone and an acorn. He was like a magical boy in a story, discovering miniature treasure.

And she wrote this on a sticky label and slapped it on the door:

'Hapless Ally. You are dead. This is *my* Wall of Yay, not yours.'

But Alison pulled it off.

There was no conversation to be had after Killing Hapless Ally.

BIBLIOGRAPHY

I have referred to, used very brief paraphrase of, or quoted where the text is out of copyright the following texts and I hope to have piqued your interest in some of those which follow. I have listed the editions I own, but where these are out of print, I have given an obtainable alternative. Albert Camus: *The Outsider,* (Penguin, 2000, translated by Joseph Laredo), 'The Myth of Sisyphus' (Penguin, 1975, 2000, translated by Justin O'Brien); *Selected Essays and Notebooks* (Penguin, 1989, translated by Philip Thody); Louis MacNeice: 'Thalassa', 'The Sunlight on the Garden' and 'Autumn Journal' from *Collected Poems* edited by I. Dodds and Eric Robertson (Faber and Faber, 1966, 1987); Simone de Beauvoir: *Force of Circumstance* (Penguin, 1987, translated by Richard Howard); Jean Paul Sartre: *Nausea* (Penguin, 1966, 1986, translated by Robert Baldick) and Annie Cohen-Solal: *Sartre. A Life* (Heinemann, 1987); Sylvia Plath: 'Superman and Paula Brown's New Snowsuit' from *Johnny Panic and the Bible of Dreams* (Faber and Faber, 2001) and the poems 'Lady Lazarus', 'Cut' and 'Daddy' from *Sylvia Plath Collected Poems* (Faber and Faber, 2002); Dylan Thomas: A *Child's Christmas in Wales* (New Directions, 2009); T. S. Eliot: 'The Love Song of J. Alfred Prufrock' from *T. S. Eliot Collected Poems*

1909-1962 (Faber and Faber, 2009), Michael Ondaatje: *The English Patient* (Bloomsbury, 1992, 2009); Samuel Beckett's 'Happy Days' and 'Waiting for Godot' from *The Complete Dramatic Works of Samuel Beckett* (Faber and Faber, 2006) and his *Collected Poems* (Grove/Atlantic, 2015); W. B Yeats: 'The Circus Animals' Desertion' from *The Collected Poems of W. B Yeats* (Wordworth Poetry Library 2000); Andre Gide: *Fruits of the Earth* (Penguin 1970, translated by D. Bussy); Dolly Parton: *My Life and Other Unfinished Business*, (Harper Collins, 1995); Peter Hogan: *Shirley Bassey. Diamond Diva* (ReadHowYouWant.com LTD, 2013); definitions given on the NHS website on its mental health and associated medication information pages and from the *DSM-5.* [An abbreviation of] *The Diagnostic and Statistical Manual of Mental Disorders Fifth Edition* (Various. Published by the American Psychiatric Association, 2013); Robert D. Hare: *Without Conscience: The Disturbing World of the Psychopaths Among Us* (The Guildford Press, 1993) and his website, www.hare.org, which is devoted to the study of psychopathy; Charles Dickens: *Great Expectations* and *David Copperfield,* (Gerald Duckworth and Co Ltd, 2005; this is the *Nonesuch Dickens six volume collection*); Frances Hodgson Burnett: *The Secret Garden* (Vintage Children's Classics, 2012); Helen Bush: *Mary Anning's Treasures* (Puffin, 1976); Charlotte Perkins Gilman: *The Yellow Wallpaper and Other Stories* (Dover Publications, 1997); John Skelton: 'On the Death of the Noble Prince King Edward the Fourth' from *John Skelton. The Complete English Poems* edited by John Scattergood (Penguin, 1992); Walt Whitman: 'Song of Myself' from *Leaves of Grass* (Penguin, 1986); Andrew Marvell: 'A Horation Ode Upon Cromwell's Return from Ireland', from *The Complete Poems of Andrew Marvell* (Penguin Classics edition, Penguin, 2014); D.H. Lawrence: *Sons and Lovers* (United Holdings Group, 1922); William Empson: *Seven Types of Ambiguity* (Pimlico, 2004); John Keats: 'The Eve of St Agnes' from *Collected Poems of John Keats* (William Ralph Press, 2014) and *John Keats. Selected Letters* (Penguin, 2014); Kenneth Graham: *The Wind in the Willows*; Robert Browning: 'The Pied Piper of Hamlin' from *Selected Poems of Robert Browning* (Penguin, 2004); Matthew Arnold: 'Sohrab and Rustum' from *The Poems of Matthew Arnold* (Oxford University Press, 1922); Moliere: 'Tartuffe', the title of which is sometimes translated as 'The Hypocrite' (NHB Drama Classics, 2002, translated by Martin Sorrell); *Father Ted*: Arthur Mathews and Graham Linehan for Hat Trick Productions and Channel 4. The poem (my own) you find in chapter one contains the first line of Richard Lovelace's 'To Althea. From Prison' from *The Poems of Richard Lovelace* (Clarendon Press, 1963) and the rest of the poem is a pastiche of its form, with a hint of its theme of confinement. The story about Eric Newby's *A Book of Travellers' Tales* (Picador, 1986) being found in Kolkata, as signed by the author, is true and the book is on my shelves at home. The story of meeting Johnny Cash in a lift is also true and happened to my husband; as with the Newby incident, I took it for the book. *Signposts* you see.

During the writing of this book I have benefited enormously from the wisdom of the articulate MH community on twitter (you are legion). If you want to know more about mental illness, then Martha Roberts's website www.mentalhealthwise.com or that of Mind, at www.mind.org.uk, are essential reading and explain where and how to get help.

ACKNOWLEDGEMENTS

The quotation 'The millstone has become a star' (used as both epigraph and in the book) from 'Prelude' by Patrick Kavanagh is reprinted from *Collected Poems* edited by Antoinette Quinn (Allen Lane, 2004), by kind permission of The Trustees of the Estate of the late Katherine B. Kavanagh, through the Jonathan Williams Literary Agency. The quotation 'Time was away' from 'Meeting Point' by Louis MacNeice is reprinted from *Collected Poems edited by I. Dodds and Eric Robertson* (Faber and Faber, 1966, 1987) by kind permission of David Highman Associates. Many thanks to my editor, Patricia Borlenghi, for her translation from the Italian of the closing lines of Canto XXIV of Dante's *Inferno*. The quotation 'Depression is a prison where you are both the suffering prisoner and the cruel jailer' from chapter one, 'The Prison', of Dorothy Rowe's seminal book, *Depression, The Way Out Of Your Prison* (Routledge, 2003) is given by kind permission of Taylor and Francis Group. The quotation from 'Faith Healing' by Philip Larkin and the quotations from *Johnny Panic and the Bible of Dreams* ('Cambridge Notes') by Sylvia Plath are given by kind permission of Faber and Faber. The quotation from W.H. Auden is from 'La Musée des Beaux Artes' and is given by kind permission of Curtis Brown Associates in New York. I am deeply grateful to Catherine Camus for permission to quote from the work of her father, Albert Camus: *Carnets II, Janvier 1942-Mars 1951*, (Editions Gallimard, 1964). I have quoted from the earliest Gallimard editions and used my own translation, but these texts are readily available in English (see below). It felt like coming full circle to receive her generous letter from 'Rue Albert Camus.'

Thank you to my beloved lads, Elijah, Isaac and Caleb, to the wonderful Patricia Borlenghi, who believed in me and in the story I wanted to tell and was not afraid to take on my strange little book, to the novelist, Alison Taft, for whose guidance and skill I will be forever grateful; to Alexi Hayward for close reading and for thinking I'm funny; to Susie Freeman and the novelist Alex Campbell, whose readings and encouragement were invaluable. To Martha Roberts, Lucy Day, Ann Saunders, Catherine Trask, Susan Case, Corinna Wells, Kath Bowland, Carole Jones, Kate and Giles Turnbull, my reading group, Bee Wicks, Sharon Denbury, Louise Darby, Mandy Andrews, Chris, Ian and Bettykins; to Sophie Langley who insisted this story be told when I baulked at it, and to the kind and determined people in our NHS which, on many occasions, has made me cry with pride, gratefulness and not a small amount of embarrassment. To all my students, most of whom are not allowed to read this book yet! Thank you to Catherine Camus and her office for wishing me well and for keeping the legacy of Albert Camus alive. But my biggest thank you of all is to my husband Ned, without whom I *could not* and because of whom I now *can*. Love, forever and thank you for the Faulkner.